The Artist's Gift

Emma Batten

Emma x

First published in the UK by Emma Batten in 2019

ISBN 978-1-9995820-5-0

Printed and bound in the UK

A catalogue record of this book can be found in the British Library

Edited by Maud Matley

Proofread and further editing by Greer Harris

Cover painting by Zoe Beardsley

www.emmabattenauthor.com

For Shaun, who was so interested to hear some of the stories in this plot as we discussed it in the heat of the Australian summer, nine thousand miles away from my home on Romney Marsh.

About the Book

The third in the series, this novel continues the story of fictional families living in Dungeness and Lydd from the 1890s to the end of the Second World War.

In the 1940s there were huge changes in people's lives wherever they lived. For now, I will focus on Dungeness, a coastal community, predominantly made up of fishermen. During the war, those working at or fishing from Dungeness could remain living there. Other property owners, such as those with second homes, were not allowed to enter the area without permission. It would have been difficult for someone not living in Dungeness to access the area. For the sake of the novel, I have allowed local families to continue living there and to have people visit them. Those living along the Romney Marsh coastline, in places such as Denge, Galloways and Lade, were not allowed to remain in their homes.

The writing of this storyline has involved a great deal of research. My main resource has been *Romney Marsh at War* by Edward Carpenter. For a detailed explanation of what is fact and what is fiction, please refer to the back of the book. Many of the stories have been inspired by actual events; however, the characters in them are entirely fictional, the only exception being the milkman and ambulance driver who were named after real characters, following discussion with their relatives.

Thanks

I would like to thank Michael Golding, Giles Usher, David Pleasants and Keith Swallow for their help with details about Dungeness, Chris Spratt for his research on pilots who survived plane crashes and Michael Sullivan-Jones for checking the flying scenes. Also, thanks to Maria Beach for helping me find information on the fund-raising and repairs to Lydd Church and to Vanessa Baker for reading the Kalamunda scene.

For the second time, I am turning to Facebook to answer historical queries. Thank you to the groups *Your Memories and Photos of Growing up in Lydd,* and *Dungeness Now and Then.*

As always, huge thanks to Maud Matley who reads my work as I write it and alerts me when she spots anything too modern, or not quite right, as well as doing the initial grammar and typo checks.

Many thanks to Barbara Shepherd who read the novel before it was published and gave feedback.

Also, thanks to Liz Grant, Louise Pyke and the team at the Romney Marsh Visitor Centre, as well as Mary Galvin from Mary's tearooms, Grant Peakall from Dymchurch Post Office and Frances Esdaile from the Chocolate Deli for being great supporters.

Artist Zoe Beardsley painted the cover image. Thank you, Zoe. I am thrilled to have local artwork on my novel.

The Two Families

The Ashford & Lydd Family in Oct 1940

Alice Stevens (Tibbs) married to George Stevens

Their children:

Richard Stevens married to Anne
Their daughter: Helen (age 21, widow of Jack Wilson)

Lily married to Charlie Scott
Their children: Elsie (age 14) & Bobby (age 11)

Henry Stevens married to Mavis
They have five children

The Dungeness and Lydd Family in Oct 1940

Emily Brooks (widow of Ed Brooks)

Her children:

Edward Brooks married to Grace
Their children: Eva (age 18), married to Dennis, & Ben (age 16)

Allie married to Ernie
Their children: David (age 13) & Michael

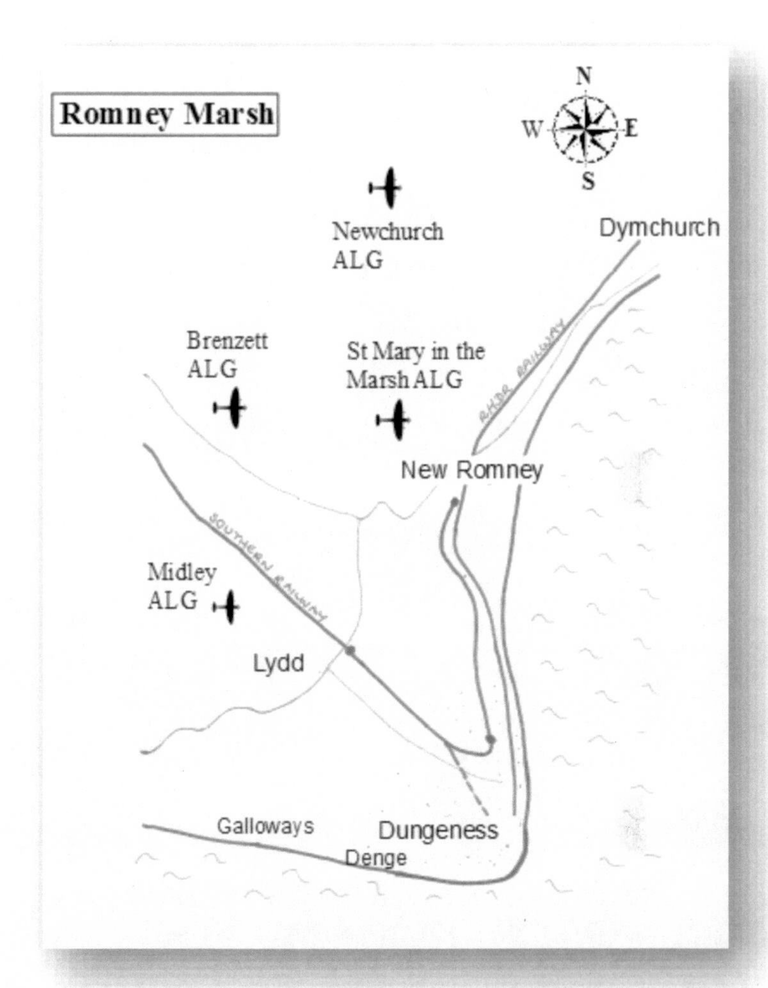

Romney Marsh
N
W
E
S
Newchurch
ALG
Dymchurch
Brenzett
ALG
St Mary in the
Marsh ALG
RHDR RAILWAY
New Romney
SOUTHERN RAILWAY
Midley
ALG
Lydd
Galloways
Dungeness
Denge

Chapter One
15th October 1940

Helen looked out across the flat lands of Romney Marsh, but she did not see the fading feather-topped reeds, the red berries on the hawthorn or majestic swans gliding on drainage ditches. The solitary arch of a ruined church and the great banks of former seawalls went unnoticed. Her face was turned towards the window, her pale hand resting on the gentle swell of her stomach, where her unborn child fidgeted.

"We're nearing Lydd now." Alice, her grandmother, tried to catch Helen's interest.

"Oh, yes." She allowed her eyes to focus. "I see the church tower."

"I wasn't much younger than you when I first came here," Alice persisted. "Of course I was going along to Dungeness, not staying in Lydd."

"You had new adventures ahead of you." Helen began to move forward in the seat, ready to stand as soon as the train came to a halt. She continued, "Starting a new life as a teacher."

At twenty-one years of age, it felt like her own adventures were over. It shouldn't seem like that, not with Jack's baby growing within her. But the vision of the telegram boy in his navy uniform, with its red piping, was emblazoned on her memory. She could see the pill-box hat and his cheeks, rosy from the exertion of cycling out to Willesborough. The paper of the telegraph was soft in her fingertips, and he lingered, waiting to see if she had a reply. None was needed. Helen had turned back into the house without saying anything to him. She was unable to say anything. Her mother found her an hour later, sitting by the fireside, numb with grief.

"Lydd Town, Lydd Town. All alight for Lydd Town," the female station master called out, her voice strong above the noise of the steam. "Next stop: Lydd-on-Sea, then Greatstone-on-Sea and New Romney."

Helen was forced into action: standing up, she straightened her dress and coat, before placing her hat on top of neat shoulder-length brown curls. Glancing across at Alice, Helen didn't know that, had she donned a Victorian black dress and coiled her hair at the nape of her neck, she would have looked very much like her grandmother when she first travelled to this remote corner of Romney Marsh. She reached for her small case and, with Alice leading the way, Helen stepped down on to the platform of Lydd Town Station.

The building was of a traditional design for those on branch-lines: an orange brick, single-storey structure under a slate roof with a scalloped canopy. The windows now sported the familiar criss-cross of tape and women replaced men as porters and guards. This rural station was a familiar sight to Helen who had visited her much-loved Aunt Lily and larger-than-life Uncle Charlie on a regular basis over her twenty-one years. Lily was the younger sister of Helen's father. Like her mother, Alice, she had ventured to Dungeness and had her own escapades there. Unlike her mother, Lily had chosen to stay, not to live on the shingle peninsular of Dungeness, but in Lydd.

With their smart shoes tapping a beat on the pavement and each carrying their own suitcase, Helen and Alice walked away from the noise and dirt of the station, then turned towards the town. They could have taken one of many lanes or roads leading to Lily and Charlie's home, but today they found themselves walking through the town's cemetery. It was here, with the autumn sun shining down upon the fallen leaves and slightly unkempt grass, Helen felt her dulled senses begin to react. Before them was a row of graves, all topped with fresh soil, so unspoiled that not a blade of grass or dandelion seed had taken root. A shiver ran through Helen's slender frame, the unborn child pressed outwards and her mouth dried.

"What happened?" she asked, her gaze fixated on the mounds, each with its own small wooden plaque.

"It was on a Saturday evening, just ten days ago," Alice told her. "Five Messerschmitt released their bombs. No one knew they were coming."

"How awful." It felt to Helen as if she had visibly paled.

"I told you about it," Alice chided her gently. "Lily wrote to me."

"I didn't hear," Helen admitted. "I'm sorry, I… It's such a small place, to have suffered so many deaths at once."

"It has an army camp," Alice reminded her. "And it's on the bombers' path to London and back."

"Of course." Helen stood, silently murmuring a prayer.

"Come on." Alice gave her granddaughter's arm a slight tug. "Lily will be waiting for us. We don't want to be late for the wedding."

The path through the cemetery led on to Mill Road,

where the site of the long-gone smock mill was, as yet undeveloped. Here plots of land were marked out – the fashion now was for bungalows with bay windows, each one a slightly unique style. About half a dozen had been built over the past couple of years and there was space for several more. But the building of homes like these had stopped for now; there was not the time nor materials for homes with bay windows or porches or pretty detailing. Helen and Alice walked past two plots where the structures had been abandoned, half-built.

A scruffy urchin of a boy appeared through a vacant window. His knees were cut, brown curls tousled, and all kinds of bits of plants and dirt clung to the woollen threads on his tank top.

"I've been up on the rafters," he called as he scampered across the rubble and weeds that comprised a front garden.

"Hello Bobby." Helen smiled and held her arms out. "Not too old to give your cousin a big hug, are you?"

"I might be…" He eyed her, perhaps calculating what a hug was worth.

"I've got some sherbet lemons!" Helen put her hand in her pocket and pulled out a paper twist with two ounces of the boiled sweets. "It's not much," she apologised.

"Nah, it's great. Thanks." Bobby swooped in and gave her a hug.

"How old are you now?" Helen asked. "You're nearly as tall as me!"

"Eleven," he replied with pride. Then he looked at Helen, his brown eyes large and said: "I'm sorry about Jack. I liked him. We'll get whoever killed him, our soldiers will."

"I know," Helen smiled ruefully. "I know they will."

"What does your father say about you running around in there?" Alice asked, giving the boy a hug too.

"He wishes he had the time to come with me!" Bobby grinned.

Helen couldn't help laughing and felt her spirits lift. No one could say that Uncle Charlie wasn't fun, but how Aunt Lily put up with him, well, no one knew!

A familiar voice rang out, and Lily was there, standing at the doorway of the red-brick bungalow. The sun glinted on her hair, which was still a beautiful auburn. She wiped her floury hands on her apron. "I'm so glad you could come." Lily offered Helen an awkward hug, keeping the apron free from her niece's navy dress, which was embroidered with white sprigs of blossom. Then, turning to Alice: "How are you, Mother? And Father, busy with the war effort?"

"Oh yes, he's been on fire-watch duty several nights a week."

They walked along the narrow hallway and into the dining room. There were already tea and biscuits set out on the table. "Mother, if you wouldn't mind pouring..." Lily stepped through to the kitchen, "...I've just finished making pastry for later and need to finish tidying up. We'll walk along to the church after a cup of tea; Charlie says he'll meet us there."

It was lovely how the families remained close, Helen reflected. It all went back to a time when her grandmother, Alice, was about her age and went to work at Dungeness. She had met Emily Brooks and learned about the hardships the young woman suffered, living not at Dungeness but in an even smaller settlement at Denge. Life was harsh there, with not enough strong men to work the fishing boats and support the families. Alice had helped to make life better for Emily and her husband. Eventually the family had moved around the shingle point to Dungeness and become part of a larger community.

Then, when Aunt Lily had grown up, she too went to Dungeness – this time to learn about the place to which her mother had gone. Lily got herself mixed up in all sorts of trouble: sometimes it was whispered that she had been married before, to a man who was murdered. It was Emily Brooks who took Lily in and looked after her. And so, the bond between the families grew.

Summer holidays were often spent with Aunt Lily and Uncle Charlie in Lydd, and always included a train ride to Dungeness to see the friends there. Uncle Charlie liked to treat them all to high tea in the café and a further train ride on the miniature steam trains that ran to New Romney and on to Hythe. Helen smiled a little to herself – she only ever recalled the sun shining over Dungeness, albeit with a brisk wind. Why were childhood memories never troubled with adult worries?

"Clean shirt, Bobby, and wash those hands… and your face, and knees." Lily gave her son a push towards the bathroom.

"I hope Elsie's ready." Bobby started to move towards the doorway, trying to remove the attention from himself.

"You know very well she is," Lily replied. "We'll be leaving in ten minutes."

Her daughter, Elsie, was to be a bridesmaid at the wedding of Emily's eighteen-year-old granddaughter, Eva Brooks, to her young man, Dennis, who was about to join the Navy. No church bells would ring out to celebrate the ceremony. It was hoped they would never ring out for the duration of the war, as to hear them would be a warning that the country had been invaded.

As the three women and Bobby walked along the roads, Alice and Helen looked at the scars caused in the year and a month since war had begun. Peeping between the houses, Helen could see Anderson shelters and extra vegetable plots in gardens. Windowpanes were criss-crossed with tape and the white lines on the lampposts helped people avoid accidents in the darkest hours of the black-out. It was the same in every town, the same in Helen's hometown of Ashford. But this was a place she came for holidays and celebrations; in her mind it had remained untouched by war. Then they were walking into the east end of the churchyard and the scene looked just the same as it always had done, with the nave and aisles of All Saints stretching outwards and, looking down on them all, the tall tower.

People were gathering for the wedding, walking down the paths that crossed the churchyard and meeting at the base of the tower. Helen spotted Emily, so thin, yet always full of energy. She was with her daughter and other members of the family. There were young women, friends of the bride, but a noticeable lack of young men. And there was Uncle Charlie, striding in from the direction of the High Street, looking around and then giving a cheery wave.

"Hello Helen, my love!" Charlie leaned down and gave her a huge smack of a kiss on the cheek. "Glad you could be here today." And then, turning to Alice with a cheeky grin: "Hello Ma, good to see you."

"Hello Charlie, good to see you too." Alice forced a

smile.

"And who's this, looking so smart?" Charlie ruffled his son's hair. "You look ready to come to the office with me."

"Not yet, Dad," Bobby pushed his hair back into shape. "I'll be going to war first, if only it lasts long enough."

"You're eleven." The smile fell from Charlie's face. "You're not going to war. There's been enough suffering already."

Lily linked her arm through Charlie's. "He's not going to war," she confirmed.

The small family group walked through the doorway, set in the base of the church tower, and into the nave. Helen paused, as she always did on entering a church. She wanted to take in the smell of centuries-old slightly damp stone, to allow her eyes to adjust to the dim light and then to let them roam over the patina of the dark wooden pews and up the tall columns to the vast roof space. The organ was playing softly in the background; there was a murmuring of voices and the shuffling of feet.

At Helen's own wedding, eight months beforehand, she too had been marrying a man about to set off to war. They had a brief honeymoon, just four days at Whitstable, and then Jack had gone to join up with the Navy, only to be lost at sea within months. Perhaps she should stay in Lydd for a couple of weeks, Helen pondered. Perhaps Eva would appreciate her company, or was Helen a reminder of the stark reality of war? Eva would want to think of her husband returning; Helen shrugged the idea aside and quickened her pace to catch up with the others.

Slipping into the pew, she sat down beside her grandmother. In the rows ahead, the Brooks family gathered: Emily; her daughter Allie, who now lived in Lydd with her husband and sons; daughter-in-law Grace and the children of the families. Smiles and whispers flowed between them all. In pews to the right, the groom's party assembled. It was to be a small wedding, or so Helen had been told. Just close friends and family. The young bride and groom did not want a fuss made when the country was at war.

Now Dennis walked in with his best man, a broad smile on his face, his hair neatly slicked into place and looking a little self-conscious in his new suit. He seemed so young, Helen thought. Foolish thoughts: at twenty years of age, he was only a year younger than her and three years younger than her own husband would have been, had he survived.

The two young men stood near the chancel; the congregation continued to murmur, and the organ played on. With his cassock flowing, the vicar walked back and forth, pausing to exchange a few words with those who waited for the service to begin. With a glance to the west end, he saw the bride and her father enter the church and sailed along the length of the nave to greet them. The organist seamlessly changed to the uplifting *Trumpet Voluntary,* and everyone turned to see the bride walk along the aisle on the arm of her father, Edward.

Eva looked beautiful: her dark hair was coiled in a chignon at the nape of her neck; the ivory silk dress was simple in style and reaching only to mid-calf length, with a sweetheart neckline, capped sleeves and an A-line skirt. The war dictated there was no material to spare for clothes that wouldn't be used again, so the two bridesmaids wore dresses of a similar style in a mid-blue. Their bouquets were large blooms of late roses. On her walk down the long aisle,

Eva gave shy smiles, but her expression was serious, as if she understood the fragile nature of this bond with Dennis.

Try as she might, Helen found it hard to concentrate on following the wedding service word-by-word. She found the rector's voice soothing, almost melodic, as he read passages from the Bible, and she responded to the prayers at the appropriate moments. Her unborn child stretched and pushed a little within her. Suddenly she felt weary, but pleased to be here in Lydd, to be a part of it.

Then Dennis was pushing back the modest lace veil and the couple kissed briefly. Helen felt a lump rise in her throat, and she wiped away a tear that threatened to make a slow descent down her cheek. The young couple moved to the vestry, holding hands as they followed the rector. While the register was signed, a low hum of chatter rose from the pews, but silence fell as the newly-weds returned to walk along the aisle. Helen moved to follow but, just as she started to leave the pew, she looked back, envying the obvious closeness between Aunt Lily and Uncle Charlie.

"I'm going to light a candle for my parents," Charlie whispered to Lily. "I'll catch up with you in a minute, darling." He bent down and kissed his wife on the cheek. She reached out and gave his hand a squeeze. Charlie turned back towards the chancel.

From the top of the church tower the lone soldier on look-out watched the trio of bomb-carrying Messerschmitt 109 fighters pass over Lydd. They would be bound for London, no doubt. He turned his back to the planes, hunkered down beneath the parapet and lit a cigarette. Unseen by him, the planes travelled on for a mile or two, before turning amongst the low clouds. As he straightened himself and looked once more towards the north-west, the soldier felt his skin go cold and his mouth go dry. The planes were returning and all three of them heading directly for Lydd. There was no time to sound an alert.

Leaning against the churchyard wall, an elderly gentleman, who had been on fire-watch duty the previous night, took out his sketchpad. He began to draw lines to represent the ornamental window of the chancel.

Chapter Two
15th October 1940

On the church tower, the look-out flung himself into the shadows of the parapet. It would make no difference, he would die if the tower were struck and survive if it were spared, but he was compelled to shelter. Not quite overhead, the fighter-bomber planes spread out a little, with the central one taking a course over the east end of All Saints.

Inside the church, the wedding party was moving along the nave towards the tower, with the rector bringing up the rear. Over the murmur of voices, some of them heard the whistle of the rapidly falling bomb. Within seconds, every one of them had fallen silent. And then they scattered, to the shelter of the solid oak pews. With her hands cradling her unborn child, Helen recalled Uncle Charlie separating from the group and walking to the far end of the church.

In the hushed silence, there came a desperate scream. It rose to the rafters, reverberated off the leaded glass windows and flew towards the chancel, where Charlie was lighting a candle for his mother. Peeping out, Helen saw Charlie fling himself under the altar and Lily's scream was cut dead as the east end of the church was destroyed by the force of a bomb. Stone fell, glass shattered, and wood splintered. And then silence.

No sound was uttered from those crouched under the pews. The baby kicked with force. A plume of dust rolled westwards and settled on the glossy brown of the well-worn seats. Then came the noise of falling masonry as part of a wall gave up the fight to stay in place. And after that, the gradual movement of one stone, then another falling. Next came the eerie creak of a medieval beam and the splintering, ripping sound of wooden joists forced apart after centuries of being bound together. The thud of the ancient beam crashing to the ground caused vibrations throughout the church and a gasp of horror to ripple through the onlookers.

One by one the church-goers emerged from where they had cowered. Best clothes were now layered in dust, hair in disarray. They clutched at one another, faces blanched and eyes wide, as they found their voices and began to express their horror. They were all there: had the bomb hit the church five minutes earlier the casualties would have been huge. They were all there… except for Charlie. Helen looked at Lily. Her aunt was standing in the centre of the nave, looking towards the shattered altar, looking towards the place where Charlie had dived for shelter.

"Charlie was there," Lily said, her voice rough. She had her arm around Bobby.

Lily's daughter, Elsie, had her fingers linked with those of Ben Brooks. *I hadn't known they were close*, Helen thought irrelevantly. *She is only fourteen*.

"Dad?" Bobby's voice was barely audible. "No, he was here with us, he was..." He looked into the stunned faces of the people he had known all his life.

"He went to light a candle," Lily confirmed.

All eyes remained fixed on the open space beyond the altar. The sunlight, softened by the clouds of dust, shone down on the rubble, shattered glass, and twisted lead in the chancel. Shapes of trees and buildings could be seen behind the slowly shifting veil of dust particles.

Like pawns on a chessboard, Alice and Emily moved towards Lily and Bobby. Helen looked towards her cousin, Elsie, and the two of them moved closer. Elsie's hand was still within Ben's.

"I must go to him," Lily said, as she and Bobby took a step forward. "He'll be fine; the altar will have protected him.

"It's not safe," Alice placed her hand on her daughter's arm.

"I won't leave him there alone," Lily scowled. "I just can't."

But as the words were said, more stone fell, sending further debris spiralling outwards. And there, amidst the dust plumes, a figure stood where the end wall had once been.

"Charlie?"

"Dad?"

The cries came simultaneously. But then there were two, no three, figures. Men in overalls with rounded tin hats. And a new sound came: the clang of the town's fire engine bell.

"It's not Charlie, love," Emily said, her thin hand resting on Lily's back. "He couldn't get out of there."

"We need to stand back now." The rector spoke with authority. No one moved.

Sounds from behind them caused the wedding party to turn and stare at the soldier who had been the look-out at the tower and who now stood before them. "They were heading for London," he said shakily. "God knows what caused them to turn back."

"My husband's down there," Lily said, her voice

shrill. “I need to go to him.”

“Down there?” the soldier repeated.

“He went to light a candle...” Lily began to walk down the nave. “Stay here, Bobby, stay with your grandmother.”

“There's not much hope.” The look-out said the words no one else had dared to voice.

“You don't know my husband,” Lily snapped at him. “He'll be fine.”

“We'll go a little closer then,” the soldier replied. “But the rest of you, get out of here, there's nothing to see. Look after the kids and stay clear of the east end.”

Helen looked on, her hand still linked with Elsie's, who continued to cling to Ben. Her unborn baby lay quietly, unperturbed by the events unfolding. As Lily walked away from the rest of the family group and along the nave, Helen became aware of the whispers now passing about. The bride, Eva, was crying into her husband's shoulder. There was the gentle swoosh of hands brushing down the material of dresses and suits. Handkerchiefs were extracted from pockets and used to wipe faces clean. Throats were cleared with discreet coughs. Helen's mouth was dry; she could taste the film of ancient stone-dust on her tongue.

Then the pain came: it started in her back, or was it her hips? Afterwards Helen could not recall, and it didn't really matter. A band of tension wrapped itself around her abdomen and radiated down her thighs. She stood, unable to follow the others through the tower and out to the churchyard. The pain began to ease, the baby lurched… and a warm gush of water expelled itself from within her. It licked around her thighs and dribbled into her shoes; the red tiles darkened as a pool of fluid gathered at her feet. Helen stood perfectly still, horrified.

It was Emily who noticed. "Oh! My Lord! She's going to have the baby."

"No, no, I'm not," Helen objected. She couldn't, she just couldn't cause any fuss, not on Eva's wedding day. And not when the bomb had only just fallen minutes beforehand. Not at the very moment her beloved Uncle Charlie lay... lay there, most likely dead. Another band of pain tightened around her immediately distracting Helen from thoughts of Charlie and the shattered altar.

"You don't get to choose when it decides to come," Emily said. "Now you and I need to get back to Lily's and..." She saw that her daughter was nearby and called out: "Allie, Allie we need the midwife for Helen."

Allie turned and her gaze travelled from the faces of her mother and Helen to the wet tile floor. She nodded her understanding and asked: "You're going to Lily's?"

"We'll have to," Emily replied. And with her arm around Helen's waist, she urged her forwards. "Just a few steps at a time and we'll stop whenever you need to."

Passing back through the churchyard, they saw the fallen east end from a new perspective. There were now several local wardens, all in their tin hats, viewing the scene, assessing the risk of further collapse. With his cassock billowing behind him, the rector moved into the scene, no doubt bearing the news of the one person who lay beneath the wreckage.

The pains came again before they left the churchyard, causing Helen to stop and cling to Emily, before giving a small, brave smile and taking another step forward. Then they turned their backs on the church, although the images of the destruction played over and over in their minds.

"Has Lily made a bed up for you?" Emily asked as they walked up the front path to the bungalow.

"I'm in Elsie's room," Helen told her. "With Grandmother."

"Alice can come back with me to Dungeness," Emily said. "Now I'll get the water heating on the stove and make us a nice cup of tea. Babies don't usually come in a hurry."

"Perhaps it's a false alarm." Helen stood rubbing her back. "There's five weeks left to go."

"I don't think baby is going to change its mind now," Emily replied as she put a small spoonful of sugar into the tea. "Damned war; you need more than a spoonful of sugar to get you through the next few hours, but that's how it is for the time being. Now I wonder if Allie will think to bring some old towels; I'll see what Lily has in her cupboard."

"Aunt Lily… things are going to be awful enough for her and the children, without me here… without all this going on." Helen slumped at the table.

"It might be the only thing they have to distract them from..." Emily couldn't say the words they were both thinking.

Helen was soon left with no choice but to accept that the labour pains were not going to ease, nor her baby wait until the time it was supposed to arrive. As the contractions ripped through her body, she focused on the smallest things: the shaft of sunlight coming through the curtains and falling on the rich brown of Elsie's dressing table; the rambling roses on the wallpaper and the book on the shelves which needed pushing back into place so as to line up with the others. Time passed: the clock in the hallway chimed the hour and at intervals in-between. But in many ways it seemed that Helen remained locked in a timeless place of rhythmic pain and fear for the baby who was not yet due. She made little fuss about the pain, but in her mind Lily's cry for Charlie continually reverberated. The whistle of the bomb was constant in her ears – she heard it more clearly now than she had done in those seconds before it plunged into the chancel of All Saints.

The midwife came, her cape wrapped around her and a smile fixed on her face. *She has heard the news about the bomb,* Helen thought, as the woman placed her capacious black leather bag on a chair. She checked on Helen, made reassuring noises, then left again, promising to return after a couple of hours. Allie came and went too, having given Helen a quick hug, and discussed with Emily the things that the new baby would need. She returned later, speaking of neighbours who had offered nappies and vests and tiny nightdresses for the child who would be born that day. Helen thought of the deep drawer at home where all the tiny things were stored, ready for the child who should have arrived in Ashford, not here in Lydd.

Amidst the women who came and went, and the whistle of the bomb, and the desperate cries from Lily, there was one constant. Emily, friend of the family for decades, remained at Helen's bedside holding her hand, speaking words that Helen didn't really take in. She ensured there was a pile of towels and warm water at the ready. There were other people in the house, Helen could sense it; they must have returned from the church. And at one time it seemed as if she heard Charlie's voice ring out. Confused, Helen turned to Emily and asked: "Charlie, is he…?"

"There's not much hope, love," Emily replied.

"I thought I heard..." Helen let her words fade.

It was late afternoon, with the midwife in attendance and Emily sitting at the head of the bed, her thin arms around Helen's shoulders, when the tiny new life forced its way into the world.

"You've done it," Emily said, as she wiped Helen's face with a damp cloth. "The baby came quickly; you were lucky."

They looked towards the midwife who was expertly wiping the new-born child clean. It let out a wail and Helen gave Emily a weak smile before relaxing into the pillows.

"He's small, but healthy enough," the woman said as she wrapped the baby in a soft cloth.

"He? A boy?" Helen looked across at the bundle; only a dark head of hair showed above the white cloth swaddling the child.

"A boy!" the midwife confirmed. "Are you ready to hold him?"

Helen looked at Emily. Was she ready? Emily gave a slight nod and asked: "Have you chosen a name for him yet?"

"I'm going to call him Jack, after his father," Helen replied.

"That's a lovely idea."

Helen cradled her son in her arms, looking down at the fine dark hair, his perfectly shaped lips and the long eyelashes resting on his cheeks. She pulled the swaddling blanket loose and marvelled at his tiny arms and slender fingers.

"He'll sleep a lot at first," the midwife told Helen. "Early babies need more sleep."

"But he's healthy?" Helen asked as she stroked

the soft skin of his cheeks.

"He seems to be, he's a good colour and breathing well. You've plenty of support around you if you have any worries." The woman was now gathering the towels stained from the birth and placing them in a bucket. "But I will stay for a little longer, to make sure he latches on for his first feed and see that you're comfortable. Then I'll be back in the morning, and we can have a chat about how you're getting on."

Just as the bells did not ring for Eva's wedding, neither did they toll for the funeral. Helen sat on her bed watching the baby sleep. His arms were flung above his head and his breathing steady, with the occasional snuffle. The midwife had decreed a week's bed rest and Helen had been told that under no circumstances should she attend the funeral with a premature baby. All she could do was lie there, watching Jack and thinking of Lily and the children. When he woke, she would pick up her tiny son and instinctively he would search for milk. Feeding him gave her a contentment she had not thought possible since her young husband had died.

The first week of being a mother passed in a haze of concern for the baby born five weeks early and being swamped with well-meaning advice, while exhausted from two-hourly feeds. She looked on as the family reeled in the aftermath of the news that Charlie's life had been extinguished when the chancel fell as the bomb exploded. Helen felt her own loss: she had loved her uncle very much, enjoying his humour as her parents looked on and shook their heads in despair. But amidst the grief, a tiny boy had to be cared for and watched over. People came and went from the house, arrangements were made. From her enforced bed rest she wondered about her future and that of her little son.

"We've been talking about you and Jack going to Wales, where it's safer," Helen's father said, when the family returned to the house after the funeral.

"Wales?" Helen questioned.

"Or some other place not on the bombers' path to one of our major cities or ports," her father elaborated. "The children are our future; they'll be the ones who'll grow up and set our country straight again."

Helen looked across at Jack cradled in Aunt Lily's arms. Surely everything would be over long before he was out of nappies. She looked at Bobby and Elsie; they would be the generation who would grow up in the aftermath.

The first order to evacuate children, pregnant women and vulnerable people had come on 31st August 1939. Children had left Ashford on crowded trains and one of Helen's friends, a young teacher, had escorted her class to new homes in the countryside. Many returned after a few months when the bombs they feared had not fallen upon Britain. Now, within the past few weeks, the Luftwaffe had persistently bombed London and other cities, causing a fresh wave of evacuations to take place.

"Of course there was a time when children were evacuated to the Romney Marsh," Helen's father said.

"That was a stupid idea," Bobby interrupted. "We've had as many bombs in Lydd as they have in London."

Helen watched as her father digested this absurd statement and gathered his momentum, having been halted in his tracks. "Not quite," he continued. "But we are rather vulnerable to any bombs being discarded as the aeroplanes make their return journey to Germany."

"I think this family have had enough of bombs and other awful things," Helen's mother said, putting her hand on her daughter's shoulder.

"Quite. Our priority now is to keep young Jack safe," her father replied.

"He can't go anywhere yet," Helen said, almost glad this was the case and her father had been thwarted.

"On midwife's orders," Lily confirmed, dropping a light kiss on his head.

"I won't… I just can't leave everyone and go off God-knows-where with a tiny baby." Helen suddenly felt incredibly young and vulnerable. It seemed that even as a widow and a mother, her parents felt it was their duty to make decisions on her behalf. She took a step towards Lily and baby Jack. "I need to stay with people I know, at least for the time being."

"I was hoping..." Lily began. "I was thinking that perhaps Helen could stay here with me for a while. It seems rather selfish, but the baby… he, well, he helps take our minds off what has happened. Not that we ever stop thinking of Charlie, but Jack has brought us such comfort. We have no choice but to care for him and be forced to put his needs before our own."

"I don't mind Helen using my room," Elsie offered, "if it helps."

Helen smiled at her cousin. "Thank you, Elsie. I was worried we were getting in the way."

"Very well, I see you can't return with us today." Helen's father paced across the room and looked out of the window across the back garden. "And despite everything that has happened over the past weeks, I doubt Lydd is any more dangerous a place to be in than Ashford."

"What Henry means to say," Helen's grandmother, Alice, added, "is that we are all pleased if Helen and Jack can bring some comfort to you all. And perhaps being here will give Helen some consolation, for none of us forgets that she suffers her own loss."

Helen gave her grandmother a smile as she felt the tension flow from her body. "I'd like to be here, for as long as Aunt Lily is happy to put up with me and Elsie can spare her room."

"That's all arranged then," Lily replied. "But perhaps, with the fuel shortages, we could look at moving the settee from the front room into here. The dining table could move up a little and we could be nice and cosy all together. Helen can have a bed in the front room and something to store things in."

"I'll send everything you made for the baby, and whatever you need," Helen's mother offered.

"Thank you." Helen reached for her son as he began to whimper. "Now, if you don't mind, I'll feed Jack and his nappy must need changing."

The family from Ashford returned on the next train from Lydd, and so a new era began in the red-brick bungalow built for the Scott family of Lydd. As they mourned the death of a much-loved husband and father, Helen and baby Jack settled into the home. New routines were formed, and family ties were strengthened; they supported each other at a time when everyone felt very vulnerable and unsure of what the future would bring.

Flicking through his sketchpad, Albert Harcourt came across the outlines of the chancel window, drawn moments before the bomb fell.

Chapter Three
March 1941

"Be good for Aunt Lily," Helen bent down and kissed her baby son's forehead. His eyes followed her as she fastened the belt on her Women's Voluntary Service overall and placed the beret on her hair, neatly coiled into a bun. Jack wasn't distressed by his mother leaving him. It was part of the pattern of his life: one day his mother tended to his needs and the next Aunt Lily cared for him. Other people came and went: Ben who tickled him and Elsie who cuddled him tightly, other relatives and neighbours who visited the family. Whoever's arms he was in, Jack knew nothing but warmth and comfort.

"I'll see you mid-afternoon," Lily said. "I'm thinking of taking the train to Lydd-on-Sea and walking along to see Emily at Dungeness. It's not quite so chilly now. But I'll be sure to wrap Jack up."

"That will be good," Helen said, as she tied the laces on her sensible shoes. "Emily will love to see you both." She looked back as she put her hand to the latch and blew the pair of them a kiss. "See you later."

Hugging her arms around her body, Helen walked down Mill Road. It had been a harsh winter with bitterly cold south-easterly winds blowing across Romney Marsh and the remote shingle headland of Dungeness. The snow had been heavy but with that peace descended on the area. Enemy air offensives were inhibited by the weather and on the ground, travel was hampered by deep snowdrifts. It was a lull that gave the people of Lydd a chance to enjoy a respite from the terror of bombs before enemy action resumed.

The wintry conditions brought their own problems: water froze, food supplies ran short, and people struggled to keep warm. Even the usually reliable supply of fish became less regular as the sea became icy and it was said that those caught in lay-lines had been found frozen.

Spring brought with it the promise of warmer weather, but also the renewed threat of bombs. In Lydd the air-raid sirens had wailed several times early in the season and the enforced hours spent in damp shelters were crushing the morale of the town's people. But they battled on, making the best of things and looking at ways to support those who fought for the country.

Not long after the funeral, and when Helen's family had returned to Ashford, Lily and Helen had decided that the care of baby Jack would be shared between them. Helping to look after the baby gave her aunt someone small and vulnerable to think about; Helen welcomed the support and advice. They were both very keen to be of some use to the war effort but had their children to care for and so nursing or working on the land was not suitable; these roles demanded more time than a mother was able to give.

Both women had joined the WVS by the time Jack was a month old, initially taking him with them to the meetings where he slept in a basket while they knitted woollen garments for the troops. But as the snow melted and there was some respite from the wind, Lily and Helen began new voluntary roles taking them away from Lydd and it was no longer practical to have a baby in tow. So, they decided that while one of them worked, the other would stay in the home caring for Jack and doing the household chores.

Turning on to Ness Road, Helen moved quickly, grateful the paths were now free of ice and welcoming the occasional glimpse of spring flowers. She scurried through the churchyard, barely glancing at the fallen chancel, and then to the High Street, occasionally nodding or giving a brief greeting to the housewives and schoolchildren she passed.

Helen heard the rattle of the Ford NAAFI van before the khaki box-like beast came into view. It was driven at pace along the High Street, then shuddered and stalled as it came to a halt, having lurched across the road in Helen's direction. Helen raised her hand and gave a brief smile before walking in front of the vehicle and opening the passenger door.

"Good morning!" Helen said, settling into the seat.

"Good morning? It's bleedin' freezing out there still!" Annie replied. She was older than Helen, about forty, with her blonde hair set in sausage curls across the top of her head and twisted into a coil at the back. Her beret was balanced so as not to cause any more disruption to her hairstyle than was necessary.

Helen grinned. She couldn't help liking Annie, but she really was making a fuss about the weather. "We'll have the tea urn going in no time and a queue of grateful soldiers. Nothing wrong with that!"

"You're right, girl. Lade first, I rather like one of the men down there." Annie gave a rough cackle as she pressed down on the accelerator and the van bunny-hopped across to the correct side of the road. "Come on *Nancy*, take us to those soldiers!"

The correct gear was selected and Nancy-the-NAAFI-van, picked up speed. Soon the two women left Lydd behind them and were heading out on the road leading to the coast. Helen clung to the edge of her seat as the old vehicle lurched crazily over bumps on the concrete surface. Annie was forced to slow down as the road changed to a single track with passing points, and to stop when they approached a level crossing on the Dungeness Southern Railway line. A policeman emerged from a wooden shed. He examined Annie and Helen's permits to enter the restricted coastal area and opened the gate.

"He does that every time," Annie said, with a scowl crossing her face. "You'd think he would recognise us by now. He's so proud of that job, fussing over every little detail."

Helen couldn't help but smile. Annie was right, of course. Now the NAAFI van neared the coastline and the bleak Dungeness peninsula, and Helen recalled her Grandmother Alice's stories of her visits to the area. She said to Annie: "I can't imagine my grandmother coming here. You don't do you? I mean you don't think of your grandparents having such adventures."

"I can think of better adventures than going to Dungeness!" Annie replied.

"Well, yes..." Helen admitted. "But that's because we know it. Imagine living in Ashford, or some other town that was rather… rather normal and going to Dungeness believing it to be a seaside village."

"It is a seaside village."

"But not exactly what you would expect. There wasn't a tea-room back then, or a road, and what must she have thought when there wasn't even a dance hall or a promenade!" Helen looked at Annie. "Oh, you know what I mean."

"I know what you mean," Annie replied. "It must have been an awful place for your grandmother to end up. A teacher, wasn't she?"

"Yes, she stayed for over a year and quite enjoyed herself in the end!"

They passed the concrete road snaking through Dungeness village and continued their route. On reaching the coast it swung to the left and followed the line of the beach. To the right was a large bay and, as the day was fair, the coastline could be seen arching around until the flat lands of Romney Marsh met the hills at Hythe. Clouds moved away from the face of the sun, and it shone down, highlighting the chalk cliffs of Dover in the far distance. The sea was a sparkling steely blue, but the shingle bank was now topped with stretches of barbed wire attached to scaffold poles. The road had the occasional bungalow dotted along it, but the area had been deserted by homeowners for some time, with the army requisitioning the properties for their own use.

Their destination was an old Napoleonic Fort that now had a row of red brick houses within its boundaries. It was here that a coastguard station also housed the lookouts for the army. The nearby beaches, with their shallow sands and proximity to France, were a likely target for invading forces.

As Lade Fort came into sight, Annie did her usual trick of shuffling about in the seat until she could retrieve her lipstick from her overall pocket and then, while balancing the steering wheel with her knees, she removed the top. Helen always marvelled at how her companion achieved such a neat slash of red across her lips, with the van travelling at speed, bounding over the ruts in the road. Helen's own lipstick was a pinky-red and a smear of petroleum jelly provided a shine on top.

"We'll show him that he ain't going to stop British women looking glamorous," Annie said with a grin. It was well known that Hitler didn't approve of make-up, and so even those who had never thought to wear it before, thinking it a sign that a woman was "fast" and it was really only for film stars, were soon defiantly coating their lips with shades of red and pink.

The two women pulled up at the roadside and saw the trail of khaki-clad men making their way across the stony ground to the tea-van.

"They must have seen us coming," Annie declared.

Moving out of the cab, and sending a cheery wave in their direction, Annie opened the back doors. Helen stepped in first. Pressing on the wall of the van, she guided the thin metal as it moved upwards and outwards, creating a canopy and a serving hatch. She then slid back small bolts and a smaller section of the side of the van swung downwards, making a shelf. While she ensured the shelf and canopy were secure, Annie had squeezed herself behind Helen and was lighting the gas below a large aluminium kettle.

"Hello ladies, a sight for sore eyes, you are."

"I bet we are," came Annie's cheeky reply. "Without our pretty faces, you'd be stuck here looking at sea and stones all day!"

And so the banter between the women and the men on look-out duty began as they waited for the kettle to boil. Helen answered shyly and smiled the best she could. She was becoming used to these men whom she saw several times a week and, once she had learned the names of their wives and children, or what interests they had, it became easier to exchange a few words with each one. While Helen asked about how Bill's son liked scouts and if Wilf's wife had recovered from her bad cold, Annie preened and pouted and flashed suggestive looks.

"Got any chocolate, love?" one of the men asked.

"Just Ration Chocolate, the same as usual," Annie replied. "If I could bring you a nice bit of Cadbury's Dairy Milk then I would, you know that."

"It's not the same."

"I know, I know," Annie said. "But what can I do about it? They can't be using milk for making chocolate. That's what they say."

"I'll have some pear drops then."

The men gathered where the van kept the worst of the sea breeze from them. They warmed themselves with tea and enjoyed a brief respite from their duties. As the tin mugs were drained and rinsed out with the smallest amount of water, the vehicle was made safe for the return journey. Then Nancy-the-NAAFI-van was turned about in the road and headed to Dungeness where further men looked forward to their morning tea-break.

"You went to Dungeness then?" Helen was at the kitchen sink, peeling potatoes when Lily came in, Jack in her arms.

"Thank goodness I did." Lily waited for Helen to dry her hands and take the baby before she began to unbutton her coat and remove her hat and scarf. "Emily's had a fall and twisted her ankle; it's all black and blue."

"Not broken?" Helen asked, concerned. Emily would be housebound, as it would be almost impossible to move about on the undulating shingle surrounding the Dungeness cottage where she had lived alone since the death of her husband eighteen months beforehand.

"No, but the sprain isn't good. She can't do much for herself, even getting to the outside privy is difficult."

Helen wondered if, not yet but in the years to come, the two families of Emily and her own grandmother, Alice, already extremely close, would eventually be united in marriage. She thought back to the day Uncle Charlie had been killed when Lydd church was bombed and she had seen her cousin, Elsie, turn to Ben Brooks for comfort. He often seemed to be at the bungalow in Mill Road; the young couple would take a walk together or go to the cinema, sometimes with Bobby in tow. But Ben was only sixteen and Elsie just fourteen, and there was a war on. You could not predict how life would turn out. Both widowed by war, Helen and Lily knew that better than anyone.

"When did this happen?" Helen asked.

"Yesterday. She tripped carrying a basket of washing out to the copper. She's doing all Grace's washing, now she's going along to Littlestone to help in the convalescent home most days." Lily referred to Emily's daughter-in-law who lived nearby.

"Oh gosh, so she had her hands full – it's a wonder people aren't twisting their ankles everyday walking about on all those stones."

"The locals don't know any different," Lily replied. "They're used to it, but she came down with a thud; she's got bruising all up one side and there's no fat on her to cushion the fall."

"She must feel wretched," Helen said. "Emily is always so busy; I can't imagine her sitting about with her feet up all day."

"She's miserable." Lily moved the kettle on to the

ring and lit the gas. “And it's only been a day. I wish I could go to help her, but there's Jack here, as well as Elsie and Bobby. I can't have you staying at home, looking after these three, and not going out with the NAAFI van either. And I can't take Jack with me, that's not right.”

Helen walked through into the adjoining dining room and placed her son on a thick blanket on the floor. He immediately turned from being on his back to his front, then reached for a wooden spoon his mother had placed just within reach. Bringing it to his mouth he began to chew on it.

“This is the problem now we're at war,” Helen reflected. “In the past there would have been any number of women in the family ready to step in and help. So now, not only is Emily lonely and in pain, but Grace isn't getting the help she needs in order to run the home and to do her war work.”

“Perhaps Emily could come here?” Lily pondered. “But she'd feel like an awful nuisance, and we are already quite full; Elsie would have to share with Bobby… or me.” She lifted a package from her bag and placed it on the kitchen work-surface, then continued. “Here's the fish, caught by Edward, but let's have a cup of tea first.”

The kettle was now boiling, and Lily poured water on to the tealeaves in the 'everyday' brown teapot. Then she took the jug of milk from the slate shelf at the bottom of the larder and placed it on a tray beside the teapot, cups and saucers. The two women settled down at the dining table, both turned slightly in order to watch Jack, who was now reaching for his rattles and the wooden bricks scattered around him.

“How was your day?” Lily changed the subject.

“Still chilly, standing there with the hatch open,

wanting to be the one next to the kettle and gas ring!" Helen looked at her hands and said, "I'll need to put some cream on these, they get so chapped, washing up in the cold. But it's not about us; think of those soldiers out there in all weathers. If we make a difference to them, then it's worth it."

"It is," Lily agreed. "Who were you with?"

"Annie." Helen gave a grin. "She's fun, isn't she?" There were four of them volunteering on the NAAFI van, fitting in their voluntary work around their family duties.

"She is," Lily replied. "But her driving..."

"I know! She gives women drivers a bad name, but we made it back safely. I'm sure she'll do the van some real damage one day."

Helen and Lily sat, sipping on their tea and speaking to Jack in sing-song voices. Each of them was inwardly reflecting on the changes in their lives since October 15th when the lone bomb whistled its way downwards and struck the chancel of Lydd Church. When Helen spoke to her aunt, she was again thinking of Emily and the family at Dungeness: "Everyone has been so good to me, since Jack came."

"You and Jack have brought us so much happiness," Lily reminded her. "I dread to think how I would have coped if this house had been empty of Charlie, without the baby to distract us."

"I was thinking..." Helen began. "What if I were to take Jack and go to stay with Emily? I can do the washing while he sleeps and watch him while I prepare the dinner and do the cleaning. It will be company for Emily; she must be so lonely. Just for a week or two... no longer, as I have my NAAFI work and you, Elsie and Bobby here in Lydd."

"And I could do your days on the tea-van." Lily

could see how this would work. “Elsie and Bobby will be fine, and you'll have Jack with you.”

“It wouldn't be for long,” Helen confirmed. “But if I could help?”

“Of course, you could. Emily would be thrilled; imagine her face when she hears of it!”

“And all the women in our family go to Dungeness for one reason or another,” Helen said as she reflected on the tales of both her grandmother and aunt's adventures. “Of course I must go!”

“It's becoming quite a family tradition,” Lily agreed with a grin.

“Shall we send a message and ask what Emily thinks?”

“No, let's not wait. Poor Emily will be thrilled to have you,” Lily spoke with confidence. “Why not leave early tomorrow morning? I'm sure to think of someone who can take you there. And if she doesn't need you, you can stay overnight and come back the next day. But she'll not let you go, I'm sure of it.”

“I'll pack up what we need this evening and be ready to leave,” Helen said. “I shouldn't say it, with Emily so fed up, but it feels like quite an adventure!”

Would it be appropriate to draw the ruined church, Albert wondered? He asked his wife, Beryl, and she felt it to be wrong. Charlie Scott had died, she said, so to make a picture was disrespectful.

Chapter Four
March 1941

Helen pushed Jack's teddy-bear into the top of an old canvas knapsack. "You need more things than I do," she said to her son, as he lay in his cot beside her bed. Her own selection of clothes was in a small carpet bag. She got a gummy smile in response as Jack stretched and kicked off his blanket.

The next morning Helen rose early, just as the sky was lightening to a steely grey. She dressed quickly, not noticing any respite from the early morning chill even though winter had passed, and they had now reached the end of March. Jack's nappy had been changed and he had been fed his milk-soaked rusk, then endured another nappy change before being dressed for the day in layers of woollen garments. After buttoning up her winter coat and pulling on stout boots, Helen swung the knapsack on to her back. Finally, she scooped Jack out of the cot and placed him into the pram, which tended to dominate the narrow hallway. Two blankets covered him and, with a hat pulled down over his ears, only his rosy cheeks, button nose and shiny dark eyes showed.

"We hadn't talked about the pram," Lily said, as she came into the hall, placing her WVS beret on her auburn waves.

"It'll be a struggle on the stones, if I need to go off

the concrete track." Helen looked doubtfully at the splendid Silver Cross model, which had in its time carried Elsie and Bobby. "But the wheels are large and should manage, although I would hate to break it."

"That's what I needed to tell you," Lily continued. "If you feel you want to take Jack anywhere off the road, then perhaps Grace still has an old sleigh. But if not, then go to the Light Railway Café, they have a couple of sleigh-prams for people to borrow. There are no visitors using the railway now, but they came in handy in the old days. It won't be what Jack's used to but will suit you better."

"Sleigh-*prams*?" Helen couldn't help grinning. "I'll see soon enough, I suppose!"

As the sun peeped through the swathes of ash-grey clouds, and the people of Lydd prepared for their day, Helen wheeled Jack along to the Style & Winch Brewery in the High Street, just as the huge geldings pulled their dray on to the main road.

"You must be the young woman Lily Scott was talking about," said the drayman, who wore his cap pulled low and his thick scarf wrapped securely around his neck.

"I am and thank you for taking us to Dungeness."

"It's no trouble for me, but I'm sure you and the baby have had more comfortable rides!" The drayman looked back at the open cart, fully laden with barrels. "Now, let's get that posh pram tied up safe; you hold the baby and swaddle him tight in the blankets."

Helen picked Jack up and expertly wrapped him in one, then two, blankets. The pram was strapped high on the cart, while the bag and knapsack were crammed in amongst the barrels. The drayman put out his arms for the baby and Helen clambered up. There was a rug on the seat. “Put that over your knees; it will be mighty cold, I'm telling you,” he said, before handing Jack to her.

The drayman swung himself up on to the seat beside Helen and tightened the reins. The geldings, knowing exactly what had to be done, barely needed prompting as they plodded along the High Street. For Helen this was a new experience, seeing the town from up high as they turned into Ness Road, and then took the road to Dungeness. Soon the houses and shops of Lydd were behind them as the dray cart left the town.

The fields either side of the road were barren; the soil sparse, nibbled by sheep who were heavy with lambs. The cloudy sky allowed the sun little chance to break through, so it offered no warmth, no golden colouring, to the landscape. It was as if Romney Marsh slumbered, still reluctant to send out fresh shoots for spring. But the one-dimensional, almost featureless land held some interest for Helen, as this was a view seen before only through the misted windows of a motorcar. Now she noted patches of shingle appear through the rough grass, and the occasional cottages and farmhouses could be viewed in more detail. Surely this was the flattest place on earth, Helen mused.

As the dray horses plodded on, in no particular hurry, and Jack's interest was focused on the wails from the swooping gulls, Helen noted the shingle patches increasing. Soon there were more stones than grassy areas and fewer sheep searching for nourishment. Bolderwall Farm was passed, and the road became a single track. Helen tightened her grip on Jack with her left arm, while her right hand clamped the bar in front of her seat, as the dray swerved into a passing place to allow a motor-lorry to pass. The landscape slowly began to change again, with water-filled gravel pits appearing on both sides of the road. As the sun broke through its cloud cover the water was no longer lifeless grey but a bold, glistening steel and suddenly the birds were not featureless dots but hundreds of glistening pearls.

Stopping at the Southern Railway crossing gates, Helen had her paperwork scrutinised and they moved on again. The dray passed over the miniature railway track, cutting its way through the road *en route* to Dungeness Station. Again, they paused, and papers were shown before they were able to proceed into the restricted area.

In a world where so many things were becoming easier, with more motorcars on the roads, electric washtubs in some sculleries and portable gramophones in front rooms, the journey from Lydd to Dungeness had been much harder since 1937 when mainline passenger trains no longer ran to the desolate coastal village. In 1894, Helen's grandmother, Alice, had been able to travel by steam train to Dungeness, via Lydd, from Ashford. In the 1920s, Aunt Lily had made the same journey. It was a comfortable trip and took only twelve minutes from Lydd. Now, here was Helen on the brewery dray, open to the wind and rain, and preparing to suffer the rough road ahead.

Helen had taken the train from Lydd to Dungeness during every holiday she had spent with Aunt Lily and Uncle Charlie. To visit the family friends who lived on the remote shingle headland had been part of the adventure. It remained a magical place in her mind and, as a child, she day-dreamed about one day having her own round-topped, railway carriage home.

And even now, although forced to arrive by cart, rather than train, she felt the old excitement running through her.

With her mind still on the steam train, Helen reflected on the last time she had sat in the carriage as the tank engine pulled into Lydd Town Station; she had been heartbroken, grieving for her husband. She still thought of him daily and missed him dreadfully, but life was busy now and full of new experiences.

The dray veered to the right and The Pilot Inn came into view: a single-storey building where the men of Dungeness could spend an hour or more with a drink in their hands. It was a strange sort of place, not at all like the ancient inns that slumbered in country villages or the taller, brick-built public houses to be found in the town centres. The roof of the saloon bar of The Pilot was formed from the upturned hull of a ship. And perhaps the skeleton of that ship was lurking somewhere amidst the ramshackle collection of extensions and annexes that had been added on over the decades, or even over the centuries, if rumours were to be believed. It was as if that original building had carbuncle after carbuncle growing upon it, until it became the absurd mixture of styles it was now.

"Here we are," the drayman remarked. "Not the easiest of journeys."

"Oh, it was fine," Helen lied. Her arms ached, one from being stretched out in an attempt to keep her balance by clinging on to the bar in front of her, the other from clamping Jack in a vice-like grip.

The baby had remained placid throughout the journey. His attention had eventually become fixed on the rise and fall of the horses' rumps and the swaying of the harness; later he fell asleep to the sound of the beating hooves and the erratic rhythm of the cart on the concrete track. The geldings didn't seem to need any commands as they slowed and came to a halt by the back door of the pub. The landlord, a ruddy-faced man of indeterminate age, appeared, as if by magic, and raised a hand in greeting. “I don't remember ordering these two,” he joked.

“She's bound for the Brooks Cottage,” the drayman replied.

“Fair enough,” the landlord said, as he stepped up to the dray. “Can I take the baby for you?” He offered his arms to take the sleeping child.

“Thank you.” Helen gave a grateful smile and passed Jack into his arms. She lowered herself until she stood on the road, feeling the solid concrete underfoot and grateful to be standing on firm ground after the journey. The pram was placed beside her, and the baby lowered into it, still swaddled with blankets.

The young woman stood, just for a moment, and took in her surroundings. Beyond the pub, a selection of single-storey wooden homes sat on the shingle. Not in rows, with paths, as they did in Ashford, and even Lydd, but placed just wherever it suited the person who built the property. There were no obvious plot boundaries and, as well as the cottages, there were various other buildings, or remains of buildings – privies, sheds for fishing equipment and brick tanning coppers. Some of the homes had ladders leading to doorways up high in the lofts; Helen knew these were where nets were stretched out to dry.

It was a familiar scene and one Helen had known all her life. Whereas her hometown of Ashford had changed as new houses were built, motorcars filled the roads and shops became filled with modern goods, the shingle headland remained unaltered. The wind from the sea was brisk and the heat from Emily's range beckoned, so Helen gave her thanks to the drayman and started to push Jack onwards in his pram.

The screech of gulls caused her to pause and look back. For a moment she studied the buildings behind her: in contrast to the traditional dwellings there was a row of terraced coastguard cottages. These would sit comfortably in any town or village, but here at Dungeness they stood out as being too tall, too regular, for the unique landscape. And, closer still to The Pilot, was the brick-built Watering House, providing a source of water, not for the cottages but for the ships using the busy lanes of the Channel.

These cottages and the Watering House were all oddities in this place where single-storey plank homes and even redundant railway carriages were the norm. The road she took would eventually lead to the lighthouse, but Helen and Jack were spared a long trek in the sharp wind. Emily Brooks lived amongst the community of fishing families whose homes gathered close to the Pilot.

The pram lurched over the tracks of the narrow-gauge railway and again Helen was recalling scenes from the past when Uncle Charlie and Aunt Lily would take her first on the mainline railway, and then on the miniature trains of the Romney, Hythe and Dymchurch Railway. They would go to Littlestone and walk to the seafront, and Charlie would treat them all to tea and cakes in Dormy House Hotel or Pope's Hotel. Helen's parents would look on, unsure if their children were being a little too greedy, worried that Charlie's extravagant ways would lead them to be spoiled! This railway was now closed to day-trippers for the duration of the war: *A phrase I hear all too often now,* Helen reflected.

At last she faced Brooks Cottage but, as she knew from her visits over the years, there was no path leading directly to it. In the past, it had been no trouble to skip over the stones. But with a baby in a pram, a knapsack and another bag, the short route from road to front door was daunting.

Helen stalled, uncertain. There was the cottage: built from tarred planks with a corrugated-iron roof and matching windows to either side of the front door. The eaves came down low, spanning a narrow veranda to the front. It was a welcome sight, but now she must leave the pram and bag, and first carry Jack. Then she could return for the pram if it hadn't toppled over in the wind. Helen gripped the handle a little tighter.

"Are you all right, love?"

Helen started and turned to see Ernest-the-milkman from Pipers Dairies with his horse and cart. "I didn't even hear you coming," she said.

"It's Helen, isn't it?" The milkman got down from his cart and continued, "You're Lily Scott's niece, who's been staying these last few months."

"That's right."

"You must be going to visit Emily Brooks, with her hurt ankle." There wasn't much that a local delivery man didn't know.

"I am, but..." Helen looked at the pram and then the stones.

"How about you carry the baby and I take that pram?" the milkman offered. "I'll pop the milk on the doorstep afterwards.

"Thank you." Helen smiled her gratitude and lifted Jack out.

And so, when the milkman rapped on the door, Emily was surprised to find the pram being delivered, along with Helen and the baby.

"Looks like you've got visitors!" Ernest announced. "Now isn't that nice?"

"If you'd like us," Helen said.

"If I'd *like* you?" A smile washed over Emily's face. "You're a sight for my weary eyes. Come on in."

Helen stepped into Brooks Cottage and a feeling of being at home spread over her. The warmth from the range comforted her chilled body and the traditional layout of an open living area in the typical Dungeness home reminded Helen of the pre-war era.

She had brought her fiancé, Jack, when they were first engaged, to meet the family at Dungeness. They had sat at the central table, with the mismatched chairs, and watched as Emily filled the large brown teapot, then covered it with a knitted cosy. That was just months before Ed Brooks had died. Once a tall, strong man with thick eyebrows over almost black eyes, he had become frail and lop-sided following the stroke.

Now, she placed the sleeping Jack in the pram, and looked about the room. It was just as Helen recalled: the knitted blankets thrown over the back of chairs, the rag rugs on floorboards, the large pine table and easy chairs. There were doors to the bedrooms but, unlike her home in Ashford and that of Aunt Lily, the privy was still outside in its own plank shelter.

Emily, seated in an armchair with a blanket over her knees and one foot raised on a stool, looked thinner than ever. Her face was pale and the skin around her eyes looked bruised. Her hair, still auburn although streaked with grey, was tied back into a loose bun at the nape of her neck. She didn't look like the woman who had taken charge when Jack's arrival seemed to be imminent, and the family were caught up in the horror of Charlie's death.

"Lily thought I could come and help out," Helen said, sitting down on a chair facing Emily. "You need to rest that ankle so it's my turn to look after you."

Helen pulled back the curtains in the bedroom Aunt Lily had used when she stayed at Brooks Cottage during her first visit to Dungeness seventeen years before. Her eyes followed the shingle ridge, with fishing boats sitting high upon it. This was her third day with Emily and the first in which the sea sparkled blue, with the promise of warmer spring days to come.

The stones, the sea, and the boats. In many ways, this was the view Lily had looked upon. But now Helen stared out upon the front-line, a dangerous and unwelcoming place for the enemy to land. The foreshore was fortified with scaffold poles, laced with barbed wire. Hidden within the shingle beach landmines littered the area and civilians were forbidden to set foot there. Already in the first eighteen months of war, this strip of beach, rich with explosives, had caused many casualties. It wasn't humans who paid the price of straying beyond the barbed wire; it was goats, brought in for food, and dogs who were the innocent victims.

Fishermen, who already faced the perils of the sea, had permits to fish between sunrise and sunset and took risks with mines in the sea and enemy aircraft flying overhead. On previous visits, Helen had seen the barriers of coiled barbed wire, which acted like a gate, being opened during the day to allow access to the boats and pulled across at night. The fishermen now played their own part in the home guard and went to sea with rifles at hand; but what protection could they give against the guns mounted in the Luftwaffe fighters?

The shared washhouse was no different from when Lily stayed here, or even when Helen's grandmother, Alice, had lived at Dungeness. A fire burned under a copper, heating water pumped from the pipe driven down some six to eight feet into the shingle. Wooden tubs were stacked ready to be filled with hot water when needed, while slender dollies were on hand to agitate the clothes as they soaked. There were a couple of mangles on the floor and a washboard hung on the wall.

Helen was now responsible for washing the clothes for the extended Brooks family, so planned to use the washhouse several times a week, rather than just on the traditional Monday. As she walked across the shingle, a bucket of nappies in her arms, she paused on hearing the familiar sound of a miniature steam engine approaching. She eyed it with mild curiosity: like an armoured beetle, it moved at a steady pace, its destination guided by iron tracks. As children, there had been some competition among her and her cousins to be the first to guess the name of an approaching train correctly. It had been the first stage of a day trip to New Romney: the glimpse of an approaching one-third size engine with its ribbon of small coaches – then waiting for it to approach near enough for the colour and details to come into focus. Helen had always paused, not called out random names, until she was almost certain of the engine.

Had she been in a group and not alone, there would have been no competition. Only Hercules served the light railway now and this was not the engine Helen knew. This was Hercules in her suit of armour, not with coaches of tourists but with two specially designed wagons, one before and one behind the engine and her tender. And from these wagons, guns poised, pointing upwards. The railway, built by an eccentric millionaire, now played its own part in the war since being requisitioned in 1940.

Hercules moved on, her pace steady, and Helen, with a basket of washing under her arm, turned and walked to the communal washhouse.

Twenty minutes later, and this time with wet washing in her basket, Helen trudged back towards the cottage. Now another sound came to her ears: a faint drone, no louder than the persistent buzz of a house fly. It caught her attention, and she studied the sky to the west. There it was: a lone speck in the sky; no larger than the fly of which it reminded her. Enemy aircraft? It was too soon for Helen to be sure. Instinctively, she backed towards Brooks Cottage, her eyes focused on it, hoping to be reassured as it neared her. The sound of the engine grew steadily louder and, as the plane neared the coast, it seemed as if it would pass directly above her.

Helen stepped on to the veranda, which ran along the seaward side of the property. The low roof and timber supports gave a false sense of safety; they shielded her a little from the pilot's sight. She kept her eyes fixed on the slender shape, with a boxy cockpit and gentle curves to the wing tips; how small it looked, how fragile, suspended there in the sky. Its colouring was a war-time camouflage of patchy grey with a splash of yellow to the underside of its wing tips and, as it tilted a little, Helen gasped. Her hand flew to her mouth as she noted the swastika on its tail.

There was no longer any doubt that this was a solitary enemy aircraft. Where was it bound for? What business did it have to be here, flying over the Dungeness peninsular? These thoughts flitted through Helen's mind as the plane passed overhead and a black cross, edged in white, flashed above her. She realised the plane was low in the sky, much lower than those usually passing over. It was going quite slowly too, almost faltering, as if the pilot had some special interest in the area. What might he be wanting in this remote corner of Kent?

Then it was gone and, still pressed close against the tarred plank wall, Helen peeped around the corner of the cottage, following the intruder's progress while the roar of the engine still beat in her ears. A feeling of dread grew within her. It caught in her throat, pressing and blocking. It blanched the skin in her face, causing it to tighten over the cheekbones. The fear forced a moment of inactivity, and an image of Jack asleep in the pram became the only thing to fill the young mother's mind.

Barely imperceivable, there came a second engine noise. Not from the sky, but the ground. It was that clanking, steaming beast Hercules on her return journey. Helen frowned to see the enemy plane lower itself a little in the sky. The engine remained unseen, but in her mind's eye, Helen visualised the guns on the armoured wagons and the soldiers from the Somerset Light Infantry who traversed this length of narrow-gauge track between Hythe and Dungeness.

Did the soldiers' hearts race, she wondered? Were their limbs flexed, poised to fire at the lone plane? Did the long barrel of their guns follow the Messerschmitt's progress as they kept it firmly within their sights?

Helen did not hear a shot; she was sure of it. But afterwards she almost convinced herself there must have been one. How else could it have happened?

However much she tried to put the events in sequence, she couldn't. It was all too fast, too unexpected.

An almighty scraping crunch of metal became the only noise to be heard. Then the ear-splitting sharp smash of the wingtip skimming the ground. Helen was racing now (how did her legs carry her?) to the concrete track. The Messerschmitt up-ended; it flipped, spun with its underbelly showing, then righted itself as it smacked down on the shingle. Yet it was not "right" – this creature should be in flight, not smashed upon the stones.

In the aftermath of the twisting, spiralling, drunken dance, there came a new gut-wrenching sound as metal was torn from metal, rivets released their hold, and the plane gave up the fight to stay whole. Helen almost felt the pain searing through her body as one wing separated and began its own erratic dance across the shingle before flopping in the throes of death and giving a final shudder.

Time slowed and still Helen looked on: Hercules came to a halt; the propeller let out a metallic "ting" as it lost its grip on the nose of the plane; the gulls let out a cynical burst of cackling laughter. Suddenly Helen was aware of the sounds of the sea: the slapping of waves on the shore, and the whoosh as the tide pulled the shingle back with it. The rhythm of life continued, as it always did. Not for the pilot though, his time was over.

As those thoughts weighed upon Helen, a tentative spiral of smoke began to rise from the Messerschmitt. It curled about itself, looking like nothing much, but enough to stop the men from the train and those from the army who had been making their way towards the wreckage. As she wrapped her arms around her body,

Helen's mouth dried. She knew it was imminent, but it didn't stop her heart from jumping when the explosion came, and the plane was finally ripped apart by the intensity of it. In the aftermath of the fireball even the gulls fell silent. After a while Helen turned her back on it, picked up the washing basket and stepped towards the washing line.

To the west, purple clouds gathered, putting an end to the promise of fair weather. As the army set out to search the wreckage for any sign of the pilot, torrential rain began to fall. It hindered their efforts as they slid on the wet stones and impaired their vision. The burned carcass of the fighter plane was hammered by the rain, washing it clean overnight. The men, on seeing the gnarled remains of the Messerschmitt, could assume only that the pilot had perished and muttered something about returning the next day to confirm this and complete the necessary paperwork.

Back in Lydd, the amateur artist strolled through the churchyard. He thought of his wife's words but was compelled to put his mark on the paper and to show his impressions of the damage caused by the bomb.

Chapter Five
A few minutes before – The Pilot

Karl Meyer fingered his newly acquired silver flying clasp. The wings of oak leaves spanning from the laurel wreath represented sixty flying missions. He traced angular lines of a tiny swastika located at the base of the wreath. He thought of the swaggering young pilots who wore their badges and clasps with such pride. Was there any glory to be gained from being a part of this war? At least he wasn't a bomber pilot; it would have been intolerable to knowingly kill so many innocent civilians. Perhaps the war would be over before he earned his gold clasp. But he doubted it; the British were proving to be formidable opponents.

He yawned and wriggled in his pilot's seat, his elbow touching the frame of the Messerschmitt. He could feel the chill of metal, even through the sleeve of his leather flying jacket. Karl had suffered a rough night; he should have been grateful to be sleeping in his narrow bed at Juvincourt. The airfield had been quiet, slumbering peacefully. He'd had a long day, looking on as ground crew made some repairs to the plane's engine, but had managed only an hour's rest before the night terrors began, wrenching him from what had been a deep sleep and leaving his heart pounding as he wrapped his arms around his body and tried to breathe slowly, drawing the air in, filling his lungs completely.

It was the same dream as usual: looking on from the boxy cockpit of his fighter to see the Spitfire on the tail of his cousin's Heinkel 111 bomber. Backing off, hoping to aim his own machine guns at the British plane while it concentrated on its own prey. Faltering, knowing that if the Spitfire began to plummet to its death, it could well take the more cumbersome bomber with it. Then, as the shadow of a second Spitfire appeared above him, his body chilled and his mouth dried before he instinctively pushed the control column forward and over to the left, kicked in the left rudder and sent his Messerschmitt down in a fast spiral to throw the Spitfire off his tail.

But, as he plunged and twisted erratically, avoiding the Spitfire's bullets, Karl saw the bomber's tail end and wings were peppered with bullet holes and a thin trail of smoke was spiralling from the fuselage. The Spitfire backed off – no doubt it was under threat from one of the German fighters. In his nightmare, which came most nights, he saw the clenched fists of his cousin as he battled to keep the Heinkel steady with half the wing hanging loose, useless and cumbersome. Then his cousin, the pilot, was no longer strong and fit, one of Hitler's prime specimens. In Karl's dream, he was just a boy, a small boy with a fishing rod and scuffed knees. And Karl was there with him, with a net for the fish and a bucket.

In the dream, just as they had three months beforehand, the white cliffs of Dover loomed, and the Heinkel bomber lost height. It was too late to turn back to France; at best his cousin would land on the fields of Kent and survive, living out the last years of war in an English prisoner of war camp. But best didn't happen: the plane lost too much height and smashed into the top of the cliffs, pounding on the chalk and sending huge shards into the air. Then, it bounced back and spiralled to the base of the cliffs, diving nose-first on to the rocks and stony beach.

Karl could see the face of his cousin, bruised but at peace, while the grey waters of the Channel lapped at the stricken bomber. And the trail of white smoke still twisted and turned upwards, all the way to heaven, taking the souls of the Heinkel's crew with it.

For how long must his nights be plagued by these dreams? Karl could speak to no one; it was not the Nazi way to show weakness. No, he must exact revenge. He must be a part of conquering the British Isles, the last great country of Europe still standing in the way of Hitler's dream of supremacy, even if his heart wasn't in it. Really all he desired was to go back home to his small village on the banks of Lake Obersee, surely one of the most beautiful places in the world, to keep chickens and a goat in a small paddock. He had simple tastes and no wish for great things in life.

Alone in the cockpit, somewhere mid-way across the Channel, Karl yawned again. He wriggled his feet in fur-lined boots, trying to keep his toes warm. A tickle on his skin irritated an area of his face under his oxygen mask; he tried to ignore it but eventually attempted to rub at it with a gloved finger. The young pilot shifted a little in his seat.

Karl had flown many of his missions during the day, then at night when the Luftwaffe changed its strategy. Today was a rare attack on Portsmouth, a naval base and town on the south coast of England. It wasn't his place to question the reasoning behind this attack when night-time raids had been in favour for some time. He was one of several fighter pilots escorting the Heinkel bombers. So far, no RAF planes had intercepted them, but there was still time. He checked his instruments as he flew into dense grey cloud.

"Do you think of me?" Karl muttered to himself, thinking of Monika, daughter of the mayor in his home village. They had been close to reaching an understanding before he had left to join the Luftwaffe. He had enlisted just before people started asking awkward questions. Before he was forced to go. "Where is the photograph you promised?"

She hadn't sent it, or he hadn't received it, making him question her commitment. Yet she still wrote him a letter every week, or most weeks anyway. Actually, there hadn't been one in the last month. The only photo in the breast pocket of his flying jacket was one of his parents. A stiff, serious likeness of them, posed for in a studio. He didn't like it; he would have preferred a more natural image.

The clouds wrapped themselves around the plane; Karl could just make out the other fighter to his left, and below them one of the larger bomber planes. The engine of his plane roared behind him and the whirring of the propeller blades soothed him; he found their constant movement comforting. Karl let his eyes close, just for a few seconds.

"*No*!" The pilot shuddered and his eyes sprang open. His heart was pounding, and he looked to his left, the bomber and fighter were still there. He hadn't been asleep; he had merely closed his eyes. Still no resistance came from the British Air force; the clouds made dull flying conditions but kept the Luftwaffe hidden. The plane was holding itself steady. Unknowingly, the pilot's right arm pressed down a little on the control wheel as his eyes closed again.

When he woke, Karl knew immediately that something had gone very wrong. The cloud cover was now light, and land was in sight: a shingle peninsular, its nose rounded, and a smattering of small buildings with a lighthouse. He frowned. He had been expecting to fly over Kelsey, but there he would have looked down on sandy beaches with groynes pointing out to sea. He was off course, and worryingly so.

"Beachy Head?" he muttered. But even as the words were said, he knew this view was far from the chalk cliffs and rolling downland of Sussex. Karl frowned. "Dungeness?" Yes, that was it. "Please God, don't let me be that far off course."

Looking to the left and right, Karl knew his search for his fellow aircraft to be fruitless. As his mind digested the predicament he found himself in, the Messerschmitt continued onwards. But what was that, moving along the coastline? A train, yes, a train. But it was so small; Karl looked at his altimeter and, reaching forward, he gave it a tap.

"Damn." It wasn't working. Hadn't he spoken to the ground crew about this only a few days ago? It was showing him to be at the height he was meant to be flying at but was clearly wrong. The train and its tracks looked to be no more than toys; he must be at least twice as high as he should be.

Karl began to let the fighter drop in the sky, while keeping his eye on the tiny grey engine. What should he do? If he were to turn about and return to the Juvincourt airfield in occupied France then, with no reasonable excuse for his not being a part of the attack on Portsmouth, he was sure to face disciplinary action. And the Nazis were not known for being lenient with those who made foolish mistakes.

There were some fishing boats out on the grey sea. He would not mind betting that the coastline was dotted with mines; they must risk their lives every day in order to continue to bring in the fish. And they would carry on; the British did not like to show their fear. He could swoop low and put some holes in their boats, but that wasn't Karl's style. He would shoot only to save his own skin, or when on a mission. He wasn't on a mission now; he was well off target and unsure about how to proceed.

"I'm still too high," Karl whispered the words. "It's so small." The engine was still moving smoothly along the track. He could see now that it had a wagon at either end, one being pushed, and one pulled. They were all grey, the engine and the wagons – well camouflaged on the stony landscape, he thought.

He tapped the altimeter again, but it wouldn't reset to give him his true height. He was swooping over the stony beach now; there was a woman sheltering under a veranda. Did she think he couldn't see her? She must be a rather large woman; in fact, she was huge in proportion to the train.

Sluggish from lack of sleep, confused by how to remedy his mistake in having lost his squadron, reality took time to put itself in any logical order in Karl's mind. As he descended over a concrete road, he finally came to realise that it was not that the woman was of gigantic proportions, it was that the train was small. Very small.

As he passed overhead, Karl looked down at the helmets of soldiers in the wagons and at the angular shape of the engine. "It's armoured," he said to himself, as he realised what a unique sight was below him.

Glancing at the altimeter, Karl suddenly became

aware that it hadn't failed, that it was he who had failed to judge his altitude, and now his fascination with the steam engine had led him to be dangerously low. The wing dipped a little; the plane didn't function so well at this height. On what appeared to be a dead flat landscape, the plane closed in on a shingle ridge and its underbelly skimmed it, sending shockwaves through the metal body and causing the cockpit to shudder violently. The last thing Karl remembered was the Messerschmitt tilting to one side, then rolling, followed by the ear-splitting noise of metal being wrenched apart as the wing was ripped from the body of the plane.

Chapter Six
March 1941

"They say there's no sign of the pilot," Edward told his mother and Helen. He had been out fishing with his son, Ben, when the Messerschmitt had flown over.

"He'd be burned to a frazzle," Emily commented.

"Oh, *Ma*!" Edward shook his head.

He was a gentle man, Helen reflected. You had to be tough, living here at Dungeness and there was no doubting Edward's strength, but his character was easy-going and friendly. With his dark hair and deep brown eyes, his likeness to his late father was obvious. But Ed Brooks had been known for his flashes of fiery temper while his son had a peaceable manner. However, when the call for the lifeboat came, Edward would show his underlying steel. He would be alongside the others, risking his life on the turbulent sea, like his father before him. Now with his son beside him, he fished the mine-ridden waters. He rolled his eyes at the image of the burned pilot, but Edward faced his own terrors on a daily basis and had witnessed many deaths at sea over the decades.

"It's what he deserved," Emily continued. "Coming over here and frightening ordinary people."

"I was doing the washing," Helen offered. "I saw him fly over. I wonder what he was thinking in those final moments."

"He was a human being following orders," Edward said. "Just like our men flying over there. It's all wrong whoever dies – them or us."

"It is wrong," Helen agreed.

Edward changed the subject. "It's good of you to come here with Jack and keep an eye on Ma. Grace doesn't want to give up her war work."

"I'm glad I could help," Helen replied. She stood at the table and reached across to unwrap the plaice, gazing for a moment at its almost translucent brown spotted scales. "This will be lovely fried for supper, thank you." The fish's eyes gazed past her – preparing it to be cooked wasn't a task she relished.

"Well," Edward said, pushing his chair back. "I'd best get home now. Ben was tidying the boat and the fish are on their way to Ashford. You take care, Ma; rest that ankle while you're lucky enough to have Helen here."

Helen's fourth day at Dungeness brought with it the urge to have a break, to stride out and explore the shingle landscape. Hampered by the lack of smooth tracks or paths, she had only been able to wheel Jack along the concrete road that followed the coast as far as the lighthouse. Now she recalled Lily's mention of some form of baby sleigh to be borrowed from the Light Railway. Helen pictured the smiles and gurgles of joy coming from her baby as he experienced a new form of travel.

"Of course, I'll mind him," Emily smiled. "You've settled him down and he always sleeps for two hours after his midday milk."

"Thank you. I just wanted to go and explore – like we used to when we were children." Helen offered an apologetic smile.

“No need to grow up completely!” Emily replied with a grin.

Helen slipped her arms into her tweed coat and tightened the belt, before pulling a hat down low over her ears. She peeped at the sleeping baby and left the cottage. The past few days had been a round of washing and cooking, while juggling the care of Jack. It was good to be helping Emily, but marvellous to be able to venture further than the neighbouring cottages at last.

Soon Helen was standing on the concrete road with her back to the sea; she breathed deeply, pulling the salt air into her lungs. The sky was vast and almost cloudless, the shingle washed clean of any debris since the heavy downfall of the previous night.

In a dip within the undulations of this stark, stone landscape was the blackened skeleton of the Messerschmitt – a foreign creature in its final resting place, slumped awkwardly on its side. One wing still looked towards the sun; the other, now detached, lay flat and submissive. Helen had seen the plane fly low over the coastline, now she felt the need to view the remains.

It was not a feeling she could justify, or even sought to understand. Curiosity drove her to step off the concrete track and select a path over the low-lying mosses and coarse grass, taking her in the direction of the crash site. At first, she walked between the scattered cottages, not taking any particular note of their features. Their unique plank walls, shuttered windows and hatches into the loft space were well known to her and needed no further examination. Then there was the narrow-gauge railway track where Helen paused, glancing both ways before balancing on first one track, then the other, as she crossed it.

The landscape ahead was almost untouched by man: ridges of shingle stretched out in all directions and, hidden from Helen's eye, gravel pits had become lakes, a haven for migrating birds. Then beyond them, the stones gradually began to mingle with soil to become a bleak, unforgiving pastureland.

Her route rose upwards, a gentle slope but challenging nonetheless as Helen's boots slid backwards a little with every step she took. Her skirt, a plain, sensible style favoured by young women of that time, fluttered about her knees. She loosened her coat buttons, feeling the heat rise in her slender body.

And then Helen was at the top of the rise, seeing the burned carcass of the Messerschmitt laid bare. There was no one else in sight so she was free to take her time, to approach it and allow her curiosity a free rein. She took small steps, her feet sliding on the downward slope. The momentum carried her forward until, feeling like a guilty child, she reached the tail fin of the aeroplane. And, not knowing what compelled her to do so, she placed her fingertips on the blistered patches of grey and khaki paintwork. The fire had not scarred every inch of the bodywork. Although the wind was light, a loose flap swung gently to and fro, further mesmerising her.

Did he still sit there in the burned-out cockpit, its acrylic window smashed and opaque? Was he forever in a world where he searched for his prey? Was he haunted by Spitfires at his tail? Or had he returned to a better place, from a time before the war? Did the pilot now think of fishing or bicycle rides or an evening in front of a black and white film?

The bold feelings that had carried Helen this far would not take her to seek out the pilot. She had journeyed beyond her usual place of comfort and, now shying away from the main body of the plane, she walked towards the detached wing. Unaffected by the fire, and washed clean by the rain, its square yellow tip was bright, reminding her of the daffodils blooming in less hostile environments than this. There were few scuffs, and a couple of dents, but it looked strangely untouched by the trauma it had suffered.

Helen looked away. What was that dark object, lying there on the stones? Too dark for a patch of moss, too flat for a young broom bush – another part of the Messerschmitt, no doubt. Turning her back on the wing, she walked towards whatever it was, as quickly as the uneven ground would allow her.

It lay draped on the shingle, a ribbon of material still sodden from the rain. Helen knelt to study it, reaching out but not quite touching the webbing of a thin scarf. She couldn't say for certain, but perhaps it belonged to the pilot. Did it loosen itself as the plane crashed and take its chance to break free? Helen frowned, knowing that the material was not designed to do that in case it distracted or hindered the pilot.

Shrugging her shoulders, Helen trudged on up the ridge and now she could see the disused school. If she were to stride out towards it, then follow the railway tracks back towards the lighthouse and railway carriage homes, she would feel satisfied. Her legs would have had a good stretch and her lungs filled with deep breaths of the salty Dungeness air.

However, before any great distance had been built up between Helen and the scarf, something else attracted her attention. This time she was compelled to hold the thin glossy piece of photographic paper between her forefinger and thumb. Having turned it around, she revealed an image of a man and woman. It was a formal picture: the pair of them stood upright, stiff, facing the camera. Helen held the photo up to the light, hoping to see more detail. The woman had a severe central parting and coils of hair over each ear. Her stare was unyielding, her mouth a tight smile. The man, a few inches taller, sported a curling moustache; his dark hair was neatly slicked into place. He too smiled as if he had to, as if it were expected. The background appeared to be rural, or perhaps they were in a studio and the scene was painted. These people were not English, Helen was sure of it.

She walked on, now drawn to a clump of stunted trees. There was no mistaking the fact that black boots were sticking out from under the bush and the brown trousers of a flying suit were lying limp over the lower part of a pair of legs.

"The pilot," Helen whispered. A German pilot: she had never seen a German before. Not that she could recall anyway. Did he look like the man in the photo with a fancy moustache and greased-down hair? "Don't be foolish," she scolded herself. If it really were the pilot lying there, then he had been through a horrific ordeal and would not be all pristine, as if in a photo.

But if it were the pilot, would he be armed? Perhaps. But would he be fit and able to harm her? She doubted it. The feet had not moved at all and it was not as if it were possible to approach in silence when the stones rattled about underfoot. Helen looked about her and spotted a short, but sturdy branch. She took a few steps and bent down to pick it up; it could offer a little protection.

Helen continued to approach the body, her own tense and heart pounding. On reaching within a yard of the boots, there was still no movement, and no more could be seen unless she were to kneel and peer right into the bushes. So instead, she sidled around the undergrowth, suspecting that there would be an opening.

Sure enough, there was a withered area of the bush, and the upper half of the pilot could be seen. He lay on his side, his head resting on his arm. The leather of his flying jacket looked to be tucked up about the waist, as if he hadn't the energy to straighten it, making his resting position awkward. His cap was missing, or perhaps it was the scrap of material Helen could see acting as an inadequate pillow? The pilot's hair looked greasy, or damp; it lay in uneven waves, some falling across his forehead. Had it been washed and dried, Helen imagined it to be a light brown colour. His skin was fair, clean-shaven, with some freckles scattered across his nose and cheeks. Eyelashes curled, thick and long.

Gazing at the sleeping pilot, for she felt sure he was still alive, Helen's heart began to calm. Sensing her presence, the young man opened his eyes and looked back at her. He held her gaze, as if waiting for her to make the next move; perhaps he saw the branch in her hand. She noted that he made no attempt to reach for any kind of weapon. Their eyes met for several seconds and, for some reason she could make no sense, Helen felt no fear.

The pilot closed his eyes again, as if this silent communication with the young English woman was as much as he could bear at that moment. It seemed that his body sagged further on to the stones. He had somehow survived through the chilling temperatures of the night and Helen feared his body could not take much more before it resigned itself to death. Most likely he was injured in some way and, without doubt, he was cold through. She crouched down a little and he opened his eyes again.

"Are you hurt?" Helen spoke slowly, leaving a pause between each word.

"Hurt?" he replied, frowning a little, as if it pained him to consider such a simple question. "I think not. Just my ankle, a little."

"Cold?" Helen asked.

"I am cold," he confirmed. "Very, very cold."

"You speak English," Helen said and then felt foolish for stating the obvious.

"A little. My Grandfather was English…" His voice began to fade away.

This was too much for him, Helen realised. She reached into the pocket of her tweed coat and pulled out a square of bread-and-butter pudding, solid and nutritious, that she had been saving for herself. Having unwrapped the greaseproof paper, she broke it into four pieces, took some in her fingers and offered it to the pilot. He reached forward and took it, giving a slight nod of thanks. She gave him three pieces before he declined a fourth.

"You have some," he said, looking at the pudding then into her eyes.

Helen considered this and then shook her head. "No, I have no need for it."

It was as if he reflected on her words for a moment before allowing himself to eat the rest.

"Thank you. This is truly kind," the pilot said, again allowing his eyes to close.

Helen gazed at him. She wondered how old he was. Had he left a wife and family at home? Had he already been reported missing, presumed dead?

"Water? Do you need water?" she asked. He must do. Even as she crouched low on the shingle, Helen could see the roofline of the Dungeness School, recently closed down for the duration of the war. There was a pump there; she could get him some.

He nodded. It seemed as if sleep threatened to overcome him.

“I'll get you some,” Helen said, pulling herself up to full height. “I won't be long.”

Turning her back on the pilot, she scurried off across the stones, walking on the patches of rough grass whenever possible, to increase her pace. Soon Helen was nearing the school, which was quite substantial, compared to the wooden homes here at Dungeness. It was a Victorian building, yet not built in the style so often found in towns and villages throughout the area. Rather than brick-built, with tall windows and a stately air, this school had white painted walls under a tiled roof. The main school room, with its slightly higher roofline, made up the main part of the building and other rooms led off the back and at right angles. There were numerous chimney stacks and a small cupola for a bell.

Closer inspection showed that in just the last year, since it had been abandoned, the building was beginning to suffer from the weather. On the main roof of the schoolroom some tiles had come loose, and part of a chimney stack had fallen, causing further damage. One of the windows of the bedrooms within the teachers' accommodation had several panes of glass missing or broken. Something else was different, and at first Helen couldn't recall what was missing. But, of course, the smart little picket fence, once surrounding the whole school, was gone. Presumably it has been taken to be used as firewood. It was no longer safe to walk the beaches in search of driftwood, and where else could such fuel be found in this landscape sparse of natural vegetation?

Passing the eastern end, Helen saw the two doors: one for boys and one for girls. She smiled, knowing they both led to the same space inside. How sad for the children who had to leave this school, many of them being evacuated to different areas of the country.

Towards the further end of the school building, amongst the privy and the storerooms, Helen could see the pump. But what could she put the water in? Opening the door to a shed, she looked at the collection of buckets, tools, rope, and any number of useful things. There, on a ragged wooden shelf, was a wide-mouthed, glass milk bottle – a little dusty and home to some dead earwigs, but nothing that couldn't be remedied by flushing it out with clean water. Helen picked it up.

The pump handle was very cold, sending shivers along her arms. She had been warm from the exertion of reaching the school. But now, standing with her hand on the metal bar, and realising that it was resisting the pressure she placed on it, Helen suddenly felt icy. She tried some short, sharp movements and the handle began to give a little. At first no water flowed but she felt sure it would come and, when it did, she allowed the first gushes to fall on the stones before filling the bottle.

Helen tightened her belt, wrapping her coat more tightly around her slim body, and turned, retracing her steps back towards the German pilot.

"What are you doing?" Albert's wife, Beryl, asked. "Nothing," he replied, pushing the sketchpad under a cushion.

Chapter Seven
March 1941

The pilot opened his eyes on hearing Helen approach. She crouched down, placing the bottle on the stones, and said: "You'll have to sit up a bit."

The look in his eyes told her how weary he was, but he still had the will to live and dragged himself painstakingly out of the hiding place under the trees. On coming into the open, his eyes flickered about, taking in the landscape.

"There is no one else here," Helen told him.

"They came looking," the pilot replied. "It was raining."

"They think you died," Helen said. "In the fire."

"I jumped out." He was sitting upright now and pointed to his ankle as he continued: "It was a – how do you say it? – an awkward…a *difficult* fall. My ankle is not well."

"No," Helen replied, uncertain of what else to say. "Drink some water. It will be good for you."

"Thank you."

They sat for a few moments, not speaking, both wondering what was going to happen next. Helen knew she must return to Jack; her walk had already been delayed. But this man needed help; he would die if left out in the cold for much longer. It was amazing he had survived the crash landing and a night of storms. She glanced towards the school; it would give him shelter at least.

"Can you walk?" Helen asked.

"I can walk," he confirmed.

"There is a building, an old school. It would be a good place to shelter."

"But the children?" he frowned.

"The children are gone; the school is closed," Helen said. "Now try to stand." She offered him her hand. She thought nothing of their being enemies; he was a man who needed help and she felt compelled to offer it. He refused her aid but gave a wry grin; it seemed he was determined to manage on his own. Watching as he stood up slowly, stiff from the cold, Helen noted that the pilot was taller than her and of a medium build; his frame was a little stocky. Curls of blond hair touched the leather of his flying-jacket collar.

Helen led the way in silence, frequently pausing. She offered no support, although she saw the man was suffering from pain in his ankle. He wanted to walk without her assistance and Helen believed it was important to him.

"My name is Karl," he said, when they were at mid-point between his hiding place and the school.

"Helen. I am Helen," she replied.

"Helen," he repeated, as if becoming familiar with the name.

It took much longer to reach the school this time and again they walked around to the back. But rather than approach the pump and sheds, Helen went up to the kitchen door and pressed on the latch; it swung open, revealing the dimly lit kitchen-cum-living area of the teachers' accommodation.

The room was still furnished with a central table

and dining chairs and a couple of armchairs. The range was still in place, black and cold, with a layer of thick dust over it. A water-stained sink housed a couple of dead spiders. There was a dank chill about the place; it was warmed by neither the sun nor the range. The curtains were drawn, but even if they had been open, only the evening sun would cast its rays into the room. Yet the pilot, Karl, nodded his appreciation. *It's better than a bed of shingle,* Helen thought.

Karl sank into a cushioned chair and began to close his eyes. But Helen, concerned about his damp clothes, would not allow him to rest yet. "Take your jacket off," she said, pointing at it and then acting out removing her own coat. He rolled his eyes but did as she said.

Meanwhile, Helen was turning the handle of a bedroom door and walking into another dark space. She pulled the curtain back a little and saw the room, as she suspected it would be, had been stripped of all bedding. *Just one blanket would help,* she thought. *He has become so chilled and needs some comfort.* There was a tall cupboard; Helen opened the door, just in case… There it was, on the shelf, a good thick blanket. "Perfect," she whispered, pulling it into her arms.

"Thank you." Karl took it. How much softer and thicker it was than the flying jacket.

Helen looked at his boots and wondered if it would be better if his feet were freed from the damp leather. Without asking, she knelt before him and began to untie the laces. Glancing up at his face, Helen saw that Karl had resigned himself to letting her help him; he allowed his eyes to close again. One of the ankles was visibly swollen, but not worryingly so. Helen felt him flinch as she eased the boot from that foot. She gazed at it for a moment before standing and going to the old pine dresser. For the second time, Helen was lucky – she discovered a first-aid tin and, in it, a roll of bandage. Deftly, she bound up his ankle; should Karl need to walk anywhere it would help.

Now conscious of the time, as it would take half an hour to walk back to Brooks Cottage, Helen returned to the pump. She filled the glass bottle and placed it on a low table beside Karl. There was nothing more she could do for him; she had neither the time nor the resources to light the range and there was no more food to leave him. But the bread-and-butter pudding had been a fair- sized portion and all she could do was hope to return with some food the next day.

"I have to go," she whispered. "I have a baby to care for, a little boy. I will bring you food tomorrow."

Karl, forcing himself to wake up, replied: "Thank you, Helen. You are very good. Your husband is a lucky man."

"My husband died," Helen said to herself, as she lifted the latch.

Helen scampered back along the path of the Southern Railway track. Sometimes she balanced on the rails, just like the school children used to do. It was quicker that way. Within ten minutes, she was warmed through and had passed the small, round-topped hut that was the station building for the Dungeness line. This is where Helen's grandmother first stepped out of a coach and started her time as a teacher at Dungeness. It was all changed now, Helen thought, and not for the first time. Why had they stopped the passenger trains, making it so much more difficult for people to travel between Lydd and Dungeness? Why would the young people want to stay here when it had become harder to reach the world away from this remote settlement?

The tracks ended and Helen passed by the curving loop of the miniature railway. This was the point where the tracks went no further across the shingle landscape and the trains returned to the small town of New Romney, then the seaside village of Dymchurch and finally to Hythe. Again, Helen was saddened by the change, but this time it was the war bringing the end of the carriages filled with holidaymakers. She felt sure they would return to Dungeness one day, fill the café with their laughter and exclaim about the unique landscape.

Suddenly, she remembered the pram sleigh. She hardly had time to go in search of it, but it would give her the freedom she craved. "Hello, is there anyone about?" Helen called, rapping on the door of the café. She had heard that a caretaker had been maintaining the buildings. "Hello..."

"Steady on," an elderly man grumbled. He opened the door a little. "We're not open for teas."

"I know," Helen attempted a smile, although he looked so fierce. "I was told you have a sleigh, or something similar, for a baby to use instead of a pram?"

"There's something like that in the store over there." He nodded towards a corrugated iron shed. "What's it to you?"

"I'm staying with Emily Brooks for a week or so, and have my baby with me," Helen explained. She really didn't have much time to stop, and this man seemed as if he would enjoy being awkward.

"Well, why didn't you say?" He began to turn away, throwing his last words back over his shoulder: "Go and have a look for yourself. You'll find it easy enough."

"Thank you. Thank you very much," Helen said, but he had already closed the door behind him.

The shed door was open and propped against the wall was the sleigh-pram, with beautifully curved runners and a box fixed on top of them – a thick blanket or two it would make it perfect for Jack. Helen pulled it out and, taking the rope in her hands, began to drag it over the stones. Within minutes she had reached the concrete road and was able to pick up her pace, eager now to return to Emily and her son as soon as possible.

"Hello my darling." Helen scooped Jack up from the floor, where he had been happily chewing on a rattle. The baby gurgled with pleasure. Helen's cheeks were red from her race along the road and the cottage suddenly felt very warm; she placed Jack down on the rug and unbuttoned her coat. "Has he been awake long?" she asked Emily.

"Twenty minutes or so," Emily replied. "He's had his bottle as good as anything and I've changed his nappy."

"Thank you so much."

"You're looking well for your walk." Emily reached across from her place at the table and poured Helen a cup of tea. "Did you find the sleigh-pram?"

"I did, but before that I went off across the shingle, like we did when we were children."

"You always did like exploring," Emily said with a smile, remembering the various members of her friend Alice's family who had visited over the past couple of decades.

"It's the best place to explore!"

"And did you see that fighter plane that got itself into trouble?"

"I did." Helen picked up Jack again and nestled her face into his chest, making him giggle as he pulled on her hair.

Although she kept herself busy during the rest of the day, including taking Jack out for a short run in the pram-sleigh, sleep was troublesome for Helen that night. She had been exhausted at bedtime, her eyelids drooping and body heavy while sitting basking in the warmth of the range. Having fallen asleep as soon as she had nestled down under the thick blankets, her mind was soon haunted by Karl's face.

In her dream Helen was back in the deserted school, and there was Karl, still sitting in the chair where she had left him. But he was no longer the young man who was able to drag himself from a shattered fighter plane, and later refuse the help of a young woman who offered her arm as he limped across the shingle. This Karl had aged until he was a faded image of his former self. His skin, originally a healthy golden colour, was now papery, translucent, lacking the glow of youth and adventure. His eyes, once a calming grey, were clouded as if cataracts had formed, hindering his vision. His body, formerly stocky and able to bear the rigours of war, was stick-like and his clothes were rags hanging over it.

She had abandoned him there in the school, unable to fend for himself. The water bottle was empty and there was little or no food. Or perhaps there was food: a few jars of preserved fruit and vegetables, high up on a larder shelf he could not reach, not with his swollen and twisted ankle. In fact, it was only the ankle, purple and yellow, which had any colour. The rest of him was ash grey; even his hair had greyed in the hours since she had left him.

In Helen's sleep, Karl gazed at her, even though his eyes were dulled. He gazed at her and moved his lips, yet no words came. She knew she had failed him, in taking him there and not being able to care for him. Everyday life would prevent her from checking on him. All he had eaten was the bread pudding, but that was now long forgotten, and his stomach no longer groaned for food. It had given up hope.

Then she was trying to reach him, slipping on the stones, making no progress. She was on the beach, with the barbed wire stretched out before her, stopping her from reaching him. Karl's face floated before Helen again, and she woke.

Her room was very dark, a dusky grey. Jack's breathing was steady; it calmed her to listen to him. But what could be done about Karl? She couldn't keep him there at the schoolhouse. Perhaps for a day or so… perhaps she could feed him and keep him warm while his ankle healed. And when he was stronger, what then?

"He shouldn't be here," Helen whispered to herself. "It's not safe."

The first silvery light of dawn was creeping around the gaps in the curtains when she eventually fell into a deep sleep. But it wasn't long before Jack was fretting in his cot and she forced herself to open her tired eyelids. She swung herself out of bed, her body heavy and head muggy. Reaching out for the baby, she felt comforted.

Five minutes later and Jack was sucking at his bottle. The gentle rhythm soothed Helen: she tried to rationalise her thoughts and fears about the German pilot. But, although she knew the night-time visions to be no more than dreams, some of the images remained vivid in her mind. As the bottle was finished, and Jack gave a milky smile, Helen knew what had to be done.

It was still early morning when Helen, with Jack on her hip, knocked on the door of the neighbouring cottage. Emily's daughter-in-law Grace Brooks, a woman of about forty, opened it. She gave Helen a smile and said: “Come on in. Is everything all right? Mum's ankle not worse, is it?”

“Emily is fine. Just fretting as she can't do everything she'd like to be doing,” Helen replied as she stepped into the living space. “But I came out early while she's still getting dressed. I wanted to have a word with you and Edward, in private.”

“Cup of tea?” Edward asked. He stood at the large kitchen table, the pot in his hand.

“Yes please.” Helen pulled out a chair and sat down, with Jack balanced on her knee. The room was warm, with heat coming off the range. She unbuttoned her coat and removed the baby's shawl.

“Something you don't want to tell Mum then?” Edward smiled. “She'd make a fuss, wouldn’t she?”

“Probably…” Helen gave an apologetic shrug.

She looked about the room. The floor was wooden with thick rugs of various colours; the furniture was solid, and the curtains hung evenly at windows looking out to the front and side. It served the function of kitchen, dining room and front parlour, all in one space and was typical of the homes at Dungeness. It was homely and traditional, yet a few modern touches were creeping in. Some of the local houses had plank walls inside, with all the ridges showing. But here they were smooth and had even been modernised with wallpaper. And, although the range remained, the old dresser had been replaced with a modern cabinet, painted in pale green and yellow, with chrome handles. The traditional butler sink and wooden draining board sat on a unit in the same green.

"I hope we can help," Edward said, putting the tea in front of Helen.

"It's about the pilot," Helen started. "The German."

"Has he been found?" Grace asked.

"Only by me, and I've been worrying about it all night." Helen took a sip of tea. "I went out for a walk yesterday, past the plane; I was going to go towards the school, and I'd only just walked by the wreckage when I saw a scarf. His scarf. Then there was a photo and then I saw him, hidden away under a thicket."

"*Alive*?" Grace's eyes were wide. Jack began to whimper. Grace handed him a finger of toast and the baby was all smiles.

"Yes, still alive, but frozen. I don't think he would have lived through another night." Helen gave an apologetic smile and looked straight at Edward. "I gave him my bread-and-butter pudding, and then I got him some water."

"He's still a human being, you know," Edward said. His expression was thoughtful, his brows knitted. "If he'd been captured, then he would have been fed."

"I know, but should I have just run off? Gone for the army or police?"

"He could have been dangerous," Grace pointed out.

"He could have been," Helen admitted. She squeezed Jack a little tighter.

"And we are the first people you've told?" Edward asked. "You didn't go to the guards?"

"That's what I must do now," Helen said. Her

stomach felt heavy. "I was going to... I was going to go to him today, give him more food. But I can't, I see that now."

"So, he's been there another night, out in the open?" Edward queried.

"No, I helped him to the school," Helen looked down at the table. "I found him a blanket and I said I would be back in the morning."

"It's not so bad, Helen. You found an injured man and you helped him." Grace reached out and put an arm around Helen's shoulders. "It doesn't matter what nationality he is."

"But I can't keep him there at the school. I can't keep him fed and warm and safe..."

"No, you can't," Edward confirmed.

"I need to tell someone," Helen said. "I feel awful about it. He trusted me, but I have to report it."

"There would be terrible trouble for you if you didn't." Edward pushed away his teacup and rose from the chair. "And this pilot, if he's a decent chap, will understand. He knows the rules."

"He is decent; I'm sure of it." Helen felt tears begin to threaten. She nestled her face in Jack's soft hair.

"We'll go and have a word with Bert; he's very active with the home guard," Edward said, now walking towards the door. "You found the pilot hiding out. Nothing more to be told. If he found his way to the school, then there's nothing to say it had anything to do with you."

"I wish I could go to him, to explain the trouble I'd be in," Helen said as she began to button up her coat. "But I know I can't. I hope he'll be all right."

"He'll get medical care for his ankle and some food." Grace's words were reassuring. "That's more than you could do for him. Now I've got to get to work and perhaps you can pop around this evening; we can have a good talk then."

"I'd like that," Helen smiled her thanks.

In his Victorian terraced house, overlooking the Rype in Lydd, Albert put the last of the pencil lines on the thick artists' paper.

Chapter Eight
March 1941

With the nappies on the washing-line and Emily dozing in her armchair, Helen was able to take Jack out in the sleigh-pram. She took a blanket and folded it several times to make a thick mattress, allowing it to curve up the sides of the box. Then she wrapped the baby in a second blanket and placed a woollen hat on his head. The pram-box was far lower than the beautiful Silver Cross pram but seemed a cosy alternative. She laid Jack down, but he immediately placed his chubby hands on the sides of the box and pulled himself upright.

"I should have known you'd do that!" Helen grinned at her son. "I know what we'll do." She returned to the living area of Brooks Cottage and took a cushion, then placed it behind Jack. "You'll be comfy now."

It was mid-morning and all Helen's thoughts were on Karl. Being stuck in the washhouse and doing the housework had been frustrating. The jobs seemed to take an age to complete, and she was tired, so made mistakes. Now she was able to move beyond the confines of the cottage and washhouse, so perhaps there would be news. *If the German pilot has been discovered, surely word of it would be on everyone's lips. But there are so few people here now; so many have gone to be somewhere safer and who can blame them? Who will I see with news of Karl?* Thoughts rattled around in Helen's mind. *The walk will do me good even if I can resolve nothing.*

There was no need to stay on the road, in fact Helen was eager to try Jack in his new mode of transport. She dragged him away from Brooks Cottage, making sure to choose a level path across the stones, before crossing the road. Then, rather than head for the open shingle, Helen decided to follow the uneven line of fishermen's cottages where there was sure to be people to talk to. Jack would enjoy any attention he got and there was always some reason to pause and exchange gossip.

The first person Helen came across was Connie Webb. "How's the young lad then?" Connie bent down and looked at Jack. In return he looked back at her and then, uncertain of the old woman with her weathered face and black shawl wrapped tight about her head, his face began to crumble, and tears gathered in his eyes.

"He's very well," Helen said, as she crouched down to offer Jack his favourite soft rabbit. "We are just trying out this old pram on runners."

"We used to see a lot of them about," Connie remarked. "But of course some of the young ones have gone now, evacuated."

"Have you any news?" Helen asked.

"There's not much I could say to interest a young woman," Connie said. "But I'll wander along to see Emily while my legs can still take me."

"She'll like that," Helen replied. "Emily enjoys a talk about the old times."

"She lived with me for a while, Emily did," Connie's eyes grew misty as she looked back over the decades. "It were a long time ago now. A very long time. Now it's just the two of us left and our husbands are gone."

"You've had some good times here." Helen tried to keep her voice bright.

"Oh, it was a hard life, but a good one." Connie nodded her agreement. "Well, this won't get me to Emily's." She began to shuffle off and then turned back and called out: "Any news, you said? There's been army people all over the place, knocking on doors and asking questions. Now there's some news for you."

Knocking on doors? They hadn't knocked on the door of Brooks Cottage, or at least Emily hadn't mentioned it. Connie had her back to Helen now and was moving at a fair speed across the stones, despite her bent spine and spindly legs.

Helen continued, taking it slowly so as not to bump Jack about too much in the wooden box. The vast sky was streaked with white clouds, but the sun shone boldly, and the wind was light. *It's good to be here,* Helen thought as she took a deep breath, allowing her lungs to fill slowly with salty air. Then she thought of her husband and his watery grave. For a moment she faltered, and then she strode on a little faster than before. *He wouldn't want us to be sad. We mustn't forget; but we must be happy*.

There were a few people at their doorways or tending the small plots where vegetables grew in soil transported to Dungeness and placed in raised beds. Helen sometimes gave a wave or nod, but there was no one who looked inclined to make conversation. With no sign of the army searching the area, Helen was led to believe Karl had been found. She needed to know for sure, but whatever news there was would not be enough, she knew that.

They were nearing the lighthouse now and Jack's eyes were heavy. He allowed himself to be laid down, with the blanket tucked tight around him and his precious rabbit against his face. Helen swung the pram-sleigh around and set off back towards the fishermen's cottages.

Halfway to Brooks Cottage, Helen saw Hazel Barton approaching. "Good morning," the older woman said. Helen knew her to be another friend of Grandmother Alice. She believed the two had worked at Dungeness School together.

"Good morning," Helen repeated. "I was wondering… about the pilot from the fighter plane." She looked towards the direction of the wreckage, and continued: "I heard that perhaps he had been found?"

"Well, they were searching all over for him," Hazel said, "and someone told my Tom that he'd been found. Not in the plane, but out on the shingle somewhere."

"Oh?" *On the shingle? Perhaps she is mistaken, for surely Karl wouldn't leave the relative comfort of the schoolhouse?* "I wonder how he managed to escape from the plane; I saw it come down, you know."

"Tom and I did too," Hazel said. "He was sitting out on the bench repairing nets and I'd just brought him a mug of ale when the plane came over. Ever so low, wasn't it?"

"It was horrible," Helen shuddered a little. "Seeing the plane like that, looking up at it." Returning to the present, she thought of Karl, alone and suffering from a twisted ankle. "But he's been found, and alive?"

"Alive? He must have been, or Tom would have said. I don't know any more, and I don't think Tom does either." Hazel reached out and patted Helen's arm, then continued: "Are you all right, love? It plays on your mind doesn't it, seeing a horror scene like that, with the flames and everything?"

"I keep busy," Helen said, looking down at Jack. "I try not to think too much. I've already lost my husband and Uncle Charlie. We just have to carry on the best we can, don't we?"

"You're right." Hazel gave a bright smile. "And you've got one of those old prams out for your little one; we all had them at one time. There's not many left now; once the babies had grown up, the boys used them to slide down the shingle banks and get up to all sorts of mischief!"

"It's lovely to talk to you," Helen said as she started to move away. "Grandmother often mentions you and the time when she worked at the school. Happy days!"

"They were," Hazel agreed. "Tell Emily that I'll be along to see her tomorrow."

"How are you, Ma?" Edward said as he entered Brooks Cottage, having given a quick rap on the door. "Not giving Helen too much trouble, I hope."

"Helen's been out for a nice walk with Jack," Emily told him. "She couldn't be happier, nowhere better in the world than being here by the sea."

"Is that right?" Edward grinned at Helen. "Well, I'm glad you got a chance to leave the washing and take Jack out. It's been a fine day."

"I did," Helen agreed. "Jack seemed happy enough in his new style of pram and I met a couple of people to say hello to."

"Connie came here for a nice chat over a cup of tea," Emily told her son. "Poor old thing. All bent she is now, but it doesn't stop her."

"You're a poor old thing yourself, Ma!" Edward bent down to place a kiss on his mother's head. "It's not going to stop you, is it?"

"He's always been cheeky, that one," Emily told Helen. "You make sure your Jack is more respectful!"

"Anyway..." Edward poured himself a cup of tea from the pot and sat down with Helen and Emily. They had been peeling potatoes, carrots, and turnips at the central table. "I've got a bit of news about that pilot. They found him!"

Helen's mouth dried. "Alive?"

"Oh yes, but he'd got himself into trouble. He'd been trying to follow the railway tracks; I don't know what he was up to. Trying to find his way off The Point, I guess."

"Probably looking to sabo...sabotage them, or whatever them spies do when they find themselves here."

"Ma! He wasn't a spy." Edward shook his head in mock frustration. "He was a pilot who crashed and was lucky to get out alive. He was stuck out on the shingle and trying to get himself somewhere safe and warm, no doubt."

"That's what he'll say," Emily replied, a frown on her wizened face.

"So, he's been taken by the army," Helen stated. "What will they do with him?"

"He'll go off to be questioned, I assume," Edward said, "then put away in a camp somewhere, until it's all over. He'll be treated well enough and know that he'll get through the war alive. He may well be one of the lucky ones."

"I suppose he will be." Helen frowned a little, her eyes thoughtful. She couldn't quite imagine what it would be like for Karl. If only she could have written him a letter, said she was sorry she couldn't help him in any way. But she was being foolish, he was the enemy. A German. Edward was right, Karl was lucky to be alive. Helen shook herself a little and turned to check on Jack, who was happily sitting on a rug and chewing his rabbit's ear.

"Come around to see us later, Helen." Edward gulped down his tea and stood up from the table. "Grace was saying she would like to see you, but she won't be back for a while."

"Perhaps when Jack is settled for the night?" Helen asked.

"Great," Edward said, as he moved towards the door. "We'll see you this evening then. Take care of yourself, Ma."

On Helen's sixth day at Dungeness, she returned from a walk with Jack to see Emily brandishing a letter. "It's from your grandmother," she announced. "It's to the both of us; Lily must have told her you were here; in fact, that's just what she says." Helen took it and sat down to read.

Dear Emily and Helen,

This morning, I received a letter from Lily, telling me about Emily's poor ankle. Helen has come to the rescue and that is marvellous news, but it can't be easy for her to manage with a baby to look after. Besides, she is a young woman and must miss her work on the NAAFI van, as well as all the company from other young women.

I have spoken with George and we both agree that I should come and keep you company, Emily. It's been five years since I last stayed with you, not long after Ed passed away. George was, at first, rather concerned about my coming to stay by the coast. But you and I know that a few bombs are nothing compared to the adventures we had when we were no older than Helen. It always does me good to remember those days, and now I look back and see them only as happy times. Although I must say, it didn't always seem like that!

I plan to arrive on the first train into Lydd-on-Sea on Tuesday. It will be lovely to see Helen and Jack before she returns to Lydd. Helen dear, please don't think I am pushing you out. I just feel that you are needed in Lydd with Lily who so enjoys your company.

I look forward to seeing you both very soon and do hope your ankle is recovering nicely, Emily.

With love to you both, Alice

"It came as a surprise," Emily said. "And we hadn't talked about you going home to Lily and the children, but of course you said a week or two when you first arrived."

"I did, and it's been a marvellous adventure to be here," Helen began. "But I do miss my voluntary work, and all the things I did in Lydd." It was time to return and Helen, who hadn't quite realised how her spirits had slumped since the discovery of Karl, followed by the worry for his safety and guilt that she had somehow been a part of his capture, suddenly felt the burden lift from her young shoulders. "I'll wait to see Grandmother and then walk along to the station afterwards."

"It will be good to see Alice and talk about the old days," Emily said. "But you've been a treasure, a right treasure and you've saved my Edward and Grace no end of bother. They don't want to be worrying about me when there's enough for them to do."

"Do you think Grandmother will be all right, with all the jobs… the laundry and the outside privy? It's not quite the same in Ashford."

"It's not the same and that's a fact!" Emily grinned, the wrinkles in her pale skin deepening. "But you'd be surprised about what your grandmother can do. She'll fit right back into Dungeness life as if she never left!"

"And your ankle is improving..."

"It is, I'm going to get myself a stick and Alice and I will wrap up and take a walk along the road and back."

"I think I'll take Jack out then; it will be his last ride in the pram-sleigh for a while."

Helen found herself drawn to the old school. She couldn't say why, and it was foolish to go all that way, but with Jack trailing behind in the pram-sleigh, she set off, taking a direct route across the shingle ridges. The sun was high in the sky, the clouds soft, with no threat of rain. If the sea-breeze was still a little sharp, then the exercise soon warmed her. Men from the army were by the burned-out Messerschmitt, and it appeared some of it had been removed from the site already. No doubt it would need to be investigated; who knew what secrets the blackened remains could offer to the British?

There was no one else to be seen once Helen left the cottages and then the crash site behind her. She was invigorated by the salty taste on her lips and the occasional swooping of gulls. The vast blue sky gave her a feeling of being very much alive and alert to all the tiny miracles of nature to be found on what at first appeared to be a barren landscape.

Soon the slate roof of the school could be seen and, as she neared the building, all the details came into focus. It saddened Helen, knowing that it stood empty; suddenly another visit seemed pointless and as if it could only dampen her spirits. It was unlikely the teachers and children would return to the school after the war, and what other use could there be for a large building so far from the normal buzz of village life? The world was changing so quickly; Helen suddenly felt very vulnerable. Nothing was certain anymore and things she believed were solid had shown themselves to be frail. People and buildings had been exposed as being fragile and unable to withstand the might of enemy bombs.

"You're nearly there now, and you never did look at the school-room last time," Helen scolded herself aloud.

And so, she found herself scooping Jack out of his unusual transport, supporting him on her hip and lifting the latch to the back door. Stepping inside, she half expected Karl to still be sitting there and her heart felt heavy when she saw the empty chair.

"Silly Mummy," she said to Jack. "He wouldn't be very happy to be left waiting all this time."

She looked about for some sign of the pilot, but there was nothing. He had left no trace of his brief stay and Helen felt saddened not to see a visible reminder of their shared time together. Not even a folded blanket on the chair. Perhaps he took it with him; she liked to imagine Karl had gained some comfort and warmth from the thick woollen cover when he decided to set off and fend for himself.

Walking to the internal door between the teachers' living quarters and the schoolroom, Helen reached out and pulled back the bolt. She pushed a little and the door swung open, revealing the cavernous space with its high ceiling. Dust motes danced in the shafts of light coming through large windows. The room smelt damp and musty, but with the familiar odour of old books and wood-smoke still hanging in the air.

Remembering a time when she had come to a church service here, Helen walked across the room to the eastern end. Her boots sounded noisy, echoing in a space meant to be full of noise: children singing, books being shuffled about, chalk on slates, the teacher's voice ringing out. Here a huge curtain hung across the room, covering the window and altar; she tugged at it a little, and peeped at the area usually revealed only for the church services. It was all rather dusty and unloved. Helen let the curtain drop.

Perhaps it was the breeze caused by the curtain that agitated the ashes in the grate, but something caused them to drift about a little before settling again. Helen frowned, aware the school had been almost abandoned with little notice, but also noting that it all appeared to be tidy, with books and slates stacked neatly. Surely the hearth would have been swept. She walked over to it, whispering to Jack as she moved about, but finding that the baby was content looking around the room.

There was something very odd about these ashes, and Helen placed Jack on the floor in order to study them more closely. They were not wood ash but – she prodded them with her finger to be sure of it – burned books. The print was clearly visible in places, along with some binding. Had Karl lit a fire? It seemed unlikely for these ashes felt damp. In fact, they had formed clumps of a soggy, clay-like substance.

Turning around to watch Jack rolling towards some desks, Helen's attention was drawn to a bundle of material pushed underneath them. She knelt and saw a collection of cushions and bedcovers, presumably taken from the teachers' bedrooms. "How very strange," she muttered. Someone else had been there, hiding out. Whoever it was appeared to have gone now, but suddenly the room felt very cold and took on an eerie feel. Helen's body felt stiff, almost frozen, and she knew she wanted to leave that very minute.

Lifting Jack, she moved towards the door and was about to step through when something caught her attention. A small object pressed up against the door jamb suddenly glinted as the sunlight caught it. Not wanting to stop even for a moment to examine it, Helen picked it up and put it straight in her coat pocket.

"Have you seen my oil paints?" Albert asked his wife. "They're not in the dresser."
"They're in a box under the stairs," Beryl replied. "But I don't know what time you've got to be bothering with painting. There's a war on, you know."

Chapter Nine
April 1941

Nancy-the-NAAFI-van plunged across the road, bounced off the kerb and came to a halt. Helen couldn't help smiling as she opened the van door. “Good morning, Annie. Nice to see you.” She hauled herself up and into the van.

“Nice of you to come back,” Annie said, as she pulled out in front of a car and raised her eyebrows at the ensuing hooting of its horn. “Have a good holiday, did you? Blimey, only just started here and you're off to the seaside already!”

“Dungeness? *Seaside*?” Helen couldn't help grinning, as she replied: “Well, you could call it the seaside, but it was no holiday. Standing in a wash-house for hours isn't much fun.”

“And you had one of them darned Mess-smitt things coming and crashing right in front of you, they say.”

“Almost,” Helen agreed. “Where are we going today?”

“I thought we'd start at Galloways.” Annie began to fling the van around in a three-point-turn. “I wonder who's there today. They were asking after you, while you were away.”

“Asking?” Helen frowned. “I don't want any man asking after me; I'm not ready for all that.”

"Just asking… wondering where you were."

"Oh, all right." Helen began to relax in the seat as Annie took the concrete track that led along the boundary of the army camp.

The sky was a blanket of white, the sun the slightest hint of pale yellow. Land on either side of the track was bleak, and the undulating shingle had little plant life on it. What flora there was seemed ragged; even the new spring growth had been beaten by the harsh salt wind, although today there was barely a breeze and the tired plants stood still. Coastguards' cottages loomed: a colourless brick terrace with outbuildings. As they neared them, they were seen to be partly broken down. More victims of the war, their inhabitants had been re-homed to Lydd.

In this lonely place there was a look-out, manned by a group of soldiers. The men very much appreciated a visit from some attractive young women, as well as a mug of hot tea, chocolate, sweets, and cigarettes. Annie brought the tea-van to an abrupt halt and the soldiers emerged from their shelter. Helen opened her door and swung herself down on to the shingle.

"Golly, what a miserable day!" They were just feet away from the sea; the air was thick with salt, but the waves could only just be seen through the mist. It merged into the low-lying cloud; a pale grey tide sluggishly rolling in and pulling back on the shingle.

"It's brighter now!" one of the men said.

"That's what we're here for!" Annie let out her familiar cackle. "But you'll have to wait ten minutes for us to get the tea made."

"Got some cigarettes while we wait?"

"Of course," Annie replied. "My mate will get them while I put the kettle on."

Helen was already lifting the hatch and fastening it, before letting the shelf fall into place. She then put out an assortment of cigarettes and hard-boiled sweets. A meagre selection, but it was all they had to offer in the army camp stores.

"No chocolate?"

"Blame Hitler," Annie called out from behind the teapot. "Have a nice cup of tea and forget about the chocolate; there's none in the store-room."

"Thought you might have some tucked away for your favourites."

"You're all my favourites, love!" Annie was now handing tin mugs to Helen, who placed them on the drop-down shelf.

Annie's cheeky replies came with ease, as the women stepped out of the van and sipped at hot tea themselves. Helen gave tentative smiles, often uneasy with the men, but aware that her role was to boost morale as best she could. Then the tea was finished, and the mugs collected; the kitchen area was tidied and made safe. Annie started the engine and soon Galloways was lost in the mist.

"Working on the land wouldn't suit me," Annie announced, as they drove along Romney Road and into Lydd at the end of the run. The comment seemed to be expressed for no particular reason. "Can you see me working all those hours, picking up potatoes or hefting dung? Imagine what my hands would look like! Shocking it would be."

"No, I can't see you working in a field," Helen agreed. "You complain enough about this old van and serving tea."

"Me complain? Not with all those army lads lined up waiting to see me!" Annie gave a low cackle.

"That's the problem with working in the fields – no men!"

"I've got to say, I'm a bit lost," Helen was forced to admit her confusion.

"It's for the land girls," Annie informed, pointing in the direction of Kitewell Lane. "They're building accommodation for them along here. That's the plan anyway: to bring the women here to work in the fields."

"Oh, I see..." Helen replied. "Lucky you have the work with the NAAFI van then."

"And that's not the only place being provided for them," Annie replied, her eyes narrowed.

"Not the only one?"

"Over St Mary in the Marsh and Brenzett. They're preparing for them there too."

"Are they?" Helen braced herself, knowing the brakes were to be applied any minute.

Annie slammed her foot down hard. "Oh yes, but poor things will be working from dawn to dusk in the mud and all sorts, I can't see them having time to be chatting up the army lads, can you?"

Understanding dawned on Helen and with a grin, she replied, "You've nothing to worry about there, Annie. They'll have no time to spend on their hair or making themselves pretty."

"Just what I was thinking," Annie said, as Helen opened the van door. "See you soon, love."

It was when Helen put on her coat the following morning that she reached deep into her pocket and her fingertips touched something cold and hard. Then she recalled the small shiny object, picked up in a hurry, as she felt the need to leave the deserted school. "What's this, do you think?" she spoke to Jack, who was sat up in the pram, waiting for the trip to the shops. The baby merely smiled and babbled his reply.

The pin, or badge, was golden in colour. With its out-stretched wings of oak leaves, it measured about three inches in width. In the centre there was a circle of leaves and – Helen had to rub it to be sure – at the bottom was a swastika. Now repulsed, she held it out a little further from her body. But what if it were Karl's? Her emotions conflicted; she was sure he was a decent man. He had done nothing to harm or scare her. Helen looked at the central arrow and wondered about the meaning of it. No, this was not a badge belonging to her pilot; she was sure of it. This belonged to another man, someone who, she was now certain, had been hiding out in the school at an earlier time. Someone who could still be in the area. The goosebumps rose on Helen's body. She took the badge and put it in a drawer in the dining room.

"Come along then," she said to Jack, as she sidled past the pram in the narrow hallway and opened the front door. "Let's go to the shops. What will Bobby say if we miss the jam ration?"

Walking into Coronation Square, Helen could not help looking at the victims of last autumn's bombing raids: a pair of dear little cottages whose roofs came down so low that the eaves rested on the ground-floor window frames, and with small dormer windows peeping out amidst moss-covered and worn roof tiles. The thick glass had not been strong enough to bear the force of a bomb and the front windows were now lifeless holes. Behind the façade, the place was now empty; the front wall and roof were a shell. The bomb had blasted into the back of the cottages, killing one old woman who refused to go to her shelter, but dozed by the fireside as the warnings sounded. If it could be seen from behind, the remains of small bedrooms under the eaves would be on show, like the view of an open dolls' house. But the staircase and beams would be charred, the plaster on the walls blistered and flaking; the furniture partly burned from the fire and mouldering from being open to the rain. Visual reminders of the war were never far away. Memories remained in people's minds and hearts.

In the same row as the houses, Hutchings General Store was an example of the endurance shown by the people of Lydd. Despite the criss-cross tape over huge windows, they too had been unable to withstand the pressure from the blast. Three had been shattered and then boarded up for a few weeks, but now they were replaced, and the window displays encouraged shoppers to come in and see what was on offer, from clothing to household goods and food. Rationing was in place, but there were still things to be bought. Helen's list included ingredients for baking and soap flakes. She eyed the display of children's clothes, but knew she had plenty of hand-me-downs in a trunk at home. Leaving the pram with two others outside the shop, Helen walked in and took her place in the short queue at the counter.

From Hutchings, Helen pushed Jack along to the post office. After all the attention he gained from passers-by at the general store, he laid himself down and cuddled into Rabbit.

"A letter to the family?" the postmistress asked, although she knew the address as well as she knew her own.

"They like to hear from me."

"I expect they miss the little man," the postmistress persevered. "Any plans to go back there? Is it any safer? It's been shocking here, as you know, what with poor Charlie Scott..."

"No plans," Helen replied, her tone a little brisk. "Four pence did you say?"

"Of course, some young mothers are being evacuated still to places like Devon. And very nice it is."

Helen pushed the coins across the counter. "Four pence."

"You feel you need to be here with your aunt, of course you do," the postmistress nodded, her expression inviting confidences.

"Good morning, Mrs Baker," Helen said, as she turned towards the door.

"They say the ghost of old Evie Stoneman haunts the cottage in Queen's Road." The postmistress gave her parting shot, as Helen pushed on the door. "And her son still walks the Galloways Road, trying to escape."

"Oh, I doubt it, Mrs Baker," Helen replied. "You know how people like to exaggerate these things."

But Helen's curiosity was fired up; Evie Stoneman and her son, Joe, were connected with the story of Aunt Lily and how she came to live here in Lydd. There had been whispers, tickling at Helen's ears throughout her childhood, about Lily having been married before. Scraps of sentences came to her young ears, things left unsaid when the adults realised she was listening to their talk.

Rather than turn the pram towards home, Helen felt compelled to retrace her steps into Coronation Square. She walked in the direction of the small cottage where Evie had lived for six months until part of it had been blasted away in the early months of the war, taking the old woman's life with it.

Having spent many hours talking with Lily, reliving

the time when she first came to the area, Helen now knew the whole story. Aunt Lily, having heard of Dungeness for the very first time, had set out to discover the place where her own mother once worked as a teacher. On arriving at Lydd, she had been given the wrong directions and walked to the remote settlement called Galloways. Having been welcomed by Evie, she was then plied with a tea known as the Galloways Grey – a special blend of leaves that grew in this coastal area and were known to dull the senses. Lily, unused to the brew, found herself confused and unaware of the significance of a forthcoming wedding. Unbeknown to her, the prospect of new blood had encouraged Evie to set her sights on Lily as a wife for her son, Joe. When Lily finally escaped from Galloways, she wore a stone around her neck labelling her as a Galloways bride. It was Charlie, a local solicitor, who had tried to sort out the trouble Lily found herself mixed up in. It took a while, but over the months Lily's affection for Charlie grew and a couple of years after her visit to the area, the pair of them married and settled in Lydd.

The army had requisitioned part of the coast, including the village of Galloways, as the war started. The inhabitants, Evie Stoneman, and several others, were forced to find homes elsewhere. The old woman, who had pressed the grey tea on the young Lily, became a victim of the war first when she lost her Galloways home and then when her new home was bombed and her life lost. She was now buried in the cemetery. The story of Joe Stoneman was a sad one: the son of Evie, he had tried to leave the area, only to be murdered before he had even left the shingle promontory. There had been tales over the years that his ghost wandered the shingle, but Helen had not heard of it recently. *What is causing the recent gossip,* she wondered. *There is sure to be some reason behind it.* Helen didn't believe in ghosts.

Jack was wheeled along the streets, passing by buildings of all ages, some war damaged and others remaining intact. Many fronted the pavement, and several had a small shop or business attached to the home. The pavements were narrow, and Helen often had to tip the pram onto the road and back up to the pavement again. She passed other young mothers and housewives in aprons, as well as older men in tin hats, doing their part for the home guard. Most had a friendly smile or a comment to share; they were determined to stay cheerful.

On passing the fire station, Helen met Emily's daughter, Allie. She was a tall, slim woman in her early forties, with a mass of dark hair streaked with grey, resting in waves on her shoulders. "How did you enjoy your stay with Ma?" Allie asked. "It was good of you to go, and I bet she loved seeing little Jack."

"It was strange to follow in the footsteps of Grandmother and Lily," Helen said. "But did I enjoy it?" She thought of the plane coming down and the discovery of Karl. "It's different, isn't it? With the war on, I mean."

"It is in so many ways," Allie replied. "But in other ways it must be just the same."

"I guess it is. But I'm back now and taking a walk while Jack sleeps."

"Isn't he a darling?" Allie bent over and gazed at the peaceful young face. "Look at him, just lying there with his rabbit and not a thought in his head about this awful war. Still, we've had a quiet few weeks since all those plane crashes last month."

"March was certainly a bad month for them," Helen

agreed. The Messerschmitt had not been the first to crash land at Dungeness that month. "It's a wonder any of them escape alive."

"It must give hope to the poor wives of the pilots," Allie said. Then her smile faded as she turned from the pram and looked at Helen. "Oh, I'm sorry, Helen. My big mouth – Army, Navy or Air Force, it's all just awful."

"That's fine. My husband has been gone over a year now, and next week it'll be six months since Lily lost Charlie. We have our children and we have to keep going." Then Helen remembered something Emily had told her. "Your mum said that you had your own loss in the Great War. You must think of it, when you see all this happening again."

"I do," Allie replied. "But it's very different this time around; it's not my sweetheart I worry over but my son. My David is leaving school in a couple of months' time; he turned fourteen in February. I can only pray he doesn't end up going to war."

"Lily told me that he is going to work at the railway station," Helen replied.

"That's right. Junior porter he'll be and as proud as anything. He's hoping to get an apprenticeship at the Ashford Engineering works though."

"That will suit him very well," Helen said. The two women spoke for a few more minutes before continuing on their way, Allie to the shops and Helen towards Evie's cottage. She walked on, past the fire station and then to the row of terraced cottages, where two on the end were now half-ruined and abandoned. There was nothing much to see: ragged curtains at windows, loose tiles, a bird taking flight from under the eaves. *What did I expect?* Helen silently admonished herself. *The ghost of Evie beckoning me in? Of course not.* But Helen had had a secret fascination with the wizened old woman since Lily had first spoken of her, and any excuse to pass by her cottage had been welcomed.

The pram was pushed a little further along the pavement. *Just so it doesn't seem as if I had come this way to look at the cottage. That is if anyone were to be watching.* Then Helen turned the pram around and passed by the cottage again, determined to give the place nothing but a quick glance. There was nothing to see but, as she turned away, it seemed as if there were some movement at the window. *It's nothing at all, perhaps an animal or a bird,* Helen scolded herself. But she could not help but feel that hidden eyes were following her. She shivered and quickened her pace.

Beryl would be queuing at the shops for some time, Albert thought. He would have time just to look at the paints and see what colours he had.

Chapter Ten
July 1941

"There's a charity ball at the Guild Hall next Saturday evening," Lily announced, as the family sat down to supper. "And I think we should go."

"Gosh, all of us?" Elsie asked.

"No, Helen and I will go," Lily said, as she manoeuvred bubble and squeak from the large pan and on to their plates. "You can look after Jack."

"You're too young," Bobby sniggered.

"Elsie can go in another year when she's sixteen," Lily said.

"I don't know if you should be going to a dance, Ma." Eleven-year-old Bobby, now man of the house, scowled at his mother.

"It's perfectly respectable, darling. And the Town Council have allowed it; they must think it safe."

"But who are you going to be dancing with?" Bobby asked. "I don't know what Pa would say."

"If Charlie were here then he'd come along with me and Helen," Lily's voice softened, as understanding dawned. "But he's not, and the war has brought terrible losses to both Helen and me, which is all dreadfully sad. Don't for a minute imagine that we don't both think of our husbands, and your father, every day."

"I don't know that I would actually want to dance,"

Helen said. Would it be awkward standing there with servicemen from all over the country waiting to partner local girls; she a widow and not quite ready for that. An image of Karl flashed into her mind, and she pushed it away. She shouldn't think of him; she would never see him again. She thought of walking arm-in-arm with Lily to the Guild Hall, rushing in so as not to let any light show at the doorway. Then the thrill of excitement to be in the room, with a band playing and low lights sparkling, and everyone having done their best to dress up for the occasion. The soldiers would still be in uniform, of course, but Helen could already see the local women, some of them in real stockings and most with carefully pencilled lines up their calves; their lips would be cherry red, and they would smell of fresh lavender or rose. "But I would like to go, if only to watch."

"Neither of us has to dance, or we could dance together," Lily suggested. "We'll go along to listen to the music and show Hitler that we can still enjoy ourselves."

"Golly, will he know?" Bobby asked, brown eyes wide.

"Of course not, silly," Elsie said scornfully. "Unless he has spies there..."

The threat of spies was, in fact, very real, with the shallow coastline of Romney Marsh being so close to France. Only last year one had even been caught in the town of Lydd, having landed in a boat at Dungeness and walked to the town in search of a drink. Doubts about this man were raised when he walked into the Rising Sun, an hour before opening hours, and asked to be served. He was one of four who had landed overnight, with the intention of reporting back the state of the coastal defences and location of the airfields. Any stranger was treated with suspicion. Looking out for spies was a great hobby for boys of Bobby's age who were frustrated about being too young to have any hope of fighting against the enemy before the war was over.

"We thought we saw a spy over in Back Lane," Bobby told them, between mouthfuls of dinner. "He was acting a bit strange, but then we found out it was Mr Whyte's brother, come to stay from Hastings."

"But *was he*?" Elsie teased. "Or was he pretending?"

"Well, he had a look about him that reminded me of Mr Whyte and his English was very good. He didn't speak funny."

"Saturday night then?" Lily looked at Helen. "What do you think?"

"I'd like that," Helen replied. "It… well, it sounds like fun."

"We'll have to make an effort to dress up," Lily said.

"Oh Ma..." Bobby rolled his eyes.

At Hutchings General Store the window displays encouraged housewives to persevere, despite the difficulties. A tailor's dummy showed a re-modelled dress, with a selection of tape measures, threads and pincushions. Bunting fashioned from dress designs was looped up high.

"Look at that old dress and what Sylvia did, smartened it up very nicely." A young mother, with a baby in a pram and another at her knees, paused alongside Helen at the window. "She's got a talent with the needle."

"She has." Helen didn't know Sylvia, but presumably she was the person who had transformed the dress with such skill. Helen had a couple of dresses she had worn in the last months of her pregnancy; with a bit of imagination perhaps they could be made into new outfits.

"We still want to look our best, even if life is a bit dull at times," the other woman said. "I've been sitting in the evenings making a new dress out of an old one of my sister's."

"We've been unpicking old jumpers to make into new ones," Helen said. "But after seeing this display, I'm thinking of making a dress."

"Are you going to the dance?"

Helen, who had been undecided up to this point, saw herself in a frock that twirled and hovered just above her knees. It would be tucked in at the waist and with a rounded neckline, or perhaps a sweetheart – yes, a sweetheart – neckline. On her feet she would wear... she considered her own sensible lace-up shoes and her neat slip-ons with box heels... she would borrow Lily's navy-blue baby-doll shoes with tapered heels and a sling-back.

"Yes, I'm going with my aunt," Helen replied. "But I'll have to hurry up if I'm to make a dress in the next ten days. I don't want to go like this." She looked down at the pre-war skirt with a front pleat, a hem touching mid-calf and a slightly worn cardigan.

"I had a nice letter from my Bill yesterday," Helen's companion informed her. "He'll be home on leave next month, or so he hopes. But there is no harm in having a dance, is there? My ma will mind the little ones."

"No harm at all," Helen agreed. "Now I had better get the shopping before Jack gets bored of sitting here waiting, and I'm going to look at patterns for my dress." She gave her companion a bright smile and stepped into the general store.

Ten days later, and feeling rather self-conscious, Helen walked into the living area of the bungalow. "Cor, you look like a cracker!" Bobby exclaimed. "I didn't know our Helen was so pretty, did you Elsie?"

"Well, she doesn't have time to go about looking pretty, like the rest of us who have to work hard," Elsie pointed out. "But of course I knew she was. She's got a lovely figure and beautiful waves in her hair."

"She's wearing Ma's shoes," Bobby observed.

"Can you two stop talking about me!" Helen laughed and gave a twirl; the hem of her frock brushed on the edge of the table as it flowed outwards.

"You really have done a fantastic job on that," Elsie fingered the navy cotton fabric, which was sprigged with small white flowers.

"A lot of it was thanks to Allie," Helen admitted. "To change a maternity dress into a dance dress was rather a lot for me to take on." The neckline was a sweetheart style, just as she had hoped. The waist was tucked in and the skirt full, thanks to the volume of material provided by the dress she had worn to Eva's wedding. The sleeves on the dress were short and showed off Helen's slim arms, bronzed by the summer sun. Her legs were finished off by the attractive sling-back shoes. Off-cuts from the material were destined to trim a summer dress.

When Lily came into the room, Bobby was more cautious in his praise, "You're looking nice."

"Thank you, Bobby."

"Nice?" Elsie repeated. "She's looking lovely."

"Well, I don't want her getting ideas."

"No one is getting ideas." Lily put a reassuring arm around her son's shoulders. "It's just a dance."

It was still warm as Lily and Helen walked to the Guild

Hall on the High Street. The sun was low in the sky, casting a mellow glow on the buildings. Helen felt a small thrill of anticipation as they saw other groups of women gathering and making their way to the dance. There were a few men, those not able to serve in the forces due to medical reasons or being in a reserved occupation.

"Look, there's Annie, with Denny and Maeve." Lily pointed in the direction of their fellow NAAFI workers. "Don't they look different without the uniform?"

"Annie will be making the most of being able to dress up," Helen commented. "I wonder if she managed to get herself a pair of stockings; she was determined she would!"

"I'm sure she has."

They watched the three women disappear into the open doorway of the Guild Hall. Soon Helen and Lily were passing the George Hotel and approaching the red-brick, flat-fronted, building where the dance was being held. The sound of a saxophone, alongside other brass instruments, was drifting down the stairs and on to the street. Excited chatter came from groups of women and talk in all sorts of accents from the soldiers stationed at Lydd Camp, who had been given a pass to go out for the evening. Even in the entrance hall, with large doors open to the street, there was a haze of tobacco smoke hanging in the air.

Having given their coats to women who placed them on hanging racks, Helen and Lily exchanged a glance before moving with the flow, up the wide staircase to the elegant room where the dance was being held. At the far end, underneath paintings of local dignitaries through the ages, was the home guard band: five men from the town in their best suits and newly polished shoes, their faces full of smiles and feet tapping along to the music. A couple of women, the landlady of the Dolphin and her sister, who now worked as an ambulance driver, stood before the band. As they belted out *Don't Sit Under the Apple Tree*, Helen smiled; it was a favourite of hers. Moving to the music as they crossed the room, Helen and Lily took a glass of shandy from a table trimmed in patriotic red, white and blue bunting.

"Isn't this a treat?" said Annie, as they joined her and the other volunteers who worked on Nancy-the-NAAFI-van.

"It's wonderful," Lily agreed. "Just what we need."

"And if we have an air raid, I wouldn't mind getting cosy in the cellar with one of them." Annie flashed a cheeky smile in the direction of a group of servicemen.

"Oh gosh, now look what you've done!" Helen whispered. Two of the men were coming across the room, encouraged by Annie's smile.

"I'm Frank and this is Donnie," the Liverpudlian introduced himself and his friend; they were tall, bronzed and athletic looking, with a confident manner. "Now would any of you ladies like to take to the dance floor with us?"

"How very kind," Annie took a step forward and linked her arm through Frank's. "I'm Annie."

Donnie looked at Helen; she lowered her eyes and twisted the stem of her glass in her fingers.

"How about you, Denny?" Annie asked the young woman with stocking seams drawn down her legs and lips carefully coloured in red.

"Thank you, Donnie, I'll have a dance with you," she replied. Her eyes darted around the room. Perhaps Denny was conscious of her reputation: should she be seen to take too many dances with these bold men?

Women in floral dresses and men predominantly in shades of khaki and sage green began to fill the floor. A jaunty tune struck up and they all started to move in time with the music, stepping and swinging their bodies in a manner that was fast becoming adopted at such dances, thanks to the influence of modern music.

As the next number began, Lily and Helen joined in. They danced together, as did other women who were unsure of accepting an invitation from a soldier.

"If you want to dance with one of them, there's no harm in it," Lily told Helen. "Or someone local, like Jim over there; he's nice and gentle." In his shirt and tank top, Jim was a lovely young man who owned a bakery on the High Street. He suffered from asthma, keeping him out of the forces, but did his bit in the home guard.

"Oh no, I'd rather dance with a stranger," Helen replied immediately. "It would mean nothing, but to give a local man attention… they might get ideas."

"I understand."

They continued to dance alongside but not with the servicemen, sometimes exchanging a shy smile or allowing one of them to teach them a dance move, but more comfortable within their group of women friends. Then the musicians and singers took a break, and some women from the WVS brought out trays of spam and corned beef sandwiches, along with Lord Woolten pies. There were rock cakes and coconut cream desert, to go alongside savoury treats.

"What a lovely spread," Helen whispered to Lily. The music still rang in her ears and her cheeks were a little flushed; she hadn't thought how wonderful it would be to be away from the daily routines. A small needle of guilt started to prod away at her, and she brushed it aside. *I am still alive and still young; I wasn't meant to live the rest of my life being sad because my husband died. I can still think of him, and I do, but I can enjoy my life too.* With a rock bun in her fingers and these thoughts in her mind, Helen gave a smile to one of the many young men who had been trying to gain her attention all evening.

"Would you like to dance with me?" he asked, having taken hope from her warm smile. His accent was Scottish: soft with a pleasant lilt to his words. "I'm Douglas Saville, and none too good a dancer compared to these from the big cities."

"I'm not much of a dancer myself!" Helen replied. "Thank you, Douglas, I'll dance with you. I'm Helen."

After the break, the band continued with slower songs; the women's voices were rich and washed over the room relaxing the dancers. A haze of tobacco smoke mingled with the streamers and bunting. The talk became less lively and some of the couples moved closer together. Douglas, with his sandy hair and freckled face, was an attractive man, with none of the over-confidence shown by many of the soldiers. Helen felt comfortable in his company. As the dance finished, they moved off the dance floor.

"Would you like a drink?" Douglas asked.

"Just a lemonade," Helen replied with a smile. She had felt a bit wobbly earlier after three glasses of shandy.

They spoke a little about his home in the Highlands, so different from the flat lands of Romney Marsh. Helen liked his gentle manner and the way he treated her with respect. She found herself telling him about her husband Jack, and the baby named after him.

"It's too bad he never got to hold his son," Douglas said. "It makes me glad I've not left a wife at home; although it would be nice to have letters from a sweetheart."

Standing to the side of the dancers, Helen watched Lily laugh as the man she was dancing with whispered in her ear. He was an older man, his uniform slightly different, presumably showing he was an officer. There were so many different styles, Helen found it hard to recognise them all. She watched the hand resting on Lily's back move down to the curve of her bottom and thought of Bobby's fears. But Lily moved the hand to the small of her back and the officer shrugged.

"Your friend will be fine with him," Douglas told Helen. "He won't mess her around."

"She's my aunt," Helen said, "And neither of us is here to make a fool of ourselves with a man."

"That told me!" Douglas laughed. "And very sensible too; there's a war on and none of us will be in Lydd for long and who knows if we'll ever come back. You're a lovely young woman and I wouldn't want you to fall for someone who'll be at a dance with another girl in a month or so, if they're lucky that is!"

Helen understood his meaning and appreciated his honesty. She found herself hoping that he would make it through the war and manage to return to the Scottish Highlands. She was sure there would be plenty of women glad to have a husband like Douglas when the conflict was over.

The evening ended and people left with their groups of friends or family members. Helen gave Douglas a hug; she had a feeling she wouldn't be seeing him again. The night air was still warm and scented with summer flowers. The moon was full, lighting their path home.

"I'm not a bit sleepy," Lily said. "Let's go for a walk and clear the tobacco from our heads. Did you enjoy it?"

"I did," Helen replied with enthusiasm. "Those new dances are such good fun, and can you believe how our home guard band learned them so well?"

"They did us proud," Lily agreed.

Their steps took them further down the High Street before they turned to the left and it was here, coming from an alleyway behind the Royal Oak, that they heard a familiar cackle. "Oi, behave yourself," a woman said, her voice husky.

A glance down the alley showed Annie's unmistakable blond waves picked out by the moonlight. Her dress was pulled up, revealing stocking tops and ample thighs. Her arms were wrapped around the soldier's neck, her face tilted upwards, and her lips pressed on his.

"Gosh, do you think she's all right?" Helen whispered.

"Oh, I don't think she's really complaining," Lily said, with a smile.

"But she wouldn't… not there, not where she could be seen?"

"I think she might!" Lily looked at Helen and raised her eyebrows. "Let's hope the moon goes behind a cloud sometime soon."

Where the road ended, they turned and, without discussion, continued to walk further from home, enjoying the freedom of being out at night. The streets were quite busy, with groups and couples heading back from the party. It was as they neared the fire station that Helen recalled Evie's cottage and the ghostly tales.

"What a sad time Evie had," she began. "I didn't know her of course, but you hear talk of people in a small place like this."

“She did, and then for all the people of Galloways to lose their homes. It doesn't seem right.”

“It's happened in several coastal communities,” Helen mused. “Imagine leaving your home and the army moving in.”

“It would be awful on top of all the other troubles,” Lily replied.

Helen hadn't mentioned the talk of Evie's restless spirit still lingering at the cottage, and she certainly wouldn't mention Joe. But she was drawn to walk past the cottage in Queen's Road before they turned for home. They passed it, silent and seemingly empty, with a boarded-up door that once opened on to the pavement, and a window similarly blocked. Upstairs, the openings were empty sockets, with curtains hanging limp at the sides. The birds were roosting for the night. But as they passed it, Helen heard the rub of wood on wood and a gentle clunk. It was as if a door was being closed. And she felt certain there was someone in the old cottage.

The colours on the painting were looking fine;
Albert loved the tones in the blue sky.

Chapter Eleven
July 1941

On a Monday at the end of July, the sky above Romney Marsh hummed with RAF planes. They flew in waves, like geese heading south for winter. But their destination was no further than France, where they sought to destroy the Germans' preparations to invade Britain from the French ports.

Helen and Denny were out on the NAAFI van that day. First, they headed off down the concrete road to the deserted settlement at Denge, where just the bases of the old cottages remained. It was a beautiful summer's morning, the sky was clear blue and the stones of the Dungeness Point almost shone in soft shades of grey, brown and white. The clumps of broom looked tough and ragged; their branches bent low from having the wind press against them for so many days of the year. At the roadside, viper's bugloss thrived in the sparse soil: its flowers were a vivid blue, growing on hairy, grey-green spikes. Equally bold was the red valerian, another shock of colour in the landscape. As *Nancy*, driven by Denny, slowly negotiated potholes and areas where shingle was strewn across the roads, Helen looked through the open window. She found a beauty in the plump grass-heads and loved to watch them sway in the breeze. She admired them for their subtle colouring and delicate fronds; some had a reddish tinge, others a pale green or straw-like yellow.

The soldiers at the first stop were in good spirits. They appreciated the tea and a bit of company from a couple of pretty young women. Helen and Denny stayed there for a short time before turning back to Lydd and then taking the Dungeness Road back to the sea. From there, they moved along the coast, stopping at various lookouts and batteries on the way. It was a lovely day to be out in the van and Helen was in good spirits. There were several miles of coast road from which there were good views of the water and the bay. In the distance, to the east, the white cliffs of Dover could be seen, looking fresh and clean in the sunshine. But reminders of the war were never far away, from the fortifications stretching along the beaches to the planes overhead. As the sand dunes at Greatstone rose along the edge of the beach, restricting the open view of the sea, it was time to turn *Nancy* back towards her home at Lydd Camp.

"There's talk of those cottages in Queen's Road being made good again," Denny said, as they drove back into the town. People are needing homes and they're not so bad."

"The ones where Evie from Galloways lived?"

"Strange old woman, she was," Denny continued. "My uncle, he lives in the same terrace. There was Evie on the end, and then the butcher's son, Mike, and then him. His house was fine, just took a bit of a shake-up. Poor Mike, he has five children and his wife to care for and they had to move out, but it's only his scullery that was smashed to smithereens and a bit of a hole in the roof. He says it can be repaired. Lucky to be alive, he says, and if it wasn't for his one short leg then he'd be off fighting somewhere."

"And the end cottage? Evie's?"

"It came off the worst, but they say it could be repaired and give someone a home."

"Then it should be done," Helen said. "There have been so many houses lost and people are living all squashed-up with family, rather than having their own places."

"They have lovely little gardens. People want somewhere to grow their vegetables and even keep a few chickens."

"Let's hope someone finds the time to do something about it soon," Helen replied.

Denny drove the van along Back Road, taking it slowly as the children were out of school and you never knew when a ball might roll across the road, or a young lad appear from nowhere on a bike. Helen thought the conversation about the cottages was done with, but Denny must have been dwelling on the bomb-damaged homes and their occupants, as she surprised Helen with her next words, "Of course, no one'll want to live in the end cottage, however smart it's done up."

"Why ever not?"

"It's her ghost, they say it haunts the place."

Helen felt goosebumps rise on her arms. It wasn't the first time the suggestion of a ghost had been made. She rubbed her cold limbs, and felt compelled to ask: "Has anything been seen? Or is it just talk?"

"A figure at the window," Denny informed. "Evie in her shawl, they say."

"But the curtains flap at the upstairs windows," Helen said. "I've seen them myself."

"You know how people like to make something of it," Denny replied, her tone dark. "I've not seen anything myself; I'm just saying what others have told."

"Let's hope the ghost moves on when there's a new family setting up home." Helen tried to make the best of it. "There's no need to let a decent little cottage go to waste."

An hour later and Helen was striding out across the Rype, heading for home and looking forward to seeing Jack. The day was still warm, and the sky hummed once more with the passing of planes overhead, now returning to their bases in Kent. *I wonder how many have been lost?* Helen mused. H*ow many more telegrams to be prepared? How many sweethearts grieving?*

Another couple of hours after that and, with Jack settled for the night, Helen went out for an evening walk. Again she was drawn to the cottage. What was it that made people think Evie's restless spirit still lingered there? Helen didn't believe in ghosts and felt compelled to see the empty rooms before local builders took charge and made it habitable again.

It was a pleasant evening, with the sun not yet ready to slip behind the hills on the Sussex edge of Romney Marsh. Courting couples and groups of boys and girls wandered the streets. Men made their way back from work; the women were mostly busy in the homes. Helen had to slow her pace a little as she approached Evie's cottage and wait for a group of servicemen to walk by; they nodded and smiled respectfully. When they passed, she slipped into the alleyway and pushed open the gate into the narrow garden.

Whereas the front of the building had been boarded up, the back had been left to fend for itself. It was a 'two-up, two-down' style, with the remains of a scullery on the rear. Made of red brick, it was like many of the homes built at the end of the last century. Plain and flat fronted, this was built for the working people of Lydd. The back door was gone, lost in the pile of rubble that was once the scullery. The inner entrance, leading to the kitchen, was an open void, also without a door. Helen picked her way over the rubble, looking up to the smashed eaves and holes in the roof where birds nested. From the threshold, she peered into the dimly lit kitchen. What was it like inside this place where Evie had lived for a short time?

The room was almost empty; it seemed someone had taken most of the furniture. The dresser and table were gone. The range squatted black and cold in the fireplace, covered in dust. There were a couple of wooden chairs and some crates. The tiled floor had a liberal coating of dust and debris blown in from outside. But Helen noticed there was almost a path, or a track, going through it, as if an animal, or a person, took the same route across the room on a regular basis. *Ghosts don't leave a trail behind them*, she thought.

She stepped into the kitchen. There was silence. Not a bird flew from a nest. No mouse scurried from its hide; not even a spider scuttled to the edge of its web. Just a few steps across the room and Helen's fingers were on a door handle. She gave a gentle tug and the door moved towards her, revealing the dark square of a tiny hallway and stairs that rose sideways across the house. A further door led to the front parlour and another step opened the room up to Helen. It was lit by gleaming shafts of evening sun. They hit the front of the building and found the many gaps in the rough boarding across the open window and doorway. Helen was dazzled with the intensity of their light and the dust motes danced before her eyes. The light-beams picked out the arm of an old comfy chair, the uneven stripes of a rag rug, the tiles on the hearth, the rambling roses climbing up the wallpaper. A pile of newspapers lay on a small side-table, a section of the print was bold in the glare. Everything else was in darkness, shapes undefined as if dusk had fallen on the room.

In the shadowed corner, a door led to a small cupboard under the stairs. It was slightly ajar. Unbeknown to Helen, someone was watching her… someone she had never expected to see again. As she turned her back on the room, the sound of a voice close by made her jump in fear. "Helen? Helen is that *you*?" She recognised the accent instantly. "Do not be frightened. It is Karl, the pilot."

His voice was rough. He had not spoken for many weeks and his throat needed clearing. Helen's heart had started racing on hearing the words, and she stood poised to flee. But almost at once, she knew she was safe, that he was no threat to her. "Karl? But how can it be? They said..."

Even as she spoke, Helen recalled the pilot's wings found in the schoolroom and placed first in her pocket and then in the drawer at home. And she remembered the burned books in the school-room fireplace, and how those books were clay-like from damp and could not have been burned by Karl. Another pilot had been there at the school, another pilot had mislaid his precious wings and perhaps… it must be so… another pilot had been caught by the military and been mistaken for the one whose Messerschmitt had crashed on the shingle.

"What did they say?" Karl asked, as he crawled out of the cupboard and straightened himself.

"They said… that the pilot had been found. The pilot from the crashed plane. They said you had been found."

"I wasn't."

"It must have been someone else." Helen stood there looking at him. His hair was longer, falling in waves and he had a beard. His flying jacket had been discarded, hidden away somewhere, and his shirt was open at the neck. He stood with a shaft of light cast on his upper arm and across his chest, revealing the torso of a man who was used to physical exercise. But in the shadows his face looked gaunt, causing Helen to ask: "How do you manage? What do you eat?"

"There is the garden with its carrots and cabbages and the beans growing from last year's seeds. They are good, the beans. And raspberries, plenty of them."

"But it's not enough."

"Sometimes it has to be enough but," he paused, not wanting to say. "...But I take food from houses, at night. Never the same house twice. It is bad; they need their food."

"They do," Helen agreed. But she understood his desperation.

Karl flopped in the armchair and pointed to the second chair. "Sit with me? I have spoken to no one since we last met. When was that? The days are becoming shorter now; we have passed mid-summer."

"It's the end of July; four months have passed." Helen sat in the other chair and leaned forwards, her elbows on her knees and her chin resting on her hands.

"I've seen you. Twice," he said. "You were walking by. Once in the day, with a pram. And at night, just days ago."

"We had been to a dance," Helen told him. "I was

with my aunt." She thought about him being there, in the miserable, boarded-up house and asked: "How long have you been here?"

"Perhaps a month, or six weeks."

"Where were you before? Not at the school?"

"No, I felt it was not safe," Karl told her. "I thought of you and your kind heart. I thought of how you wanted to help, and I knew if you were caught by the army, you would be in trouble. Big trouble. So, I slept there that night and the next morning I left early."

Helen was touched by his concern. "But where did you go?" she asked, picturing the open landscape and the pilot struggling to move. "And your ankle? It was hurt."

"I went slowly, crawling most of the way, until I found a farm. And when evening came, I crawled into an old shed. I was lucky, it had some old sacking I could use as blankets and some grain. It was feed for the animals, but good enough for me. I stayed there for several weeks, resting my ankle and going out at night. Then I moved on; I could have stayed there but I was bored and decided to look elsewhere."

"And how long do you plan to stay here?"

"I don't know. Until the war ends?"

"But the builders are coming to repair these houses," Helen told him.

"Then I will find somewhere else, another house, or a barn." He shrugged his shoulders, as if he were used to the battle to survive.

They sat for a moment in silence, Helen not knowing how to help the man before her, but very much wanting to bring some comfort to his life. She knew she mustn't protect him, and he knew it too. *He will leave now I have seen him; he did it before and he will do it now. This is no life for him, lonely and having to steal food. He deserves better than this.*

"Tell me about the dance," he said. "Did you enjoy it?"

"I wasn't sure that I should go," Helen admitted. "But I did enjoy it. There were men from all over the country. They are training here, of course." She stopped; she shouldn't have said that; shouldn't talk of what the Allies were doing. But she was being foolish: Karl was not a spy; he was lost and afraid, just trying to survive.

"Soldiers?" He raised his eyebrows and grinned at Helen. "Were they fun?"

"Fun?" She considered her answer. "I suppose so, but I didn't want to dance, not at first. The band was good. If you were closer, you could have heard them."

"I would have liked that," he said.

They sat in silence for a moment. Helen wondered what his life was like in Germany. Did he have a wife, or a sweetheart who worried over what had happened to him?

"You can't stay here, Karl." Helen said. She leaned forward a little more; their knees were nearly touching. "It's just not safe and this war could go on for years. The winter will come, and it will be so hard."

Karl sat there for a moment, studying her face before finally admitting: "I know." He ran his hand through hair which was greasy and now curling on his collar. "I'm ashamed of myself. I am dirty and I cannot shave properly or have a decent haircut. I am ashamed that you see me like this."

"None of us are how we want to be," Helen said. "I wear a uniform, but I would like to be in a pretty dress and to be at home making supper for my husband."

"Your husband? He is at war?"

"He was in the Navy; he was killed over a year

ago."

"I'm sorry." Karl shook his head. "Too many deaths. Too many good men lost."

"Yes, but you are not lost. You are here in England and you can't return home, but you could hand yourself in."

"Hand myself in?" he frowned at the unknown phrase.

"You could go to the police, or the home guard and tell them you are here." Helen paused, checking that she was saying the right thing, that he wasn't recoiling from the thought. Satisfied Karl was listening, she continued: "Then you would go to a camp. The conflict is over for you whether you stay here or become a prisoner of war."

"I want the war to be over," Karl said. "It's not my war."

"I understand." She considered him being in a camp. "They would tell your family if you went to a camp. They would know you were alive."

"That would be good."

Helen got up from the chair and, looking down at him, she said: "Karl, this may sound foolish, but please let me do this one thing for you. It's a small gift to you; I want to bring you some food and then, in the morning, I will tell the home guard that I have seen you, and that you mean no harm. They will take you to a camp and you will be safe."

"Thank you." He stood up and reached out to touch her arm. "Food is no small gift. And I will do as you ask; I will wait for the police or the home guard and be happy to go to the camp, to be amongst my countrymen."

"I'm glad," Helen said, as she left the room.

He watched as she stepped lightly over the rubble

at the open doorway and into where the scullery had been. Then Helen was gone, and he raced to the upstairs front bedroom, hoping to see a glimpse of her moving down the street.

On seeing her niece's flushed face and worried expression, Lily asked: "Has something happened? I was getting worried and was about to ask Bobby to go and look for you."

"I'm sorry, I didn't expect to be very long," Helen replied. "I… Yes, something has happened and I'm sorry I need to rush out again and take just a little food with me, and I know how precious food is, and I wouldn't do this unless I had to." She walked through to the kitchen and cut two thick slices of bread, then spread butter very thinly on them and added slices of cold mutton and cucumber from the allotment. She wrapped the sandwich in greaseproof paper.

"Can you tell me?" Lily asked.

"I want to tell you properly," Helen replied. "I'll be back in twenty minutes. No, it will probably be half an hour, no longer. Then I'll explain it all, I promise." She gave Lily a quick hug and was running down the hallway, around the pram, and out of the front door.

It was time to put finer detail on the fallen stones, perhaps some thin white lines and a little shading in a charcoal grey.

Chapter Twelve
July 1941

The sun had just tipped below the horizon when Helen picked her way through the former broken-down scullery for the second time that day. Karl stepped forward and waited in the doorway to the house. "You came back," he said. "Thank you."

"I said I would," Helen replied. "I came back before, to the school. But it was too late."

"Sorry," he replied. "I knew you would, but I thought it best that I leave. It is very dark in the other room now. Sometimes I sit here." Karl gestured towards a couple of upturned crates. "They are like chairs without backs; what is the word?"

"Stools?" Helen perched on one and held her hand out, offering the sandwiches.

He took the packet and, had they not been in virtual darkness, she knew she would have seen the pleasure on his face.

"This is good," Karl said. "Very good."

"We have an allotment, a vegetable garden," Helen told him. "We grow some of our food there. Sometimes it is difficult to buy food now. We have to queue for it. Because of the war..."

"The war..." he repeated. "It is a terrible thing."

"You didn't want to fight?" Helen asked.

"No, I didn't. But I had to... I had to pretend to

believe in it, to protect myself and my family." That he would have been shot had he objected to fighting was left unsaid, the words seeming too harsh even in this war.

"I see," she said. But she didn't really.

Karl ate half the sandwich and paused, perhaps wondering if the rest should be saved. Then he continued: "We grow vegetables at home. It is a good thing to do. Very good."

"What do you grow?"

"Cucumbers, like this. Tomatoes, potatoes, onions and green vegetables," he replied. "I would like to tell you about my home. But you have to go?"

"I have to go," Helen repeated. Her body felt heavy. She wanted to stay there, as dusk fell, and hear about a life in a different country. "My family are waiting for me." She forced herself to stand up; he stood as well, the half-sandwich in one hand.

"I will sleep, and in the morning they will come for me," Karl stated. "Thank you. This is a good thing to happen to me. I appreciate your help."

"Goodbye then." Helen faltered and held out her hand.

Karl gripped it and said: "Goodbye, Helen. It was very good to meet you."

Helen turned and left the house. Karl followed her to the garden and, when she left, he stayed there for a while, looking up at the stars.

"It was the pilot! The one from Dungeness." Helen launched into the story as soon as she saw the concern on Lily's face.

"The pilot? The one from the plane crash?" Lily poured a cup of tea and placed it in front of Helen. "I think you need to tell me from the beginning."

"I do," Helen sat down. "I can't believe it; I really can't." She had been so busy rushing about, her head full of plans and her eagerness to help. Now her body felt weak and, as always, Lily was there to provide a listening ear.

"So, the sandwich, it was for the pilot you found when you stayed with Emily?" Lily prompted.

"They were. It's all so crazy, so unbelievable." Helen took a sip of hot tea and began to explain, "They didn't find him, Karl I mean. It was another pilot they found that day. Goodness knows where he came from. And Karl, well, he was hidden somewhere at a farm. Then he moved on and he's been sheltering in Evie's cottage."

"He *has*? All this time?"

"Yes, for months. It's been miserable for him." Helen, whose life was full of people and love, felt wretched to think of the loneliness the German endured. "Imagine what it's like for him, stuck in that cottage. He's an enemy to our country hiding out. But he means us no harm."

"An enemy to our country," Lily repeated. "I wonder what he is to you?"

"To me?" Helen frowned and her throat tightened. She didn't want to think about what was meant by Lily's words. "He is Karl. He's not a Nazi or the enemy. He is someone who needs help."

"He can't stay there, at the cottage," Lily said. "But you want to help him, and I understand that."

"There is no one else to help. I just wanted to feed him; it seemed like the only thing I could do for him. And tomorrow I will go to the police station and tell them he is here. Karl knows, and he will wait for them. In a prisoner of war camp, he'll be safe with food and company."

"A good option, compared to Evie's cottage."

"I think so."

Helen couldn't imagine what it was like in a camp where the captured enemies were placed. She envisaged rows of metal bunks, thin grey blankets, wooden tables, and benches strewn with packets of cards and old newspapers. She pictured great cauldrons of watery stew and thick slices of brown bread. The men would work in the day, on the land or making roads. That was how she saw Karl's life. She hoped it would be a time spent free from danger and that he would be treated well by his British guards. Then, one day in the future, he would be released and sent back to Germany. What would he do when he was home? Helen didn't know. She hadn't asked about his job. She knew only of his vegetable plot, and the parents set in a formal pose within the sepia photograph she found on the shingle. To think of Karl back in Germany, and to know nothing of his life there, made her feel very empty.

Lily began to gather the teacups. "This pilot, Karl, has had a very lonely and difficult few months; he'll leave tomorrow having had his heart touched by the English woman who gave him a sandwich. I'm sure he'll never forget the gesture."

"I don't know. It will be just one of many experiences from the war."

"Let's get to bed now," Lily said. "You've a difficult day ahead of you." She gave Helen a quick hug as they parted.

That night the sirens wailed not long after the grandmother clock in the dining room passed mid-night. Helen sighed and swung her legs out of the bed. It seemed as if she had only just drifted off to sleep, having rested for a couple of hours with thoughts of Karl running through her mind. She pulled on her dressing gown and slipped on her shoes before lifting Jack and his bedcovers out of the cot.

Lily, Elsie and Bobby were ahead of Helen as she walked into the hallway. They trooped through the bungalow, with Lily pushing the pram, while Elsie picked up a box of blankets and Bobby took the tea, milk, biscuits and lantern. It was a well-rehearsed routine, and one that had been put into practice several times over the last month.

Outside the air was still warm, scented with the summer roses rambling along the fence. The sky was bright with millions of tiny pinpricks of light from the stars, as well as a sliver of a crescent moon. The wire of the chicken coop glinted, but the birds were silent, roosting for the night. The corrugated-iron front of the Anderson shelter shimmered in the light from the night sky; the top was a murky green, covered in well-established turfs.

"Good light for a bomber," Bobby commented. "I don't hear them yet."

They paused for a moment, gazing up at the sky, torn by appreciation of its beauty and fear of the enemy planes searing through it. From the coast came the *tck-tck-tck* of the anti-aircraft guns.

"Time to go inside," Lily said, sliding the door to reveal an opening. She pushed the pram in and moved to one side, allowing Bobby to enter with the lantern. Helen and Elsie followed, and the door was manoeuvred back into place. A black-out curtain was lowered over the doorway, ensuring no light penetrated outside; in the colder weather, it kept the drafts at bay.

As always, Jack slept through it all and was placed

in the pram. Cocooned in his warm blankets, he stretched out a little, made a snuffling noise and continued to sleep. Elsie poured water into a kettle and put it on the small gas hob that stood on a low table. Lily prepared the teapot and cups. They stood with blankets thrown about their shoulders, then perched on the edge of the bunks, soothing their tired bodies with the tea before attempting to sleep.

It was not so bad in the summer; at least the damp was kept at bay. But in the winter, the Anderson shelter was a miserable place to be. The thin rolls of mattress were frequently taken into the bungalow and rolled out by the fire to be thoroughly aired. The floor was muddy, despite the planking being raised a little from the earth. But the very worst thing about the shelter was that it attracted slugs and snails, which Bobby removed on his regular checks. There were large colonies of woodlice too, enjoying their life under the boards, and making regular outings into the shelter.

"I hear the fighters now," Elsie said, looking towards the roof.

"I wonder where they're going." Helen dunked a biscuit in the scalding tea.

"And if we're over there too, giving 'em hell," Bobby added.

"Ben says he'll join the RAF when it's time," Elsie said.

Helen had noticed that seventeen-year-old Ben Brooks was still a regular visitor to their home; he frequently took Elsie, and sometimes Bobby, to the cinema in an evening. They had been close for some time and it seemed that, even with all the servicemen about, Elsie had her heart set on the fisherman from Dungeness. He was a lovely young man, good humoured and hard working. It was certainly a relief to see that there would be no soldiers taking advantage of Elsie who, at sixteen, needed to be protected from their dubious charms.

"Doesn't he want to go in the Navy?" Bobby asked.

"No, he says he knows about being at sea. If he's got to go to war, then he'd like to try something different."

"I hope he gets the choice," Lily said, as she gathered the cups. "Now you know the rules. The lamp is going out and we must try our best to sleep. It does not sound as if they are planning on dropping anything on top of us tonight."

It wasn't long after when the all-clear sounded. Lily was right – Lydd was not their target that night. Just as they had got comfortable in their beds, the routine was followed in reverse: blankets folded and taken back to the bungalow; teacups gathered and placed in the kitchen; Jack picked up and returned to his cot. The baby stirred though, and Helen changed his nappy before soothing him with milk. It was about two o'clock in the morning before she fell into a deep sleep. By five o'clock the sun was rising over the roof-tops of the bungalows across the road and within the next hour Jack was waking. Helen put him in bed with her, but there was no chance of another hour's sleep.

On leaving the house later that morning, Helen turned the pram towards the police station. It wasn't the direction she wanted to walk in; she felt a need to see Karl just one more time, to make sure he was still there and was willing to wait for the police. *If I report he is there, and he isn't, then I'll look foolish and there will be all sorts of questions,* she told herself.

The police station, a substantial Victorian building

on the main road, came into view. "It's a lovely day. Mummy would like a long walk," Helen said to Jack, who was sitting up in the pram, his hands clamped on to the sides. "Let's just pop back into the town first." She swung around and strode off, convinced that to check on Karl was the right thing to do.

Helen wheeled the pram into the alley and then into the back garden of the old cottage. Jack was wide awake, so she didn't like to leave him; she lifted him out of the pram and perched him on her hip. Karl was standing at the back door as they approached.

"I saw you from the window," he said. "You should not be here… the police?"

"I just wanted to be sure," Helen began "Sure that you were all right."

"Yes, I am good. Just waiting for the army or the police, but instead you are here," Karl replied. "I am happy to see you, but it is time for me to go. I am ready."

Helen gave an apologetic smile and said: "I must tell them then."

"You must," he smiled. "Thank you. Thank you for everything you have done for me."

She replaced Jack in the pram and said: "Good luck, Karl. I hope they treat you well." Helen felt him watching her as she negotiated the rough ground and the narrow gateway.

"There's a man… a man living in the bomb-damaged house in Queen's Road," Helen said to the policeman at the desk.

"A man?" the policeman said, pulling his notebook towards him.

"A German," Helen volunteered. Then she paused, unsure of how much she wanted to say. The words had gone round and round in her head since the evening before, but it was no easier now she stood there. "I think, I mean to say I think he is a German."

"What makes you think that?"

"I spoke to him." Helen looked about the reception area. The walls were painted a dark cream and there was a large, gilt-framed print of King George VI and Queen Mary on the wall. There were notice boards and she edged towards them, seeking the distraction they offered.

"You spoke to him?" the policeman queried. "Did he threaten you in any way?"

"Not at all," Helen replied. "I don't think he is that type of German. I mean to say, he isn't here to cause any trouble to us. I saw him and asked who he was, and he told me that he had come down in a plane some time ago."

"He'll be on the run by now then," the policeman remarked. "A job for the army, this is."

"Yes, it probably is." Helen began to edge the pram towards the door. "But I thought I should come along and tell you, and you would know what the best approach was. Maybe he will run, but perhaps he is weary of this and would rather await his capture."

"And which house was this?" the policeman asked Helen. "I believe there is more than one bomb-damaged in that road."

"It's the terraced house where Evie Stoneman from Galloways lived."

"Ah, I know it. Thank you, Miss. You've done the right thing reporting this." The policeman picked up a telephone receiver. "I'll pass it on to the army. And, if I have any further questions, I'll find you at…?"

"Mill Road, I live at Mill Road with Lily Scott," Helen said. "She's my aunt. Now, if you don't mind, there are long queues outside Hutching's, and it's no better at White's. I need to get the shopping before it's too late. I'm just thankful that we have the allotment." She wheeled the pram back on to the pavement and walked a hundred yards or so before pausing for a moment. Her heart pounded and she could feel the heat rising through her body. "It's over now," she told Jack. "Now let's use our coupons for some tinned fruit; we have enough sugar and margarine for a crumble topping."

Helen spent the next hour queuing at both Cole's the butcher's shop and Hutching's Grocers. The conversation between the housewives helped keep her occupied, but her replies were sometimes vague.

"We're all tired, love," one woman said, as Helen apologised for her lack of concentration. "In and out of our beds, not knowing when the siren will go off."

"At least we were spared the bombs," another added.

Helen agreed and, as one customer left the shop, they all shuffled along, another place up the queue.

Helen turned towards the Rype when her shopping was completed; she enjoyed walking across the large green on her way home. It was a pleasant day; the summer sun still beat down upon Romney Marsh and there had been no threat of rain in the past week. Those children who had not been evacuated were on school holidays. They ran free on the grass with balls, hoops and carts made of crates on wheels. The rattle of a diesel engine behind her prompted Helen to turn the pram on to the parched grass and step off the road. Turning around, she saw it was an army van approaching. She stood and watched it drive towards her and then pass by.

Helen sensed it would be Karl in the back of the van, on his way to the next stage in his life. She closed her eyes briefly and sent a short prayer: *Dear God, please take care of him and the prisoners of war. They didn't all choose to be a part of these dreadful hostilities. Give them comfort and hope for a better future. Amen.* She wondered where Karl was going and what would happen to him now. She felt in her heart that she would never see him again, and watching the van disappear into the distance brought the chapter to an end for her.

Albert held the oil painting up to the morning light that poured through the kitchen window. He was quietly pleased with the result. There was a sheet of thick paper on the table. The painting would be safe wrapped within it

Chapter Thirteen
May 1942

"It's a glorious day for a celebration," Lily said, as they walked down the front path.

"Fancy them naming a mine-sweeper after Romney Marsh," Bobby said for the umpteenth time since the local towns had reached their fund-raising target in Warship Week. "I wonder if I'd like it better in the Navy or the RAF?"

"You're *thirteen*," Lily replied, the exasperation clear for everyone to hear. "It will be over before you're old enough to worry about it."

"You do so much to help us at home," Helen said soothingly. "How would we eat so well if you didn't spend all those hours at the allotment?"

"It's not the same," Bobby complained.

"You're just being stupid," Elsie shouted at her younger brother. "It's not a game and I hate this war. I hate it." She stormed off, walking in front of the family group.

Lily looked from her daughter to her son. She understood Bobby's need to do something, to feel as if he had been a part of winning the war. And, although she had never suffered as Elsie did, Lily could imagine the pain her daughter was going through, as her sweetheart prepared to leave.

"Sorry, Ma," Bobby put his hands in his pockets

and bowed his head a little.

"Just try and be a little more considerate towards your sister," Lily replied.

"I won't ever fall in love," Bobby said. "It's all just rubbish."

They walked along in silence for a few minutes, taking the footpath through the cemetery as they made their way to Lydd Station. Jack sat up in his pram, his hands gripping the sides. Although his face had begun to crumple as he heard the harsh words between his much-loved cousins, he was soon absorbed with the birds, the trees and a passer-by with his dog. At eighteen months old, he was a cheerful little boy. With no sense of the dangers around him, his life was secure and happy within his family group.

The winter had passed, and the first few months of 1942 were quiet. Spring brought further threats from the Germans; families lived on tenterhooks, never able to relax while going about their daily business. You never knew when a lone Focke-Wulf or Messerschmitt would take the opportunity to fire a round of bullets at civilians, or when bombers would choose to drop their load on the coastal towns, rather than the more significant ports or cities.

Earlier in the month, Messerschmitts had appeared through the sea mists at Dymchurch, dropping bombs and machine-gunning the village. One person was killed and several injured; the horror of the incident was felt across the Marsh. The month before it was other coastal towns in the area that again suffered the bombs when planes were chased away from their targets of Folkestone and Dover. The family in Lydd once more endured restless nights in the Anderson shelter and Helen began to wonder if she should have followed the advice of her family and taken Jack to live in a safer area of the country.

It seemed that every week stories of terrifying incidents in their patch of Kent were reported. And, when Lydd camp was raided, the ground their home stood on trembled. In the queues at the shops, during a conversation with a passer-by, or while sitting with other women knitting for the soldiers, stories of the atrocities flowed.

People stopped believing the war was going to be over in 1942; they could only hope that 1943 would bring an end to it. Elsie was suffering the imminent departure of her love, Ben Brooks, from Dungeness. Having just turned eighteen, he was due to join the RAF and would be leaving within the next few days. Mothers looked at their young sons, such as Bobby, and prayed the war would finish before it took them.

The station was crowded with the people of Lydd who were eager to grasp at any opportunity to celebrate life. "I wish we didn't have to take the pram," Helen fretted when she saw how everyone would have to squeeze in.

"Oh, we'll manage," Lily replied in her usual positive manner. "And isn't it marvellous that so many people are going? Didn't Lydd do well to raise all that money?"

"We did," Helen agreed. "Can you imagine it – more than six thousand pounds! It should be celebrated; the whole of Romney Marsh has made a wonderful effort. All that money raised for a warship!"

"There goes one of the extra motor-buses." Lily looked towards the bridge spanning the railway tracks. "Thank goodness Turks thought to run them today."

A distant whistle heralded the arrival of the train and soon its steam could be seen. Then the great beast itself came hissing and clanking into the station. A few people got off and the guards started ushering people into the carriages, even stepping inside to ensure the elderly and infirm were seated. Jack was lifted from the pram, and it was taken to the guard's van.

Helen was seated with Jack on her knees, but the others stood and held on tight as the guard blew his whistle, the wheels began to turn, and the coaches jolted against one another. They headed towards the coast, with the Dungeness peninsular to their right, necks craned to spot the familiar buildings and landmarks.

Elsie, whose face had retained a sullen expression, began to fret over her stocking seams as they drew closer to Lydd-on-Sea Halt.

"Darling, he won't notice," Lily said.

Elsie raised her eyebrows in response. But as the train slowed, she was all smiles to see the Brooks family on the platform and stood at the carriage door waving. Edward and Grace, with Ben and Eva, stepped inside, exchanging greetings, and raising smiles with baby-babble from Jack. The wobbly seams were forgotten as Elsie slipped her small hand into Ben's. Within ten minutes the train arrived at New Romney Station, the end of the line. All the passengers stepped down on to the platform and, as if pulled by an invisible current, they flowed out of the station before turning towards the town.

It was a short walk along a tree-lined avenue before they reached the High Street. Spirits were high amongst the throngs of people who were joining to watch the big parade. For Helen, it was a struggle at times to manage with the pram, but it almost gave her a holiday feeling to be amongst the crowd, with smiles and banter passing all around her. She followed Edward who led them down a back road, in the hope of finding a good spot midway along the High Street.

"There's no such thing as a quiet space today," Edward commented as they looked in dismay at the milling crowds. "But, if we cross the road, at least we'll have the sunshine on us."

"That's perfect," Lily said. "The sun is glorious, and we'll find that people will move up for us. I'm not complaining – just glad to be a part of all this."

Soon silence fell upon the crowds as, in the distance, the barked commands of an officer could be heard, and then the drum rolls began, followed by the uplifting sounds of the brass instruments. They could not yet see the Band of the Royal Marines, but the parade had begun, and onlookers jostled to have the first view of it. The very rhythm of the music encouraged Helen to envisage herself marching and she felt an excitement build; to witness these celebrations was going to be wonderful. Jack was held up high and passed amongst the two families; his round face showed enthusiasm for the moment and chubby hands pointed.

The marines came into view, marching in lines, giving the music their absolute best effort and looking proud to be leading the procession. As the band neared the friends from Dungeness and Lydd, the brass instruments ceased and an impressive drum solo beat through the High Street; Helen found her body moving to and fro, and then the trumpets once again joined in. "Gosh, look how smart they are," she whispered to Lily. The men wore their ceremonial uniform of a dark blue, with red banded peaked caps.

The marines passed, but their music continued to fill the air. Next came groups of soldiers from various regiments, backs straight and bayonets fixed to their rifles. Their lines were neat, and they marched in time to the beat of the marines' drums.

"If Romney Marsh can put on a parade like this, imagine what London or one of the big cities could do," Grace commented.

"Makes me proud to be a part of it," her son, Ben, replied.

"I know," she said, her enthusiasm waning a little. "But I wish you didn't have to be."

Then the sounds of drums and brass, to which they had all felt the need to tap feet and sway in time to the music, was replaced with a less exuberant sound: that of the engines rattling and roaring within the vehicles used for the war effort.

"Look, there's Annie and Denny," Lily yelled, and they all waved with enthusiasm, calling out as Nancy-the-NAAFI-van came into sight.

"Thank goodness Denny is driving!" Helen laughed. "Look, Jack, look at Mummy's and Aunt Lily's van coming along. Wave, darling, wave."

The van drove along slowly and following on behind was the khaki-painted ambulance. Both vehicles were driven by the women who volunteered their time in order to help out during the war. Annie, having spotted Helen and Lily, reached across to the horn and they saw Denny scowl, as *Nancy* let out a loud "parp-parp". But Denny was soon waving along with Annie and smiling broadly to her friends looking on at the parade. Next it was the fire engines, four of them from local towns and villages, all freshly washed and polished. Some of the crew walked alongside the vehicles, waving and cheering, and encouraging others to do the same.

Following on, but just as important, were the familiar faces of local people who worked tirelessly for the home guard, and the wardens who checked the civilians were safe from the dangers of air raids, as well as making sure no light showed at windows and doorways of homes and businesses. In their tin hats, they were not as smart as the military, but received just as much appreciation from the crowd. Then there were the scouts and guides, the older children whose parents hoped they would never serve in the war.

Trundling behind came the Bren Bren carriers – light-weight tanks with mounted guns. They caught the imagination of young boys as they snaked along on their caterpillar tracks. Behind the procession came the people who spilled off the pavements and into the road. Men in their Sunday suits and women, in new dresses made from old outfits, swept along as they became caught up in the joy of the moment. They had worked hard to raise thousands of pounds towards the minesweeper HMS Romney and were rightfully proud of it.

The Royal Marines Band had turned off the High Street and marched on to the patch of open land known as St Martin's Field. As the vehicles moved on, the rhythmic beat of the drums and the all-powerful blast of the brass instruments could again be heard.

"Shall we go and watch the band?" Helen suggested.

"I'd love to," Grace replied, and the others started to move off the pavement, in order to join the flow of people who seemed to have the same plan in mind.

"How was Dennis' leave?" Helen asked Eva, who had married the day Jack was born. It was better to remember it like that – the day Jack was born – rather than recall it as the day the church was bombed.

"It was wonderful… hard though, very hard," Eva replied. "To know that we had such a short amount of time together – just five days – but to try to enjoy every minute."

"Counting the hours," Helen mused. This was only the third time Dennis had been home in the eighteen months since they had married. The young couple had no place to call their own. Initially, two rooms had been set aside in his mother's house. But Eva had soon returned to her own family and so, when Dennis returned, they had to move around. They had spent a night with Eva's family, two with Dennis' mother and then taken the train to Hastings where they had stayed in a guest house for the remaining two nights. Helen's husband, Jack, had returned home only once on leave; she was glad Eva had this time with Dennis, however short it was.

The splendour of the Royal Marines Band once again came into view as they rounded the corner and saw them on a makeshift stage. People gathered to watch, some of them sitting on picnic rugs or chairs brought from nearby houses. Grace and Lily pulled blankets from the rack under the pram and the picnic was laid out; packets of greaseproof paper were opened, revealing food to be shared. The days of sugary cakes were gone, but honey from local bees made a good substitute and Bobby kept chickens at the end of the garden, as well as tending the allotment. From Dungeness, there was a ready supply of fish and so both families managed better than those who lived in the cities.

An hour passed, with the warm sun shining upon them, and music to accompany the food and conversation. The marines had a break, and some local groups took turns to provide the entertainment. They were not as professional and were accompanied with a fair amount of light-hearted banter from those who knew them.

Much as they tried to avoid it, before long there was more talk of the war when Bobby recognised a farmer from the Greatstone area. “Ben, do you see Sid Gosnells over there?” Bobby pointed in the direction of a young man. “It was his bullocks that got caught up in a mine-field at Greatstone; did you hear them go off – the mines I mean? Blimey, I'm sure I heard them in Lydd, and even Ma said so.”

“I didn't just hear them,” Ben replied. “We were out at sea and felt it too.”

“Caused quite a wave, they did,” Edward added.

“Gosh, I'd have liked that,” Bobby narrowed his eyes as if imagining the scene. “They need to sort out their fences down there; were you out on the boat when the sheep got into the minefield?”

“You're right they do; what a carry-on and a shocking waste of livestock too. No, we weren't on the boat that time, I think we'd just brought it back on to the beach.” Ben reached out for a slice of honey-flavoured sponge cake. “This is lovely, Lily. Very tasty.”

“You're welcome, Ben. We weren't far away with the tea-van when the sheep got themselves into that bother,” Lily added. “It certainly made me jump.”

“Ma, what time are we going back?” Elsie changed the subject.

“I think another half an hour, and we need to start walking to the station,” Lily replied.

“Shall we go for a walk, just around the town?” Elsie asked Ben.

"Yes, let's." He pulled himself up and reached for her hand.

They kept their fingers linked and strolled off along Fairfield Road. Lily and Grace watched the young couple, their expressions serious. Nothing was said, for as mothers to Elsie and Ben, they had discussed their fears at length over the past year. If they were to marry, the families who had known each other for decades would be joined. It should be something to celebrate but, at only sixteen and eighteen years of age, there was bound to be heartache in store for the pair of them. Grace had already looked on as Eva struggled to accept Dennis' absence and knew her son would now suffer as he left Elsie behind. Lily found herself worrying about Elsie being too young to commit herself to a future with Ben. She had been a full ten years older when she met Charlie and had very much enjoyed her young adult life before marriage.

As the crowds moved back down the avenue to the railway station, chattering and laughing, there came another sobering reminder about what the day was all about. As had been the norm over the past weeks, the first wave of RAF bombers passed overhead. All talk stopped and people slowed to gaze up at the sky.

"Off to France again," Edward muttered.

"Why not Germany?" Bobby asked.

"It's still the Germans they are after," Edward replied. "They've set up factories producing military supplies, or so they say. And they're in France."

"I wish we didn't have to see them today," Grace said. "It's silly, I know, but I was forgetting this was all about the war."

"It was a good day, Ma." Ben put his arm around his mother's shoulders. "A nice family day to remember when you're feeling glum over the next few weeks."

"You're right, Ben. You had to go and I'm glad you got into the RAF like you wanted."

"He's got so much training to do, and there are plenty of jobs on the ground, as well as those in the air," Edward said. "No need to worry, not yet."

"And I'll be back on leave in no time," Ben said. "Think how glad you'll be to see me striding along in my uniform."

"I don't know about that," Grace replied. "I'll just be happy to see you back home."

The bombers were gone, and overhead the sky was clear once more. But with Ben soon going off to war, spirits were now deflated as the two families rounded the corner and prepared to find a space in the over-crowded carriages.

Chapter Fourteen
November 1942

"Be good for Aunt Lily, my darling." Helen leaned down and, having swept back the dark curls, planted a kiss on Jack's forehead.

He looked up, his face streaked with sticky porridge, clasping a spoon in each hand. "Mumma, bye, bye."

"I hope you enjoy your day," Helen said to Lily.

"I'm sure we will," Lily replied. "We are going to the allotment."

"A two-year-old and mud, sounds like fun!" Helen grinned as she fastened the buttons on her khaki jacket before pulling on a woollen hat, scarf and gloves.

It was one of those days when it wasn't properly raining, but the misty drizzle in the air would leave a wet sheen on anything it touched. Pavements were damp and dead leaves slumped in piles against walls and kerb stones; their autumn splendour was over. Helen wrapped her arms around her body and walked briskly, her head down.

Annie was waiting at the roadside in *Nancy*. She gave a wave and, leaning across, opened the passenger door. "Jump in – airfield run today."

"You sound cheerful," Helen remarked.

"RAF pilots flocking round us? Of course I'm

cheerful!"

"Not going to complain about the weather?" Helen asked as they pulled away and turned a sharp left opposite the church.

"I could complain about the weather all day, especially how it will play havoc with my hair." Annie patted her victory roll, now a glossy red and carefully pinned into place, her hat balanced on the back of her head.

They were heading out into the countryside now. The view from the grubby window was uninspiring: grassy fields stretching out on both sides; twisted hawthorn trees with dark green leaves; drainage ditches at right-angles to the road and lined with faded reeds, their heads bowed from the wet. Isolated farm buildings appeared and fell away behind them.

Rather than work their way along the coast, there was a new route for the NAAFI van and its team of volunteers. A second tea-van had joined the service and took its turn with the job of catering for the soldiers manning the look-out posts on the beaches. The original van and its team could enjoy a change of scene when they toured the Romney Marsh countryside, offering a welcome distraction for the men constructing four new airfields.

Annie was being optimistic in imagining there would be pilots stationed at the part-built airfields. For the past month, the women had been greeted only by disillusioned workmen, their clothes sticky with mud and often wet through from the persistent rain. With the ground not fully levelled and drainage ditches still needing to be filled, there was no chance of a Spitfire or Typhoon being able to make a landing before the following summer.

The muddy road was slippery as the vehicle turned

a corner and Helen was grateful to note Annie slowed a little. Another corner and the site of the airfield could be seen in the form of a tented area for shelter and stores, along with patches of disturbed land. Sheep still grazed there; it was important that to any enemy aircraft there was little sign of disturbance or clue as to the intended purpose of the site. Annie steered the van down a track, taking it slowly and coming to a stop not far from the collection of canvas shelters.

"They've heard us coming," Annie remarked. Men were appearing from all corners of the construction ground and trudging towards the tea-van.

"No pilots yet," Helen laughed, as she opened the cab door.

"You never know when one will come visiting," Annie replied. "A girl has to live in hope, you know!"

While they prepared the tea-van, opening the hatch and putting a kettle on to boil, the men gathered. Annie and Helen chatted as they placed mugs on the shelf, but it was awkward from the confines of the van, with the clatter of tin mugs, the hissing of the gas and the need to keep busy with jobs.

There was something about these workers: a desperation, a loneliness, perhaps resentment. The camaraderie was missing, and this concerned Helen. She saw it on all the airfields. They had come to Romney Marsh to be faced with weeks of appalling weather. It was bleak and muddy; they lived in tented camps and the only entertainment they had was the daily visit from the NAAFI van. There was no town nearby; if they were lucky there was a village pub. Their shoulders were slumped, eyes dulled, and they took little care of their appearance.

It was different on the coastal run. The men there were mostly local and amongst friends as they manned the lookouts. When their shift finished, they went home to their families. And at the army camp, where many troops came and went, there was also entertainment, as well as a cinema in the town and dances to attend.

Much as Helen enjoyed the countryside drive, despite the weather, these men made her feel uncomfortable as she tried to talk with them and exchange pleasantries. However, she saw the effort Annie made both with her flirty chatter and glamorous looks. As the war entered its fourth year, the lipsticks and mascaras women were encouraged to wear in order to boost morale were in short supply as cosmetics factories had long since turned to manufacturing products needed for the war. Annie now saved her precious lipstick for the dances and died her lips with beetroot for day-to-day use.

As the last of the tea was poured, the two women stepped out of the back of the van and offered tins of rock cakes. The men grunted their thanks and chatted a little with the women. Helen, standing with a tin mug of tea in her hands, found that the conversation became easier as cakes were enjoyed, and the men became more at ease. However, she was grateful when she drained the last of the warm drink; she could now tidy up before moving on to the next airfield.

They made good time in the NAAFI van that day, with St Mary-in-the-Marsh being the last stop. "Midley is the worst of them all," Annie commented as they headed towards home. "I filled up with water and there's plenty of milk left; shall we go back and give them another cup of tea?"

Helen, who was feeling rather glum, agreed with Annie, "Do you know, I think that would really cheer them up, and make us feel a bit better too."

So, as mid-afternoon came, the two women were following the same road they had used that morning but this time returning to Lydd, having cheered up the men based on the Midley airfield. There had been some light-hearted banter, not often heard on the airfields, and plenty of tea to go round. Tired, but with their spirits lifted, it was agreed it had been a worthwhile detour.

Neither Helen nor Annie heard the pair of Focke-Wulf fighters flying low over the coast and machine-gunning various targets. The van rattled about so much that even when the planes were above Lydd, they heard nothing. It was Helen who spotted the two dark objects in the sky, flying over the trees and rooftops. In the poor weather conditions, it was impossible to recognise the aircraft from their shape or markings, but their presence above the small town immediately alerted Helen to the danger before them.

"*Planes* – over Lydd," Helen said, the words pouring out in a rush.

Annie glanced upwards. "Looks like they're coming this way," she muttered. "Be glad of this bloody drizzle; it might be the thing that saves them from spotting us."

Helen craned her neck forward, watching their movement in the grey sky. The fighter planes were bearing down upon them, and now she could hear the occasional crack-crack of their machine guns.

"Watch out girl, I'm going to turn here," Annie took a sharp left into a side road. There were some tall trees alongside it, which offered shelter and camouflage. The van slid and the planes were momentarily forgotten as the ditch at the side of the road became dangerously close. A jerk of the steering wheel and *Nancy* veered in another direction, this time coming to a stop in the entrance to a cottage. The engine stalled.

With the van now silent, the roar of the Focke-Wulfes' engines indicated how close the planes were. Helen thought of Jack and Lily; she wondered what they were doing. Annie looked down at her nails and picked out a bit of dirt. A burst of machine-gun fire seemed to hit the road behind them and, before there was a chance to react, to say anything, the sound of metal on metal pierced their thoughts. One, two, three, four – the bullets seared into the side of *Nancy*, the fourth coming through the passenger door and exiting through the foot-well. Helen, whose legs were usually stretched out in this space, had at some point drawn them back against the seat, probably as her whole body tensed with the fear of what might be to come.

Helen looked at Annie: the older woman's beetroot-stained lips looked shocking in her white face. She stared down at the floor and the bullet hole. Her sturdy, lace-up shoes rested just an inch from it. Slowly, Helen turned back towards Annie. "We're all right, aren't we?" she asked.

"Yes, we are," Annie stretched out her hand and held Helen's. "I think he's done with us."

But, as they lifted their eyes and looked through the windscreen once more, an incredible thing happened. The planes, one in front of the other, had turned and were swooping towards Lydd again, following the line of the railway tracks. Once more their machine guns fired but, before either Annie or Helen could even think of saying anything, there came an almighty explosion, which rocked *Nancy's* metal body and sent shudders through the horrified women. As the planes veered away, one of them exploded, part of it becoming an orange fireball that propelled itself across the sky in the direction of the town, while the remaining debris was left falling the short distance to the ground.

The other fighter was gone and there was silence. The crows that had flown from the trees in a squawking mass had settled. There were no other vehicles on the road, or planes in the sky. The day was as it had been before the incident, damp and seemingly uninteresting.

"Gosh, what was that?" Helen was the first to speak.

"I've never seen a plane explode just like that," Annie replied, her voice low.

"But the bang, or blast, or whatever it was?" Helen tried to express her thoughts. "It came before the explosion."

"Did it?" Annie queried. "It all happened so fast. We'll find out soon enough though."

At that moment, a policeman appeared in the lane. Later Helen told Lily that it seemed rather odd for him to just appear, but his presence was soon explained.

"Are you girls all right?" the constable asked, pausing to look at the side of the van.

"Yes, sir," Annie replied. "Just a bit shaken up."

"I was at Westbrook checking the sheep dipping," he said. "Heard it but didn't see a thing. We had just gone into the barn."

Helen and Annie fell into step beside him, walking in the direction of the Caldicot Crossing. "Have you heard the three-fifteen train pass by?" the constable asked.

"No, but with the shock of being shot at, and then the explosion, I thought nothing of it," Helen replied.

"Perhaps it was kept back in the station," the

constable said.

Just then the scene changed, from there being just the three of them to figures appearing at the crossing gates. They spilled out, coming from the tracks, and between two of them came a Southern Railways fireman, his jacket sleeves in tatters. He slumped at the roadside, most likely in shock and people moved forward to help ease his arms from the ruined garment.

"Thank God, the ambulance is here already," someone said, noting the uniforms.

"No, sorry, we're from the tea-van," Helen was forced to reply, "But I'm sure the ambulance isn't far away." She looked at Annie. "Perhaps tea would be welcome though?"

"I was thinking the same," Annie replied. "But I'd like to know for how many and what on earth has happened. If that was the fireman from the mid-afternoon train, then it looks like it was shot at."

They reached the crossing and looked a short way down the track to see wreckage spread out before them. "Well, I never expected that," Helen whispered. There was the tank engine, the internal workings on display, twisted and blackened, and clearly the result of the explosion. Behind it the carriages, both derailed and slumped in a drunken manner. Carriage doors were open, and the police constable rushed ahead, but there were a couple of senior army personnel on hand already helping passengers from the wreckage. They exchanged a few words with the policeman, who returned to Annie and Helen.

"It seems that no one is hurt, except the fireman who has been scalded. A miracle really when you look at what's happened. It appears that the boiler was hit by machine-gun fire and blew up, taking the Focke-

Wulf with it."

Helen and Annie gazed at the policeman and the engine, speechless for a moment. Finally, Annie spoke, "We were thinking that perhaps tea...?"

"I am sure that would be much appreciated." The police constable gave a brief smile.

They returned to the lane, walking in silence, thoughts on the horrific scene. Annie and Helen became two amongst a trail of passengers, many dressed in army uniforms. The noise of an engine was heard in the lane, and everyone stepped to the side, allowing the ambulance to pass, but it slowed, and a woman leaned out of the window.

"Any injuries here?" she called.

"No love, we're all just a bit shaken up," one of the soldiers replied.

"Hoping for a cup of tea," another added.

"Aren't we all!" the woman replied.

"The fireman, he's in a bit of a mess," one of the soldiers added.

"Right-oh, we'll go along to him." She pressed gently on the accelerator and the ambulance picked up speed before coming to a stop just before the railway crossing.

Annie opened the back doors of the van and stepped in. She lit the gas while Helen poured water into the huge aluminium kettle.

"They'll have to be small cups of tea," Helen remarked. "We're lucky to have any water left."

Within ten minutes the NAAFI tea-van was providing tea in tin mugs to the passengers. The initial shock of the explosion and destruction of the fighter-bomber was wearing off. No one had witnessed the accident. Like Annie and Helen, they recalled snapshots of the event: the sound of the Focke-Wulf bearing down upon them; the feeling of being helpless, confined in the carriages; the condensation on the windows so only the vague outline of the planes could be seen; the ting of metal on metal; the explosion and the great jolt to the carriages causing them to jump off the rails.

"Never heard of such a thing."

"It's a first – a steam engine taking out a fighter plane."

"Miracle no one got hurt, apart from the fireman."

"And the pilot."

"The pilot – he was the one who started it."

The first mugs of tea were handed to men huddled up in their overcoats, feeling the chill of this late autumn day. Then Helen thought of the fireman and asked if someone could take a mug to him. "And to anyone else still over there," she said.

Willing hands reached out. "You're heroes, you two women," said the young soldier who took the first teas for those still with the train. "It's people like you who will help us win this war."

Tears pricked at Helen's eyes and her heart swelled. She could not find the words to give a reply, but it didn't matter; he had turned away in search of the fireman.

"It seems so insignificant, what we do," Helen said to Annie.

"It keeps them going: a friendly smile, a cup of tea and a bit of cake if they're lucky," Annie replied, as she washed up the tin mugs in the meagre amount of water they allowed for the task. "They get lonely, and we make them smile."

"I know, but to think of everything *they* do." Helen could hardly imagine what they did do, all these brave men she saw on a daily basis, whether as lookouts on the coast, workers on the airfields, or troops in Lydd. They had different lives she didn't see when they faced all kinds of dangers but pushed on stoically with the fight for the freedom of their country.

With their tea finished, the soldiers gathered and, under orders of the officers, they walked back along the lanes into Lydd. Helen and Annie began to pack away the mugs; tipped away the tea leaves and made everything secure in the rear of the van. They were about to get into the cab when the police constable arrived. “You've done a great job there,” he said.

“Did you get one, sir?” Helen asked.

“I did and thank you.” He looked tired and pale.

“Was the pilot…?” Annie asked.

“We found him by the edge of a dyke,” the constable replied. “Bit of a mess he was in, and not surprising considering the way the plane went up. His parachute was open, not that he stood a chance of it helping him at all. Too low he was.” He paused for a minute, looking across the flat fields towards Midley, as if seeing it all again. “Bloody amazing that he got out of the plane at all; excuse my language, ladies.”

“That's fine,” Helen smiled at him. “We hear all kinds of things when we stand at the serving hatch!”

“Would you like a lift back to Lydd?” Annie asked.

“I've got my bike at the farm.”.

“Sling it in the back,” Annie suggested. “What an afternoon! Come along with us and save yourself some time.”

“It's women like you who keep us going through these dark days,” the constable said. “Has anyone ever told you that?”

Annie licked her beetroot lips and flashed him her best smile. “Well, actually they have!”

Chapter Fifteen
A few minutes earlier – The fighter-bomber pilot

Hans Bauer looked down on the patchwork of fields and thin trails of water, a sneer on his thin lips. The town of Lydd came into view – he recognised the huge barren green and the tall church tower. His eyes narrowed and mouth formed a half-smile, as he saw the bombed end of the church. That had been a good day! A small detour before a successful raid on the East End of London. He had been flying a Messerschmitt then. But the Focke-Wulf he now piloted was a superior plane. It excelled at low altitudes and Hans got immense pleasure from going as close as he dared to the ground. It gave him a chance to see the fear on the pale faces of the British people.

Back on that day in the autumn of 1940, it had been his good friend from childhood, Josef Kohler, who had dropped the bombs. Hans and the third fighter-bomber pilot watched as the chancel and the ends of the two aisles were shattered. These places in which God was worshipped should all be destroyed. Hans felt very strongly about that.

In his hometown, the church had been stripped of all things encouraging good Germans to worship the saints or God. Now a cloth emblazoned with a swastika was draped over the altar and all those old-fashioned pictures of miracles and martyrdoms had been replaced with carvings and paintings depicting scenes of strong young men and healthy young women in rural scenes. His father, an amateur wood carver, had played a part in creating them.

There were no bibles or crucifixes on the altars of Hitler's churches. The priest read from *Mein Kampf – My Struggle* they would call it in this country spread out below him. How many English bibles and religious icons would have been destroyed by the bomb from Josef's plane? He had done well!

It was a shame to see the tower standing proud, but these things served as a useful landmark. Turning his plane slightly to the right, Hans veered towards the church, noting there was a fair amount of shattered homes below him. Lydd had not been spared from the bombing raids.

He was in a playful mood; a letter had come from his wife just before they had left for England. She was expecting their third child.

"Well done, my love," he said the words out loud. "Another child for Mein Führer!"

He had chosen well when he selected Gerda for his wife. With her fair hair and blue eyes, she was the perfect vision of Aryan beauty. Her frame was sturdy, built for bearing children and she had no desire to make herself look foolish by painting her face. Those English women with their red lips and lines drawn down the backs of their skinny calves; did they have any idea how ridiculous they looked?

"Shall we go for gold?" he asked his wife and imagined her nodding in agreement as he laid his hands on her ample breasts. Medals were awarded for women who provided a good number of children for the German nation. She was twenty-four now, two years older than him; could they achieve six children and the silver medal before Gerda was thirty? He hoped so. And by then this war would be over and the British subdued; he would be there to provide her with the gold medal in no time!

Nearing the tower, Hans allowed his finger to press on the trigger and his machine guns fired: for a few seconds a flood of cracking filled the air. He was having fun with the look-out on the top of the building. He could well imagine a middle-aged man from the home guard in his round-topped helmet cowering there. Wouldn't it be entertaining to destroy those spindly stone things pointing upwards on all four corners. Hans tipped the plane slightly and tried again; he missed but it hardly mattered. It was time to go home and stop wasting his time on these trivial amusements. He was due a week's leave and would soon be travelling home to Gerda and his beautiful children.

Swerving away from the church, Hans noticed a second fighter-bomber was taking pot-shots at the vehicles on the High Street. He followed his comrade, not firing, but his very presence would instil fear in the Britons below.

Hans allowed his thoughts to turn to his best friend from school: the bomber pilot who had successfully destroyed the church he had just looked down upon. Josef and he had very much enjoyed their school days during the early and mid-1930s. The Nazis had dropped all the subjects they considered pointless, just sticking with the basics in subjects such as maths. Physical Education had played a big role and that suited the two friends very well, giving them the skills to pass the trials for the Hitler Youth. They had relished the military activities on offer with the organisation; there was a certain thrill to be found in a perfectly organised parade!

For Josef, his skills at throwing, football and running eventually led to him being a part of the Olympic team when the 1936 games were held in Berlin. He had run in two races, the 100 and 200 yards, as well as taking part in the long jump. This should have been a chance for the athletic young German to shine, but Hans thought of the growing horror he had felt as his friend was beaten again and again by the team from the United States of America.

As they became young adults, the friends remained close, enjoying football together as well as their military training. They had barely started military service when an even more glorious opportunity presented itself – a chance to serve in the Luftwaffe and show the world how powerful their nation was, as well as make good all the injustices served on Germany since the end of the last war. Hans planned to do his duty in all ways and ensured he made a good choice when he selected his wife. He was only 19 when they married, just days before he left to train as a pilot. Being loyal to the Führer, Gerda shed no tears but was proud to let him go.

How his mind wandered as he left Lydd behind, but what was this? A little truck of some sort was coming towards him. It swerved into a narrow track, and he dipped his wing to make a neat turn before peppering the side of the vehicle with bullets.

Now the other plane had moved ahead, and Hans followed at a short distance. A steam engine was moving away from the station with a couple of carriages behind. It was travelling inland, and it seemed as if the other pilot had the same idea as he turned to face the train, flying above the tracks. Hans followed; he could have some fun here. It would be something to tell Josef about as they packed up their kit bags at the end of the day and prepared to go on leave. His bullets lacerating the metal of the engine would make a terrific noise. And if the roofs of the carriages were riddled with holes, then it would make travelling a little uncomfortable for these Britons who were being so awkward about surrendering.

The tank engine was picking up speed as it left Lydd behind it, but it was no match for the Luftwaffe fighters. Hans allowed the other plane to maintain the lead; it flew low over the train, machine guns leaving a smattering of holes in the carriages and ricocheting off the cab and boiler. With his mouth twisted into a smirk, Hans followed in the tail of his fellow pilot.

With his finger pressed on the firing button, Hans felt his own machine gun spring into attack. But the exhilaration he experienced soon changed to a terrible fear: a terror that froze the smile on his thin lips. As he swooped before the engine, and then began to turn for a second flypast, he glanced down to see a sheet of flame coming from the great metal beast, and the next he knew was that his own Focke-Wulf had been struck by something at such a speed that the whole of the plane shuddered uncontrollably. And before Hans could even consider he had been assaulted by the very steam engine he had chosen to play games with, his plane was on fire and the heat coming through the metal wall between cab and engine was a thousand times more intense than any he had ever experienced.

Chapter Sixteen
November - December 1942

"We were out shooting on the ranges when the planes came over," Bobby announced. "The army had us running for the shelters, but we still heard it."

At thirteen years old, Bobby was in his last year of school in Lydd. Once or twice a week the older boys were going for training at the army camp. The girls were learning first aid skills, as well as knitting socks and scarves to help keep the troops warm over the winter months.

"It was terrifying." Elsie's voice was sober. "We had no idea what we would find." She had recently started working with the Lydd-based Ambulance Brigade and was still wearing her thick woollen A-line skirt with a white blouse. The jacket, with three brass buttons and a wide belt, was thrown over an armchair. The hat was on a hook in the hallway, and Elsie's dark waves bobbed around the nape of her neck.

Lily dished up a meat and vegetable casserole. "That must be the worst of it, not knowing what you'll come across," she said.

"What you're doing, Elsie… it makes me think I should have trained to do something more worthwhile." Helen cut up the bowl of food for Jack who was waiting in his highchair. She blew on it and pushed it around the bowl. "It's still too hot," she said to the eager child.

"No, you shouldn't think that," Elsie was quick to reply. "It was different for you. The war came and then you had Jack. I had time to think about what I wanted to do. And I can't be with Ben now, but I can help other people who are injured through this war."

"At least Ben is coming home for Christmas," Lily said.

"I can't wait." Elsie grinned. "Four weeks to go..."

They started to eat, glad of the winter greens Bobby grew in the allotment and the rich gravy which disguised the lack of meat. "Ma, I've got no meat at all," Bobby announced after a minute; he was moving his casserole about with his fork.

Lily grinned. "None at all? You know you won't get much. I'll give you a bit of mine." She looked at Elsie.

"All right," Elsie said, rummaging through her own meal. "There really isn't much though."

"I should have shared it out more fairly," Lily said. "I usually do but my head was full of the accident and to think of Helen and Annie being shot at; it's just awful."

"It was over so quickly though," Helen said, passing a piece of mutton to Bobby. "We hardly knew it would happen and then he had flown over and then… well you know about that."

"The ambulance wasn't needed," Elsie reminded Helen. "It was the cups of tea which saved the day!"

"I suppose they did," Helen grinned.

"Did you put the body in your ambulance?" Bobby asked.

Elsie rolled her eyes. "No, he went in a van. The policeman would have called for it when he got back to Lydd."

As plates were scraped clean, Lily suddenly

announced: “I’ve just remembered – I heard from Grandmother Alice today: she has invited us for Christmas. How do you feel about that?”

“I'm happy to go,” Bobby replied immediately. There were several cousins of his own age in Ashford, where his grandparents lived. The younger of Lily's brothers, Henry, had five children.

Lily looked at Elsie, knowing her response. Elsie looked back, with horror in her eyes. “I can't, I just can't… not with Ben coming back. And work, I might be needed, it wouldn't be right not to be here.”

“Of course, I didn't expect you to come,” Lily replied. “You can stay here or go to Allie's house, whatever is best.”

“Oh, I'll decide nearer the time,” Elsie replied. Her relief was clear to see.

Out of the blue a feeling of being alone washed over Helen. Christmas was a time to share with someone special. It felt a long time since her romance and marriage with Jack's father. The little boy was two years old now and her husband had been gone for two and a half years. She often went to dances with Lily and occasionally met a pleasant young man, one with whom, in different circumstances, she might have enjoyed a few dates and the possibility of a relationship developing. But these soldiers were all passing through, spending time in Lydd before their duties took them elsewhere. Helen wasn't inclined to start a courtship where she would be forced to say goodbye as her sweetheart left to fight and live in dread of the black-edged telegram once again.

“Jack and I will come,” Helen said. “We'll stay overnight with Mother and Father. It's been a few months since our last visit to Ashford, and it’ll be nice to go as part of a family party.”

Helen's mother pushed the pram along the pavement. It was Christmas morning, and the sky was heavy with snow; there was no wind and it seemed as if the town was at peace. Thin spirals of smoke rose from chimneys and meandered across the rooftops. The birds were silent as if waiting for the snow. Windows of red-brick houses were criss-crossed with tape and winter greens grew in tiny front gardens. Bomb-damaged houses lay slumped amongst their neighbours. The two women passed other family groups and exchanged Christmas greetings.

Richard, Helen's father, was on fire-watch; you never knew when the enemy may decide to strike. He had not moved far from his childhood home, and they walked from one red-brick Edwardian semi-detached house, across the railway tracks and towards a house of the same era and style. Helen's paternal grandparents still lived in the house in Jemmet Road, opposite the park; the same house she remembered from her childhood and the one where her father, Aunt Lily and Uncle Henry had grown up.

It felt odd not to be pushing the pram, as if Helen were the child again and her mother had taken control. Lily never took over when Helen was there to do it. She felt irritated to be robbed of her duty, and then ashamed that she could barely allow her mother the pleasure of pushing her only grandchild. Jack didn't mind. He sat up, cushioned by a pillow and so well swaddled that only his dark eyes, button nose and red cheeks showed. His little hands were in mittens and his dark curls were hidden beneath a woolly hat.

On entering the hallway, Helen felt there was something incredibly special about returning to her grandparents' home; it made her feel warm and safe. Nothing much changed: her grandfather ensured the paintwork and wallpaper were kept in good condition while her grandmother tidied, and polished furniture. Occasionally they bought a new appliance, like the electrically heated tub for the washing of clothes and a modern gas cooker. This caused a lot of interest in the family, and soon it was not just the grandparents displaying these, as family members followed suit.

"Come along in," Grandfather was saying. "Now look at this splendid little fellow." He reached out to Jack, patting his head in its knitted hat.

"Happy Christmas, Grandfather," Helen gave him a kiss on the cheek before turning to lift Jack out of the pram. "There's a bit of sleet in the air; I didn't want to leave the pram outside."

"That's absolutely fine; it will do as somewhere to place the coats!" Grandfather took the layers of winter clothing being discarded and laid them over it. "Now, remind me: how old is this fine chap now?"

"He was two last October," Helen told him, keeping Jack in her arms as the hallway was rather crowded.

"He'll have a marvellous day then!" her grandfather proclaimed. "Now come on through to the parlour."

Helen placed Jack down on the parquet floor at the entrance to the room. "Bob-bob-bob," Jack shrieked, as he spotted his cousin and ran to him. "Jack's here!"

"Hello Jack, how's my little soldier?" Bobby held the small boy up high.

Jack's laughter prevented him from replying and he settled himself on Bobby's lap, wanting the protection of the boy for there were other cousins here, faces he had seen before but not so well known and loved.

Helen glanced around the room. It was decorated in the style of the last decade: low-slung armchairs with curved backs and arms; a fireplace with glazed tiles; strips of dark wood making floor-to-ceiling panels on the walls and inserted with embossed wallpaper painted in cream. Pride of place was the wooden wireless with the shape of a sunburst across the front; Helen knew that her grandparents listened to the nine o'clock news without fail, and today the family would hear the King's speech at three o'clock in the afternoon. Grandmother's tapestry bag with her knitting was placed on the lower shelf of a side table and newspapers printed on thin paper were folded in a rack, along with patterns for knitting and dressmaking. In recognition of the Christmas season there were paper chains, a nativity scene, and some cardboard angels, decorated by the grandchildren several years ago.

Helen wished her cousins a Merry Christmas and said to Bobby: "I'll leave Jack with you then; Grandmother might need some help." She joined the women in the kitchen but, with Lily already there, as well as Uncle Henry's wife, Mavis, and her own mother, all preparations for the early afternoon dinner were in hand. There was space around the pine kitchen table, and she was grateful for a cup of tea. It was Grandmother Alice who poured a cup for Helen; in her mid-sixties with her iron-grey hair pulled back in a knot at the nape of her neck and her skirts still reaching mid-calf, she was still very much in charge of the Christmas meal. Her daughter and daughters-in-law were welcome company and assistants, but it was Alice who ruled the space between gas cooker, pine dresser and Belfast sink.

Talk amongst the women soon turned to those who were not with them and especially their friends in Dungeness and Lydd. "I went to see Allie last week," Lily said. "She's worried about her mother – Emily has struggled with her breathing over the last few months. All this damp weather is no good for anyone. She wants Emily to move to Lydd and be with her."

"She won't like that," Alice commented. "Although I must say that I agree with Allie. George and I drove to see Emily just last month and she wasn't her usual self."

"No, she isn't the same as she was before she hurt her ankle. But Emily is determined to stay where she is," Lily continued. "With Grace busy working and Edward out at sea, it's a lonely life for her. So many of the families have gone."

"They had to go, especially those with young children," Alice added. "It's no life for them with barbed wire across the beaches and areas of shingle full of mines. Children at Dungeness are used to being free."

"The shop has closed and the post office too," Helen said. "And she can't even walk along to the church on a Sunday, not with it being closed down. She has so little company."

"I don't think she could walk to the church now, not since she twisted her ankle." Lily was lifting the lids on pans and checking to see if the vegetables were cooked.

The church had been part of the eastern end of the school building – a stained-glass window, an altar and altar rail behind a curtain, only revealed on a Sunday. The school closed in 1940 when the children were evacuated to Sussex. So, both school and church were lost. An image of Karl the pilot sheltering there came into Helen's mind. Although surrounded by family, she felt a sense of loneliness wash over her.

"How sad to think of the school no longer being used." Alice thought back to her own time there. "It was such an oddity; rather a substantial building to be placed out on the shingle. I wonder if the children will ever come back?"

"They'll be back," Lily said. "After the war. Whenever that is."

"They'll travel to Lydd for schooling," Alice suggested. "There's a good road now and with all the opportunities young women have had during the war, however would they find a teacher prepared to live out there? It's a lonely place, and no one knows that better than me." Alice had been only nineteen years old when she had first arrived to live and teach at the school.

"Even Tom and Hazel Barton have moved into Sussex," Helen commented. "You would never think of that happening." The Bartons were a long-established family of fishermen who lived and worked at Dungeness.

"We had a Christmas card from them; that was kind," Alice told them. "Hazel said they've settled in nicely and she's not missing the wind!"

"I told Allie," Lily said, returning to the original subject, "that she should invite Emily for a week over Christmas and see how they all got on. Then perhaps she could suggest that Emily stays with them over the winter, on the understanding she goes home in the spring."

"Then she is free to choose, and her home will still be waiting for her," Helen said.

"That would be perfect, Lily," Alice agreed. "I know Emily won't want to be a burden and no doubt she is set in her ways, so she won't have lost her own home forever."

"I'm sure we'll have news of them soon enough." Lily moved to the kitchen sink. There were pans to be washed as Alice drained the vegetables and placed them in serving dishes.

"The meat is ready to carve," Alice said, having glanced at the clock. "Helen, if you wouldn't mind fetching your grandfather..."

Christmas dinner was a noisy affair and rather crowded, with an additional table brought into the dining room to help accommodate everyone. Bobby and his cousins kept the atmosphere lively, and Jack was clearly now happy to be a part of the larger family group. A small roast chicken was placed in the centre of the main table; there were large dishes of potatoes, both roast and boiled, but the vegetables were sparse: cabbage from Grandfather's garden and a selection of carrots, swede and turnips provided by the different branches of the family. The roast potatoes lacked a crispy skin as there was little fat available, and while mashed swede and carrot was flavoured with salt and pepper, it suffered for a lack of butter. The chicken was tender, but with portions so meagre, there was some light-hearted banter.

"I thought we had chicken, not sparrow!" Grandfather joked.

"Mother said you'd been trying to scare the birds off your seeds," Uncle Henry added. "We didn't know you'd taken to shooting them for the dinner plate!"

"I hope I've not got the shot in mine," Bobby started prodding the white meat.

"Take no notice, Mother," Lily said. "These men are just being cheeky and Bobby, show some respect to your grandmother."

"Sorry Gran," Bobby grinned. "It's lovely, really it is. Very tasty. I hope it doesn't leave you short of eggs though."

"Oh no." Grandmother smiled across the tables. "I

bought this one from the butcher. We still have our hens in the garden, but they've not laid many eggs now the weather is so cold."

There was no Christmas cake that year, not with sugar and fat rationed and fewer eggs. Icing on a cake would have been seen as an extravagance. But Alice had been saving her dried fruit and sugar to make a wartime pudding, with breadcrumbs from the National Loaf to add more substance. The mixture had been fed a generous amount of brandy over the past months and when it was placed on the table, the room filled with its rich aroma. Served with a jug of custard, the pudding had mouths watering.

The men now enjoyed beer as the meal ended and Lily brought in a pot of tea. Jack was put down for a sleep in the pram. Chairs were pushed back a little, legs were stretched out and the family relaxed more on the hard wooden chairs. The talk now turned to Uncle Henry's daughter, Polly, who was not there with her parents and siblings.

"I wonder what Polly's doing with the WAAFs?" Grandmother said.

"We had a letter from her just last week," Aunt Mavis, Polly's mother, replied. "She didn't say what they would do for Christmas. She can't say much about work; it's all about the dances and the other girls there."

"I'm not at all sure that Helen needs to be out in that van," Helen's mother commented. "There's no need at all, not with a young child at home."

"I wanted to do something useful," Helen replied, her spirits slumping a little at the return of this well-worn conversation.

"There's plenty to be done. I'm with a lovely group of women who meet and knit for the troops. No need to be out in all weathers mixing with soldiers and the sort."

"Helen wouldn't get shot at if she was just knitting all day," Bobby commented. "It would be boring, wouldn't it?"

Helen and Lily exchanged a look, both knowing there was nothing to be done to prevent the onslaught of maternal worry.

"Shot at?" Helen's mother's voice was high. "I'm sure I would have been told about this...Helen? Lily?"

"Not me, mother," Helen began. "It wasn't me being shot at. But the van…"

"Helen was fine," Lily added. "You can see she was. The van took a few bullets, that's all."

"*A few bullets*?" Helen's mother repeated. The room went quiet, the cousins now listening in. Teacups and beer glasses stayed on the table or poised in mid-air.

"We'd been out on the Marsh," Helen explained. "To the airfields, and a fighter came over, it took a few shots and was gone." She waited, hoping Bobby wouldn't say another word about it, but he had seen the stern look from his mother and concentrated on scraping the remains of pudding and custard from his bowl.

"Well, I just wish you would think about doing something a little less dangerous."

"This is important, Mother." Helen said, determined to make her views heard. "It makes a difference and it's a job that suits me. I can help with the war effort and still spend time with Jack. Knitting socks is...well, it's useful, of course it is. But it's not for me."

"We all do our bit to help," Lily added. "With Father on fire-watch and all of us doing something. You must be proud of Polly going off to the WAAFs."

There was a general murmur of agreement and the talk moved back to Helen's cousin who was stationed somewhere in Suffolk. She hadn't been home on leave yet, so they could only wonder what her role was and look forward to seeing her in a smart blue uniform.

The day ended with the men asleep in armchairs, unaware of all the cousins playing at their feet. The rug was strewn with hand-me-down cars, bricks and books for Jack. The wrapping – layers of thin newspaper – had been smoothed and folded, ready to be used to light the fire. Presents this year were kept to the minimum: home-made sweets, knitted clothing using unpicked wool, calendars re-made from those collected over the years. The younger generation were given savings stamps to add to their National Savings Certificate.

The women sat talking quietly around the kitchen table. Pots, pans and crockery had all been washed up and the kitchen was once more in good order. Left-over food had been packed up in grease-proof paper and would be taken by Helen's Aunt Mavis; the whole family were due to be in her home for dinner the following day. From the scarcity of coal and food, to the black-out pulled across the windows as dusk fell, there was no forgetting the war as British aircraft still flew overhead on bombing raids. But for this family, Christmas day passed peacefully.

Chapter Seventeen
January 1943

Nancy-the-NAAFI-van, with Denny at the wheel, had just turned away from Lade Fort when a lone plane appeared in the sky. Helen felt her body tense as both women craned their necks to watch it pass over.

"Hurricane," Denny said. The relief was clear in her voice.

The aircraft's underbelly was a pale beige; its wheels were tucked up inside, and towards the rounded wing tips there were the circles showing the RAF's red, white and blue roundel. As the plane tilted a little in the sky, the top was visible – a camouflage effect of brown and khaki, again with the patriotic circle showing it as a British plane. They could just make out the tiny figure inside the cockpit, with his flying helmet and goggles.

"He's made it home." Denny turned away and pressed her foot on the accelerator.

"Imagine what it must be like to cross the coastline and know you've lived to see it again." To see the pilot there, not knowing where he had been, but that it had been dangerous, beyond terrifying most likely, had caught Helen's imagination.

"In the summer they'll be heading to our airfields, but this one has a way to go before he's home for his supper," Denny replied.

"But he *is* home; he's flying over British soil."

The tea-van was pointed in the direction of Dungeness now and they could no longer see the plane as the Hurricane had passed behind them. For Helen and Denny, he had passed out of their lives, or so they thought. But above the rattle of *Nancy's* engine, there came the unmistakable sound of bullets being expelled from an Ack-Ack gun. They exchanged glances and Denny was compelled to swing *Nancy* around. "Not the Hurricane?" she breathed in disbelief.

There was no other plane in the sky. What had led the soldiers who had been drinking tea and eating rock cakes only minutes to fire at a British aircraft?

"No," whispered Helen.

Their eyes tracked the Hurricane, with the spiral of smoke coming from its rear and another from behind the cockpit. It appeared to be losing height but kept moving away through the clear sky. Denny turned the key, switching off the tea-van's engine and, if they strained their ears, the young women could just hear the hum of the plane's engine. Was it severely damaged? They couldn't tell as now a couple of miles separated them. Then something happened: a speck in the sky, something coming away from the plane, or someone…

"He's bailed out," Denny gasped.

"He was in trouble," Helen added, "and couldn't make it home."

"So close, and just as we were saying..." Denny started the engine again and did a U-turn in the road. As she did so, the pilot-less Hurricane seemed to have changed course a little and could still be seen in the sky, but now rapidly losing height.

"God help us," Denny breathed. "Please no."

With *Nancy* picking up speed, they watched as the

plane disappeared from sight and, within seconds, they knew of its fate. A double boom resounded across the Marsh: not of the Hurricane crashing to earth, but a pair of landmines exploding in the fields to the north of Lydd as the plane landed on them.

"How much longer must this go on for?" Helen questioned. "Isn't it bad enough when *they* come down, but what did this pilot do to deserve the horror of being fired at when he should have been safe? Then the terror of having to bail out... He's lost his plane and there will be all sorts of trouble, even though he did nothing wrong."

"I just pray he's not hurt, and the plane did no more harm than setting off a couple of mines," Denny said. They were rounding the corner now and had turned away from the coast.

Within minutes *Nancy* had passed the coastal checkpoint at Halfway Bush and Lydd was only minutes away. Before turning left towards the army camp, they had to pause as an ambulance raced by. In the distance the fire-engine's bell could be heard. For Helen and Denny there was nothing to be done but return to the camp and prepare the tea-van for the next day.

Helen walked home from the army camp, her thoughts absorbed with the Hurricane and the pilot. Who was this young man? Was his accent Scottish, or Welsh, or West Country? Was he young, in his first months of being a pilot, or one of the more experienced men? She wondered what it was like at the aerodrome as they counted in the returning planes, and imagined the looks exchanged between the staff as the time came when he should have landed, yet didn't.

"Did you see it? The plane coming down?" Helen

asked Lily even before she reached out to her son who was contentedly stacking bricks on the floor.

"I heard it," Lily replied, she had been sitting in the armchair darning, but put her work aside. "We went out in the garden and saw all the smoke coming up from north of the town."

"We saw him, Denny and I." Helen placed a brick on Jack's tower. "We were at Lade and his plane flew over, then he was shot at. How could they make a mistake like that?"

"Oh gosh!" Lily's eyes widened. "I can't imagine… just when you think we couldn't see any more horrors..."

"I know." Helen drew Jack on to her lap. "Hello darling, aren't you clever with your bricks? One, two, three – all in a tower."

"Big tower," Jack said as he wriggled from her lap and pushed it down. "Again!"

"Has he been dry all day?" Helen referred to their attempts to introduce Jack to underpants.

"He has!"

"That's wonderful; what a difference not to be washing all these nappies." But Helen's thoughts strayed back to the pilot. "We saw him bail out, so hopefully he's all right. The pilot, I mean. But I'm not sure where the plane landed."

"If it set off mines, then out of town somewhere, but there still could have been people or livestock nearby." Lily walked through to the kitchen and stirred the stew on the gas hob: she looked back towards Helen and said: "Bobby is sure to have heard something; he's out doing deliveries for Whites, and you know what that boy is like for sniffing out a story!"

"You're right," Helen gave a brief smile. "He'll have all the news and he won't be late for supper. And where's Elsie? I saw an ambulance going by, but it was Ted at the wheel; I didn't spot her next to him; it was an older woman, I think."

"She went to see Emily." Lily lit the gas under a pan of potatoes. "Allie is disappointed that her mum went back to Dungeness last week. Elsie took the train to Lade, and then she was going to pop in to see Allie afterwards. She'll be home soon."

Elsie and Bobby arrived within minutes of each other. Elsie was looking so grown-up now, at nearly seventeen years old. Her cheeks were glowing after a brisk walk across the Rype from Allie's house. She wore thick woollen tights and a plain dress with no embellishments. There was no point in painting lines down the back of tea-stained legs and pretending to wear nylons when everyone knew that the wind was sure to be howling at Dungeness and, in January, it was bound to be laced with an icy chill. Her cardigan had been created from re-used wool, but her coat was a new one, bought from much-prized rations.

Bobby was still very much a boy to look at, although he wore long trousers as a concession to being in his last year at school. His jumper was re-worked as well, but already showing signs of wear at the hem and elbows. His hair had been cut just the week before and although neat at the back and sides, it curled in all directions on top.

"What's for supper, Ma?" Bobby asked.

"Rabbit stew," Lily replied.

"Rabbit stew with rabbit, or vegetables with a bit of gravy?"

"With rabbit!" Lily smiled, as she mashed the potatoes in the big aluminium saucepan. "I've done extra potato so we can have it fried tomorrow," she told Helen.

Bobby, with Jack now clambering on to his lap, sat at the table and asked: "Did you hear the mines going off earlier?"

"We were just talking about it," Helen told him. "It was a Hurricane, shot at by our own anti-aircraft guns."

"Blimey, that's not right." Bobby shook his head.

"I saw it from the train," Elsie added.

"Did you know the pilot bailed out?" Helen asked. "We saw him, but I don't know what happened after that."

"Gosh no," Elsie said. "That's good news."

"Hope he's all right." Bobby handed Jack over to Helen; his mum was bringing the supper in and he wanted to be ready.

"I imagine there's a good chance of him surviving," Helen said, as she strapped Jack into his highchair. Her thoughts were on her German pilot, Karl, who had walked free after coming down hard on the shingle at Dungeness. Where was he now, she wondered. It had been so long, eighteen months since she had last seen him.

Throughout the night, Helen's dreams were disturbed by the man whose features she hadn't seen. His face had been obscured by the cockpit as he soared over the beach at Lade. In her dreams, he remained hidden behind an opaque acrylic screen, or a plume of smoke; at one time it was the parachute blocking his features. Had he looked down on the NAAFI van? It would have been clear to see as it moved along the coast road. Just as Helen and Denny had gazed up at him, perhaps the pilot had looked down at them and not quite been able to see the young women in the old vehicle.

In the morning, Helen woke tired and frustrated with herself. Busy with the daily chores, she left Jack too long without a reminder to use the potty. He wet himself and she muttered her frustration: “Oh blast, more work to do now.” She washed and pegged out the night-time nappies that had been used over the last few days, glad of the brisk wind. *If only they dry, then we won't have them on a rack in front of the fire all evening.*

Elsie was there, entertaining Jack with a soft ball in the long hallway of the bungalow, while Helen swept the area underneath the dining table, moving the chairs to and fro. “Elsie, would you mind putting him on the potty?” Helen called, suddenly remembering. The fire had already been cleared out and re-laid by Bobby before he went to school, but the rug in front of it needed a good shake in the garden. Everything seemed as it were too much bother, but Helen wasn't the type of young woman to shirk her tasks. If only she knew how the young man was, her mind would be at rest. *How foolish I am to allow myself to dwell on these things,* she thought, *there are so many of our men dying every day. This pilot is just one of many. But he is the one I saw.*

“Elsie…?” An idea had popped into Helen's mind. “If I were to come along to Elm Grove with you, perhaps someone would know about the pilot who bailed out yesterday?”

“There is bound to be someone there who can tell you,” Elsie replied, coming back into the room with Jack. “I could ask for you?”

“No, I'll walk along, if that's all right?”

“Of course, it is.” Elsie gave Helen a warm smile, showing an understanding of Helen's emotions, despite her young age. “These things stick in your mind, don't they? I see some terrible things and so often we don't know the outcome. It would be good to know, even if it were the worst news.”

“That's how I feel,” Helen said, her face serious. “I'll get myself and Jack ready, then we can come with you.

The day was bleak: the skies grey, the wind brisk; the houses and gardens colourless. It seemed unlikely the sun would remain any more than a pale glow behind the curtain of cloud. Gardens looked unloved and houses tired. It was the kind of January day where you felt as if the bulbs and tight buds had no intention of blossoming for a long time. But, as Helen and Elsie walked through narrow streets from Mill Road to the High Street, a glimpse of cabbages in a well-tended vegetable plot or a freshly scrubbed front step showed that the townspeople still took pride in their homes. It just wasn't easy to manage all the jobs that needed doing with the men away or on local war duties, and the women out at work as well.

They crossed the High Street, bumping the pram on to the far pavement and turned into Dennes Lane before turning once more into the driveway at the back of Elm Grove, the house now used as the Ambulance Brigade Headquarters. There were two boxy ambulances parked there. The rear doors of one were open and a man looked around on hearing their footsteps crossing the gravel.

“Hello Helen, what brings you here?”

“Good morning, Ted, I've got something on my mind...”

“Got bored of serving tea?” he asked.

“No!” she grinned. He was a lovely man, with a

daughter a bit younger than Jack. Helen often sat with his wife at the women's groups where they would chat and knit, while the children played around their feet. "It's silly really but I keep thinking of that pilot who was shot at yesterday. The one who bailed out."

"That's not silly," Ted replied. "These things play on our minds. Over and over sometimes." As an ambulance man, Ted knew all about that. He saw a lot of things and often had to deal with incidents he hadn't been trained for, sometimes volunteering for jobs beyond his role.

"It's just that we saw him fly over, Denny and me. We were thinking how it must feel to be up there in the sky and to see the coast, and to know you are safely home. But he wasn't, was he? He got shot at."

"It's a terrible business," Ted agreed. "Not just for him. Those men on the ground made a mistake and think how they'll suffer for it."

"I hadn't thought of them," Helen admitted. "Not like that, not about how they felt. We saw him bail out, and that's it. Do you know… have you heard what happened to him?"

"I can do better than that," Ted gave a grin. "It was me and Ernest who went along there and picked up the poor bloke. James, his name is. Comes from just over the border in Sussex. We took him through to the Victoria in Folkestone. He had a broken leg and his shoulder was a bit dodgy. Came down a bit awkwardly."

"But he'll be all right?"

"He'll be all right," Ted confirmed.

"Oh, thank you." Helen gave a big smile. "That's marvellous!" Suddenly the day didn't seem so grey. "I'd better get to the butcher now before it's too late."

"Have a good day then, you and little Jack."

"We will." Helen turned the pram around and manoeuvred it over the gravel. As she turned back into the High Street, she saw one of the ambulances had followed her, and as it passed her, Ted gave a wave. "Another incident," she said to Jack, who pointed with glee at the vehicle.

The depressing January continued, and February began with dark clouds bringing many days of rain. If the icy cold of previous winters had seemed bad, then this was even more intolerable. At least the washing would part-dry on the garden line with a wind and an Arctic chill. At least people could wrap up warmly and take a brisk walk to the shops or work in freezing weather, and not return muddy with a coat that would take all day to dry on the clothes horse in front of the fire. It was a miserable time, made only a little more bearable by the fact that the air-raid siren rarely blasted out at night.

The airfields could no longer be worked on, and farmers were struggling with flooded fields. The RAF squadrons went to do other duties and did not return until the springtime. In the skies, Allied bombers regularly flew in formation towards the coast: grey shapes partly concealed by clouds and their engine noise muffled by the rain.

It was on one of those days, when the rain fell steadily from dawn to dusk and the nappies steamed in front of the fire while woollen jumpers hung limp from the airer on the kitchen ceiling, that Allie brought heart-breaking news.

"Grace found Ma this morning," she told them, her face pale as she slumped in a chair at the dining table. "It looks as if her passing was peaceful, and she was where she wanted to be. Ma wanted to go home, didn't she?"

"She did," Lily said, tears brimming in her grey eyes. "Emily was an amazing woman, honest and loyal."

"She was a good mother," Allie agreed. "Firm with us, but full of fun and love."

"Can we go at the weekend?" Lily asked. "To see Edward and Grace, and... well it's where I first met her; I'd like to go to Dungeness."

"Of course," Allie said. "I'll tell them you'll be calling on Saturday."

Chapter Eighteen
February 1943

Casting concerned looks at the black clouds to the west, Lily and Helen scurried along the main road towards the railway station. They wore raincoats and the pram had a water-proof apron. "But however water-proof it is meant to be, it's hardly going to do much good at Dungeness," Helen had said. She was right, of course; a combination of rain and driving wind would force its way through most materials.

Although it wasn't raining for once, the gutters on the station building dripped. Pale channels showed though the grime on the brick walls where rivulets of water had trailed over the past weeks. The station master and porter had their collars up and hats pulled low; their expressions were those of people resigned to the wretched weather. There were no flowers in the window boxes or tubs; there hadn't been any throughout the spring and summer of the previous year. The station was tired and neglected. The steam trains passing through were no longer magnificent clanking beasts – they were cumbersome targets for agile fighter planes.

"Lydd Town, Lydd Town. All alight for Lydd Town," the female station master called out, her voice listless, unable to compete with the hissing of the engine. "Next stop: Lydd-on-Sea, then Greatstone-on-Sea and

New Romney."

A dozen passengers emerged, and Lily walked forward to hold a carriage door open. She stepped in and, leaning down, took the front of the pram to help lift it into the carriage. Helen stepped in behind her. Nodding a greeting to the other passengers, she noted that there was an air of defeat about them. None of the women had a slash of bright red or pink on their lips, a pretty scarf or fancy brooch. They were tired of this war: beaten down by the constant fear for loved ones, and the suffering they endured.

It will be easier in the spring when there is sure to be some good cause needing fund-raising and the communities will pull together. It will be easier when the dances begin again and the RAF come to the airfields, giving us new interests. Helen looked across at Lily and they gave each other a brief smile. It all would have been so much worse without the mutual support shared between the two women.

Within minutes the train slowed and stopped at Lade Halt. They stepped onto the platform, lifting the pram between them. Having passed the small wooden station building, Helen and Lily began their trudge along the coast road to Dungeness, with the dark clouds still hanging ominously above the Sussex hills to the west. They followed the route taken by the NAAFI van on a daily basis, turning off the main road and taking the concrete track that eventually led to the lighthouse on the shingle promontory. Homes changed from modern brick or rendered properties to the wooden dwellings. On passing the pub and the miniature railway track, Emily's tarred plank home came into view.

Helen paused for a moment looking towards Brooks Cottage as memories flooded back: those childhood holidays and outings; Emily beside her on the day Jack was born; the week spent here back in the spring of 1941. Suddenly it felt as if she had been holding her breath; she exhaled slowly and pushed the pram onwards.

"You didn't have to come," Grace said, "but it's lovely to see you."

"We wanted to," Lily replied.

"It felt like the right thing to do," Helen added.

They took off their coats and undid the straps holding Jack in the pram. He began to clamber out, with Helen holding it steady.

"Look at him, so independent!" Edward came into the room. "Good to see you both."

"Come and sit down," Grace walked to the range and pushed the kettle on to the hotplate.

There was always a feeling of coming home when Helen sat down in the living room of a Dungeness cottage. It was strange really, because she had never actually lived there, not like Lily who had stayed with Emily for several months, or Grandmother Alice who had lived at the schoolhouse for over a year. But the stories of Dungeness were passed down through the family. It was a place that held wonder and mystery for young minds; a place so unlike anywhere else that Helen and her Ashford relations ever visited. There were so many stories attached to both Lily's and Alice's visits: tales untold, adventures not fully explained.

The Dungeness homes didn't follow fashions or have the latest modern conveniences. Yet they moved with the times a little – Grace had chosen the green and yellow kitchen units just before the war broke out; and Emily had once spoken of one young housewife having an Art Deco sideboard. But these twentieth-century touches sat beside the central tables with mismatched chairs, the ranges used to cook and heat, and the old armchairs with re-stuffed and patched cushions. This is what Helen liked about these homes: the welcoming comfort; the not needing to conform to the latest fashions.

"I went to see the vicar in Lydd," Edward told them as Grace poured the tea. "It will be a graveside service in the cemetery. Perhaps a small gathering in the Hardy Hall, or a room at The George. Not much of a send-off, but that's how it is at the moment."

"And Ben?" Lily asked.

"He sent a telegram to say he'll be here."

"Oh wonderful," Lily replied.

"When is it?" Helen asked, imagining them all standing in the churchyard, heads hung, rain settling as a damp sheen over their coats.

"Next Thursday," Grace told them.

On the day of the funeral Grandmother Alice and Grandfather arrived from Ashford by steam train. Grandfather's car could no longer be used as petrol for private use had been withdrawn completely. Helen went to meet them at the railway station. Leaning forward to give Grandmother a kiss on her powdered cheek, it was clear Alice was suffering the loss of a dear friend. She looked tired, her face pale and eyes dull. Walking along to the cemetery, she needed the support offered by her husband's arm.

When they arrived in the cemetery, the sun sent shafts of warm light through the clouds, lifting Helen's spirits. The family and friends were coming together at the graveside, heads bowed and voices low. Lily separated from the group and went up to her parents, taking her mother's free arm and linking it with her own.

Ben Brooks was there, his hand wrapped around Elsie's. *It is wonderful that he can be here today,* Helen thought. His sister, Eva, had not seen her husband since late last summer; his family ties were not close enough to warrant leave. Besides, he was goodness-knows-where on a naval ship.

Jack was with another young mother for the morning. Helen was relieved not to have to keep him at her side, his small handheld within her own, or strapped in the pram. A funeral service was no place for a two-year-old. Later, at the small gathering in the Hardy Hall, he would be free to run about, and her grandparents would be pleased to see him.

A hush fell over the small group, and the rector began to say a few words about Emily. Helen listened, but felt the words wash over her, and her mind filled with memories of all the people lost over the last few years. The sunlight gathered strength, giving warmth to the mound of freshly dug earth, casting short shadows around the headstones, and perhaps giving a little hope to those huddled there.

“In the name of God, the merciful Father, we commit the body of Emily to the peace of the grave." The rector allowed his voice to rise a little and all eyes watched the lowering of the plain coffin into the ground. Leaning down, he scooped three handfuls of damp earth and let them drop on to the casket; each one fell with a dull thud. "From dust you came, to dust you shall return. Jesus Christ is the resurrection and the life." Standing back, he continued, his voice a monotone, compelling the mourners to listen to the gentle rhythm of his words: “The Lord Himself shall descend from heaven with a shout, with the voice of the archangel as he welcomes our loved one. And we, her family and friends left on this earth, shall rejoice in the knowledge that Emily is at peace, as her spirit returns to God who gave it."

The family moved forward to pick up a little of the earth and murmur their final goodbyes as it fell on the wooden lid of the coffin. Then old friends had their turn and Helen took some earth in her fingertips. It fell all at once, not scattering lightly as she felt it should, for it was wet and pressed together. *Goodbye Emily, thank you for your friendship.*

Afterwards, trailing along the pathway through the cemetery, Elsie turned and said: "The pilot – the one who bailed out. He is back here in Lydd. Recuperating."

"Oh?" Helen frowned, pulling herself to the present. "Gosh; it would be wonderful to meet him. Although perhaps he would think it a little odd?"

"I should think he would be very glad!" Elsie replied. "There's no petrol to spare to take him home to Sussex, so the poor man is stuck here with nothing much to do. It will be a lonely time for him while his leg heals."

"Perhaps I will then… with Denny." Helen thought about it for a moment, then confirmed: "Yes, I'll go with Denny; she'll want to be a part of it."

The following week, Helen took advantage of Elsie being at home while Jack had his afternoon nap and arranged to meet Denny outside the town hall. Both young women wore their winter coats and scarves. Plain skirts peeped out from under coats, the hems touching their knees. The February chill meant that woollen stockings were essential unless they were to be going to a dance, when cold legs were better than woollen-clad ones!

Denny was a couple of years older than Helen. Now in her mid-twenties, she was mourning the fact that *all* the local young men had gone to war. She kept desperately hoping to attract one of the visiting servicemen and she now thought the outing to the convalescent home might provide an opportunity to meet someone suitable. "One with just enough injury to keep him safe at home," Denny suggested to Helen, as she patted her victory roll, which sat above her forehead atop brown waves of thin hair. "I wouldn't mind moving away, perhaps to the West Country. That is if he had prospects..."

"There are some lovely men right here in Lydd," Helen replied. "They couldn't all go, not if they worked on the land, or had some medical reason."

"I don't know about someone with medical reasons," Denny said with a frown. "Anyway, let's see how it goes today; I might become a regular visitor. Someone who does reading or just pops in for a chat."

"Of course, you could." Helen tried to suppress a grin. "If you go every week there are sure to be new men arriving all the time."

They were now nearing Shrubbery House, a long brown-brick Georgian house set at the end of the High Street and fronting the pavement. Helen felt her pace slow a little as she wondered if they were doing the right thing in calling to see a stranger? But how would it feel to be placed in a nursing home, albeit a very pleasant one, and not have a friend or family member nearby?

"Nice and posh for those poor men," Denny commented, eyeing the impressive façade. "I'm looking forward to having a look inside, aren't you?"

Helen considered this as she raised her hand to

the brass knocker and rapped on the door a couple of times. “Yes… well, I hadn't thought, but it will be interesting. I hope it's all right for us to come calling… that they won't mind.”

But her last words were lost as they door swung open and a nurse in a blue dress and starched white apron stood before them, her expression both kindly and curious. “Hello. Can I help you?”

“We wondered if we could see… if it was possible to see the pilot, James...” Helen shot a worried look towards Denny. “Gosh, I don't know his surname, do you?”

“I don't,” Denny replied.

“He's not been here long,” Helen told the nurse. “He has a broken leg… from bailing out of his plane a couple of weeks ago.”

The nurse stood back, allowing them to enter. “I know who you mean; a nice young man, he is. But I take it you aren't family or friends, as you don't know his surname?”

“We saw him get fired at,” Helen informed.

“We were in the NAAFI van on the coast,” Denny added.

“And you're worried about him? Wanted to meet him?” The nurse gestured to a couple of chairs in the entrance hall. “Take a seat and I'll see if he is up to seeing visitors. I'm sure he is.”

The two women sat in silence, their eyes following the elegant handrail rising up the staircase and wondering what lay behind all the panelled doors. Kitchen sounds came from the rear of the house and a smell of boiled cabbage mingled with the scents of a hospital ward and tobacco smoke.

“James would love to meet you,” the nurse said when she returned. “This way.”

They followed her into a large room with a high ceiling and lamps suspended from it. The fire glowed in the grate and the walls were adorned with framed paintings in all shapes and sizes. It was busily furnished with lots of chairs and small tables covered with newspapers, books and puzzles. Most of these upright wooden chairs were vacant but the room was clearly able to hold quite a crowd. On one, a young woman sat by the piano, as if ready to start playing.

Then there were the men, in their blue cotton pyjamas and a smart tweed jacket or a comfortable cardigan. There were about eight of them and they all turned as the nurse and two young women came into the room. *How will we know who he is?* Helen panicked. But of course the nurse knew that the pilot, James, was a stranger to them and they were not going to be left without an introduction. But then there was no need, for sitting by the fire was a young man with his foot raised on a stool and his leg strapped up. His left arm was in a sling, propped on the arm of the easy chair; he raised his right hand in a greeting.

"Visitors! These chaps will be jealous; how lovely of you to come to see me."

Helen could not help but smile to see the pleasure on James' face and the warmth in his eyes. "We hoped you wouldn't mind..."

"Mind? Why would I?" James replied. "Do sit down, I'm sorry I can't stand to welcome you properly. It is no good having a broken leg and having to ask for help all the time." He waved his free hand in the direction of some chairs, and his expression sobered a little. "It could have been a lot worse though; I'm not complaining."

The young women weaved their way around the chairs and tables, then busied themselves with handing over their coats and scarves to the nurse. “I'm Helen and this is Denny,” Helen said as they sat down. “You must be wondering why we're here.”

“Well, it doesn't look like you're here on official business, which is a relief!” James replied.

“We wanted to know how you were… to see for ourselves,” Denny began.

“Because we saw it happen – the guns firing at you,” Helen continued.

And so they told their story of being in the NAAFI van and the horror felt when the Hurricane was hit.

“I don't really remember it,” James admitted. “No reason not to, I didn't get a bump on the head or anything.” He gave his head a tap; his fingers ruffling light brown hair.

“It must be the shock,” Denny said.

“Must be,” he agreed. “And I've lost my Hurricane. We'd been together for a while.”

“It wasn't your fault,” Helen reminded him.

“No and I imagine there will be one hell of a stink over it.”

“It killed some sheep,” Denny said.

“Denny… there was no need to say,” Helen felt herself become a little anxious, she leaned forward a little and said to James, “You couldn't help what happened. We must be thankful the plane missed the towns.”

“Still not nice though.” He looked towards the doorway and smiled. “Thank you, nurse. Kind of you to bring tea. It will be weak of course, but perhaps they'll come back if we can offer them a cup!”

“He's a lively one,” the nurse replied with a smile.

“Do you have any other visitors?” Denny asked.

“Not yet, but I'm expecting my parents at the weekend.”

Helen poured the tea and conversation turned to James' family who lived near Brighton and would travel by train on the Saturday. He asked about the work on the tea-van, and about life there in Lydd during the war.

"And will you be going back to war?" Denny asked.

"I should think so," James replied. "I can't see me getting away with this." He nodded towards the leg. "They say it will fix itself."

There was a moment's silence as the three of them pondered the risks of James returning to his squadron. They all knew his life was in the balance. Every time a plane set off, there was a chance it would be one of the ones that never returned.

"But before I go, perhaps I might get to one of those dances you told me about?" James said, his tone bright. "Will you save a dance for me?"

This brought smiles to their faces and with the clock showing an hour had passed, it was time to leave him. He asked if they would come again, and it was agreed that one or both would call the following week.

Chapter Nineteen
March-May 1943

“Another poster,” Helen muttered to Jack as they queued at the doorway of Cole's for the meat ration.

The little boy pointed at the images of planes on the sky and squealed: “Look Mama. Look. Air-planes in sky with man.”

“That's right, darling,” Helen forced some enthusiasm into her voice. “Shall we count them?”

Winston Churchill's head and shoulders were set before a backdrop of sky with planes. The words below offered communities the chance to show their gratitude to the Royal Air Force by contributing their support during the Wings for Victory week.

“If we raise money now, it will be thanks to us when we win the war,” another woman in the queue remarked, disbelief in her voice.

“...Ensuring a final victory,” Helen read. Just to see it depressed her; she shouldn't feel like that. This poster was meant to encourage positive feelings.

A couple of people left the shop and Helen, with her hand firmly around Jack's, moved forward in the queue.

“I don't think they'll make much of an aeroplane out of this.” Grace looked at the two saucepans, the battered frying pan and a couple of baking trays.

Helen and Jack had gone to help her sort through Emily's belongings. They were tidying out the kitchen cupboards, aware of the need to collect aluminium pots and pans to melt down.

"Maybe not, but with a few from Lily's house and Allie's and… well, you know what I mean," Helen handed Jack a wooden spoon. "Do you want to play drums?"

"We'll leave the rest of the household goods for now," Grace said. "It will be up to the next person who lives here to decide if they want them. It's not so easy to buy new at the moment and they might well be grateful. For now, we'll keep an eye on the place and do any repairs that need doing."

They had already filled boxes with Emily's and her husband Ed's personal belongings – photographs, letters and books. Now it was time to go through her clothes and for Helen to take a bag back to Lydd; the Women's Voluntary Service welcomed garments and material of any kind and passed it on to those in need. But, before that happened, there would be jumpers and cardigans whose wool could be reused within Grace's and Helen's families.

Emily's bedroom was dark and cold. Grace pulled back the curtains and opened the window. "That's better," she said. "It's horrible having to do this, isn't it? I really appreciate you coming to help."

"I know," Helen said, as they opened the wardrobe. "But it's not right for you to do it on your own. It brings back so many memories."

They worked for an hour, side by side, reminiscing and chatting about their daily lives. Four piles emerged on the bed. One for Helen, one for Grace, one for re-use in the community and the last for fabric recycling. As they closed the window and tidied up after Jack, Helen gave Grace some news.

"I'm going to see the pilot, James, on Friday. I've been once since I went with Denny, just to see how he was getting on..."

"And he asked you to go again?" Grace prompted.

"Yes." Helen busied herself with Jack's coat. "It must be lonely for him."

"Or perhaps he liked you for yourself, not just for the company?" Grace suggested. She didn't probe further; Helen usually kept her feelings to herself.

Helen walked across the Rype on the way to Shrubbery House. It felt good to have the open green around her. Spring had finally arrived, heralded by clumps of daffodils in front gardens, pale pink blossom on the branches of cherry trees and bright yellow forsythia flowers. The sun warmed her face and at last the breeze lacked a sharp chill. Helen allowed her pace to slow a little, telling herself it was pleasant to linger, but knowing it was due to her uncertainty about visiting the pilot.

James was a very pleasant man, she told herself. He was agreeable to the nurses, not demanding as she had heard some of the men being. When they spoke, he showed an interest in Helen, but did not intrude, seeming to sense that she was a little reserved. He talked with affection about his family and told her a little about his hometown and former occupation as an optician. Physically James was not particularly striking but, with his tawny brown hair and hazel eyes, he had a gentle look about him. His eyes were warm and smile friendly. There was nothing not to like about James, or nothing that Helen had discovered during their two meetings. She smiled to herself and picked up her pace; her husband had been dead for nearly three years and she was still a young woman. Would it be wrong to have a little romance in her life?

A nurse opened the door to the house and this time Helen did not have to wait in the hallway. “Come in; he's waiting for you,” the woman said, leading the way through to the room they called the reading room.

James was looking towards the doorway. “I hoped it would be you,” he said, the pleasure clear to see in his face. Using the arms of the chair and then putting his weight on a crutch, he managed to pull himself to his feet.

“Please don't get up on my account,” Helen gestured towards his chair. “Sit down again; it looks so difficult, juggling the crutch and balancing.”

“But I must make the effort,” James explained. “It will do me no good at all to be sitting about all day. I did three laps of the garden this morning!”

“Well done!” Helen couldn't help herself from smiling, to see this man who flew a plane across Europe, now so proud of walking a few yards around the garden of Shrubbery House. “And the doctors, they say that your leg is able to cope with the pressure put on it?”

“The bones are fusing together nicely,” James told her. “And so now I must use my muscles and not become lazy.”

“I see, well as long as the doctor said so, then it must be the right thing to be doing!”

“I wondered if you'd like to sit in the garden now, or is it too chilly?”

“I'd love to,” Helen told him.

She followed as he moved around the tables and chairs in the cluttered room, sometimes pushing a chair aside with the crutch. Resisting the urge to help him, Helen felt that James needed to manage on his own, not to be seen as dependent on her. It took a few minutes but finally they were sitting on ornamental metal chairs within the walled garden.

"Isn't it lovely here?" James said, gesturing to the spring flowers with his crutch. "Quite perfect."

"It is," Helen agreed. "Someone works very hard to keep it so attractive."

"Some of the chaps work out here," James told her. "I'd like to do something myself, when I can."

They spoke about the garden, and the allotments in their respective lives. Both their parents were growing vegetables in their hometowns and, here in Lydd, Bobby was in charge of the family vegetable plot. Tea was served on the table, and Helen opened her handbag to pull out a grease-proof paper package. "Only rock cakes," she apologised.

"Better than no cake at all!" James replied.

Looking at the metal garden furniture, Helen said, "There are all sorts of posters going up around the town. The latest is a pilot, just like you, sitting in the cockpit and smiling out at us. They want metal you see, to make more planes with."

"I've seen it in the papers. I guess my Hurricane needs replacing, and we must do our bit. I'd be sorry not to be able to sit out here though if they take our furniture."

"We offered a couple of saucepans," Helen said. "It's not much, but what can you do?"

"But just think: if everyone in Lydd gave two pans – I should think that would make a new plane, don't you?" James paused and grinned at her, "Especially if they took this garden furniture too. And the railings in front of houses!"

"There's to be a parade." Helen paused and took a

sip of her tea. "Around the town. It will be in May; it's to celebrate the fund-raising efforts."

"To boost morale."

"Yes, that's it."

"If I'm still here, I'll be able to watch from outside," James said, "if it goes the full length of the High Street."

Helen sat with him in the garden for about half an hour, finding that conversation flowed easily between the pair of them. When she rose to leave, James said: "I can't offer to take you dancing, but would you care for a walk around this green I hear about? Bring your little boy, perhaps on a Sunday afternoon?"

"A walk around the Rype?" Helen stalled. "It's not pretty like your Sussex villages or the Weald; it's not even as attractive as this garden."

"But it's here, on the doorstep, as they say, and I wouldn't want to venture out on my own." He gave a rueful smile "In fact they may not let me! Save me from another day stuck in here. Say you will. If only to make the other chaps jealous!"

Helen couldn't help but smile and her confusion melted away. "Oh, very well then. But a walk with a two-year-old is anything but restful!"

The people of Romney Marsh gathered pots and pans with enthusiasm throughout the early spring. They raided kitchen cupboards then turned to the garden sheds, as the urge to provide the metal for aeroplanes was spurred on by the posters throughout the towns and adverts printed in thin newspapers. As piles of cookware, tools and railings grew; they saw that they really could provide a wealth of metal if they all pulled together.

"Showing your legs, are you?" Bobby threw the

cheeky remark in Helen's direction as he walked through the kitchen on his way to feed the hens.

It was the first of May and promised to be sunny. “Time to put on a summer dress, I think,” Helen replied. Just to put aside the tweed skirts and worn cardigans in favour of a pretty, light outfit had lifted her spirits.

“I love that frock,” Lily commented. “You'll borrow my sling-back shoes, won't you? They'll be just right for today.”

“Yes please!” Helen said as she spooned porridge into bowls for herself and Jack.

The dress she wore was an old one from the days before the war. Allie's expertise in sewing had helped create something new by shortening it and removing the fussy bow at the neckline. A fresh scooped style, trimmed with a contrasting polka-dot material in navy blue, settled against Helen's collarbone. The new material continued to trim the hemline and sleeves. Not comfortable with the flamboyant victory roll worn by some women, Helen chose to pin her hair back at the sides and let it fall in natural waves on her collar. A small bow had been created from spare material and was clipped to the side of her head.

There was to be a parade that morning, starting in Coronation Square, before following the High Street and turning towards the Rype. It heralded the beginning of Wings for Victory week in which civilians were tasked with raising money to help the RAF.

“How much is it they want us to raise?” Bobby asked, returning with four eggs cradled in his hands.

“Ten thousand pounds!” Lily told him. “That's between us and Dungeness; it will pay for two Spitfires if we manage to do it.”

“I don't know how, what with everyone struggling,

but we'll do it," Bobby said. "We're not ready to give up yet."

"You're right," Helen agreed. "Winston Churchill has set us this target and he believes in us; I know he does."

"I see those posters and it makes me proud to be a part of it," Bobby said. "I can't go and fight, but I can do my very best."

"It will be over before you reach eighteen," Lily said. "We need to think of your education. Work hard when you move on to the grammar school and look to a better future."

Helen left early with Jack; she wanted to give him the opportunity to run and play on the Rype before having to stand and watch the parade. She chose not to take the pram and held the little boy's hand as they moved away from the green and followed the narrow streets along to the High Street. "We're going to watch the parade with James and the other poor men who've been hurt," she told Jack.

"He couldn't play ball," Jack recalled.

"He couldn't," Helen agreed. "But he can when his leg is better." The High Street was becoming crowded, so Helen lifted Jack and balanced him on her hip. As they approached Shrubbery House, she could see a row of wooden chairs lining the pavement, their backs to the brown brick wall of the house.

James was there, his crutches propped against the wall. On seeing his guests, he turned to drag the crutches forward and pulled himself up. Balancing on just one support, he attempted a wave. "Hello!"

"Good morning." Helen couldn't help smiling to see him there. "How are you?"

"Getting along quite nicely," James replied. Then

he raised his eyebrows a little and grinned before saying: “Golly, you do look lovely and summery today.”

“It is May, so it seemed like time to be summery.” Helen looked into his sparkling eyes, then turned her attention to Jack. “Listen darling, can you hear the music? It's the soldiers coming along the road.” In the distance there was the merest hint of drums and brass instruments; the musical notes flitted in-between the chatter on the streets, the scraping of chairs and footsteps on the pavement.

“The band's still too far away,” James said. “But we'll see them in no time; they must be on their way. Listen, I appreciate you coming here to be with me. It was good of you.”

“Thank you for inviting us,” Helen said.

“I was hoping to meet the rest of your family.”

“They are going to follow the band,” Helen told him. “They'll not be far behind.” *But do I want him to meet my family?* she wondered. *Will it mean...mean that he is more than I meant him to be? And if he were to become important to me, then would that be so terrible? I just don't know.* She smiled at James, hoping he didn't read the concern in her eyes.

“Is this them coming – the band, I mean?” James craned his neck to look up the street where the pavements were lined with on-lookers.

Sure enough, a jaunty tune was now clearly audible and the first of the soldiers could be seen. They marched, looking straight ahead, heads held high. Just to see them made Helen's heart swell with pride. They were so brave, facing death and fighting for their country. She must smile her encouragement and do whatever needed doing to support them. And if serving them tea, cigarettes and Ration Chocolate helped cheer their day, then Helen was more than happy to play her small part in the war.

The music from the brass now filled the air and radiated through her body. At her feet, Jack stamped his shoes on the pavement, and she smiled to note that he was trying to march like the soldiers did. As they passed, Helen lifted the little boy so he could watch them until they reached the end of the street. Following behind were the mayor and other dignitaries, then representatives from the police, fire and ambulance services. Finally, there were the boy scouts and girl guides with their own band. Although not as compelling, their drums, trumpets and trombones led to smiles and shouts of encouragement from those gathered at the side of the road.

The people of Lydd soon spilled off the pavements, becoming part of the procession. They waved paper flags, and some carried their own instruments, while others launched into song. Helen hung back, waiting for Lily and Bobby to appear. She soon spotted them, walking with friends and neighbours. "Over here!"

They moved towards Shrubbery House and the line of patients, now slowly dispersing since the parade had passed. Helen, unsure of how to introduce James to her family, need not have worried.

"Hello, I'm James." He stepped forward and, balancing on one crutch, made an awkward attempt at offering his hand.

"Lovely to meet you. I'm Lily and this is Bobby," Lily replied with an easy smile.

And then Bobby was asking about the Hurricane and the crash and James was explaining that he didn't really remember it. Bobby was hopeful that he would in time, and so the conversation flowed. Helen felt herself relax a little.

"We're going to the fête," Lily told James. "I don't know if you're able to...or if you'd like to come?" She eyed his leg and the crutches.

"It might be a bit much for me with all these crowds." James offered a rueful smile. "I've been getting about a bit, but I'll wait until it's quieter. The nurses are going to take a few of us out later, and I'm hoping to get myself along to the Rype. They say that's where the action is!"

"We need to raise ten thousand pounds," Bobby informed him.

"I'll make sure I bring some money then!" James gave him a grin and continued, "If you'd like to, but don't feel you must, they are serving tea and fruit cake in the garden here. Donations for the cause, of course."

"I think Jack would rather be running about and I..." Helen's words trailed away. This was too soon, not what she was looking for.

"Of course," James agreed. "It's not the sort of place for a little boy."

Lily looked towards Helen, a slight frown on her face as she tried to understand. "Perhaps later, if we see you?" she suggested.

"That would be perfect," James agreed.

Chapter Twenty
September 1943

"Newchurch next, and then I wonder what Brenzett will have on offer." There was a gleeful tone to Annie's voice, as they drove through the pretty village of St Mary in the Marsh. "I've got high hopes! I'm telling you, Helen, I'm going to find my pilot there!"

Helen grinned and rolled her eyes. Annie would never give up and she liked that about her. In her own life she had no thoughts of finding herself a pilot, a soldier or a sailor!

Three of the airstrips had become operational in the early summer and the long-awaited pilots and ground crew were in place. There had been delays at the fourth, Brenzett, and the men had only just arrived, hence Annie's enthusiasm to meet them.

Romney Marsh drowsed in the late summer sun. The fields were parched and the grass thin, offering little sustenance to the sheep. Helen spotted a heron which, startled by the noise of the van, soared upwards, its body awkward as if flight did not come naturally. The bent willows by the sides of the waterways were in full leaf, giving a romantic look to the drainage ditches and, to make the vision complete, elegant swans sunned themselves.

There were very few properties set alongside the narrow road; the area was sparsely populated and sometimes the duo would drive for miles without passing another person. However, land girls were becoming part of the landscape and Helen spotted a small team turning hay with long pitchforks. Others manoeuvred low carts pulled across the fields by heavy horses, who then waited patiently for them to be filled.

Bordering this flat land, the distant line of hills was featureless in the heat haze. The van windows were open, and the air was thick with the dust from freshly harvested hay. Occasionally the rich smell of manure wafted in. The only thing to disturb the peace of such a pastoral scene was the sound of *Nancy's* engine clattering and roaring along.

The square church tower and cottages of Newchurch came into view. Annie drove into the village and swung around to the left, then on to a track leading to the airfield.

"The planes are here then," she commented as the airstrip and its buildings became visible.

The Spitfires sheltering within the four hangers could just be seen through open doors. There was some movement around one of the planes and, as the tea-van come to a stop, men emerged, blinking as their eyes adjusted to the bright sunlight. A couple of them were wiping their hands on rags and it was clear they had been working on one of the planes.

"I don't recognise those two," Helen pointed to a pair of men walking over from the stores.

"Oh, I saw them yesterday," Annie said. "New they are. Nice blokes. Right, let's get the kettle on the boil or we'll have complaints!"

There was a different atmosphere to the airfields now, Helen thought, as she went about her duties, automatically lifting the canopy and dropping the shelf down on the side of the van. Whereas the men working on the sites over the winter were disgruntled by the miserable working conditions and lack of entertainments, the squadrons of pilots and ground-crew were cheery and good company. Here in Newchurch, they frequented the Black Bull in the evening during the week and the village hall on a Saturday, when a dance or some other form of entertainment was held.

The men were now milling around the van.

“Hello girls, what have you got for us today?”

“Victoria Sponge?”

“Cadbury's bar?”

“Apple pie and cream?”

“You'll be lucky,” Annie replied. “There's a war on, as if you hadn't noticed.”

“But we thought you'd have something special, something put aside for us.”

“That's what they all say,” Helen replied with a grin. She was getting used to the banter; it was becoming easier.

“Actually, we have got something today...” Annie gave a big grin.

“Not Ration Chocolate!” One of the men groaned and others joined in. “Come on love, bring out the Cadbury's.”

“I would if I could.” Annie poured water into the huge enamel teapot.

“What have you got then?”

“Hold on, hold on. You can see I'm busy.” Annie raised her eyebrows.

Helen was pouring a splash of milk into each of the tin mugs. She looked back towards Annie. “I'll get them, shall I?” Reaching down to pick up one of several large tins on the floor, she lifted one up and opened the lid. "There you go – rock cakes!" She put the tin on the shelf. "Only one each mind – we've still got to go to Brenzett and Midley."

"And here's the tea," Annie announced, putting the first of the mugs on the shelf.

The men moved forward, taking a mug of tea and a bun. Grateful for the diversion, and the female company, each one gave his thanks. One had an unusual accent which led Helen to give him a second glance. It wasn't American, or South African; she couldn't quite place it. He moved aside and the next one reached out for his drink.

"Let's spend ten minutes standing in the sunshine," Annie said, pouring tea for them both when all the men had been served.

They stepped out of the back of the van and stood in the warm air. It was a pleasant spot to pause for a while, with far-reaching countryside views and, closer to hand, the airfield still held an interest for the women who had been visiting it for a couple of months now.

"Where's the red-head?" It was the man with the unusual accent again; Helen still couldn't place it. "Will she be here tomorrow?"

Helen looked at him. He was in his forties, she imagined – tall with brown hair and soft blue eyes. Under the RAF shirt, his shoulders were broad, and muscular arms were revealed where his sleeves were rolled back, His hand, still holding the tin mug, was large. This was a man who could chop down a tree or wield a hefty mallet with no effort. His face was kind and his smile gentle. "The red-head?" Helen repeated with a smile. "You must mean my aunt."

"Oh, is she?" He looked genuinely pleased to hear of the connection. "Does she work regular days on the tea-van?"

“We take it in turns,” Helen told him. “But she might not be on the airfields run tomorrow. We go along the coast too.”

“I'll just have to hope she is.” He raised his eyebrows a little and gave an apologetic smile. “I thought she was nice!”

“She is.” Helen found herself smiling back. “I can't place your accent, where are you from?” she asked.

“Western Australia,” he said.

“Oh gosh, and you've come here to help us. How wonderful.”

“You can't beat them on your own,” he replied. “I'm Ian, by the way.” He held out his hand.

“Helen,” she said, placing her small hand in his huge one. “Nice to meet you.”

With her tea finished, it was time to start rinsing out the mugs. Helen poured a couple of inches of hot water in a bowl and took a cloth from the side. Yet again the women had to be economical with the water as storage in the van was restricted. “It's more of a wipe than a wash,” Denny would often say when out with Helen.

Some of the men returned to their work, but several hung around until the van left. Many were lonely for female company and took the opportunity to chat while the women tidied up.

As Helen fixed the shelf back in place, one of the men spoke to Annie as she stood by the doorway, wiping out the mugs. His accent was strong, perhaps from Birmingham.

“There's a dance here at the weekend. Why don't you come?”

“I'd love to but how can I get over here for an evening?” she asked.

"How about you cycle over, and I borrow a truck to take you home?" he suggested.

"Can you see me messing up my hair on a bike?" She put a hand to her victory roll and, looking flirtatiously at him, ran the tip of her tongue over her lips.

"Well, have a think about it, darling," he reached forward and placed a hand on Annie's buttock. Helen turned away, but not before she saw him give Annie a squeeze.

Annie gave a low cackle. "Easy, I'm not that kind of girl."

"Are you sure about that?" the man laughed as he moved away.

After speaking to Ian and thinking what a pleasant man he was, Helen felt quite sick to witness this scene. She said nothing to Annie as they drove away; the older woman enjoyed any attention from a man, regardless of his intentions. "On to Brenzett and another squadron," Annie said, with relish.

It was not far to the next airfield, but the journey was nerve-racking for Helen who would have preferred Annie to drive a little more gently along the narrow, winding lane. After a sharp swerve to the right, seemingly without checking the new road was clear, then a turn to the left, they neared the newly opened airfield. As if to confirm it was indeed up and running, the rattle of *Nancy's* engine was overpowered by the sound of a Spitfire overhead. The plane swooped over them, skimming the tree-tops, and was soon bumping along the landing strip.

Annie found a suitable place to park the van and as they got out, an officer approached them. "Oh, my word!" Annie murmured. "There's all my dreams rolled into one!”

He was a tall man, and his RAF uniform fitted him very well, showing off long legs, a trim waist and square shoulders. His dark hair was neatly slicked with a side parting and the closely cropped sides were greying. His skin was tanned, emphasising the blue of his eyes. He exuded confidence; Helen stepped back a little, allowing Annie to take the lead in talking to him.

“Good morning! A tea-van – my men will be pleased. I'm David Mason.” He was well spoken, as Helen expected. A lean hand was offered first to Annie, who grasped it.

“I'm Annie.” Letting go she put her hand up to check her hat was in place and lowered her eyelashes a little. “And this is Helen.”

Helen moved forward and forced herself to look into his eyes “Nice to meet you.” She gave a brief smile.

“We'll be here at about this time every day,” Annie told him. “Perhaps not us… unfortunately, but the van will be here with tea and chocolate, cigarettes and sweets. Sometimes an extra treat. We do our best.”

“I'm sure you do.” He appraised Annie's rounded breasts and curvaceous hips.

“Send the men over any time.” Annie flashed a smile. “They enjoy a chat as well as the refreshments.”

“Very well, I'll spread the word.”

The women on the NAAFI van enjoyed the route taking them around the country lanes that summer and autumn. They watched the crops being harvested and the lambs mature until they were fully grown. Hawthorn berries ripened to a rich, glossy red as autumn progressed and reeds withered at the edges of the dykes.

There were a few exceptions, but the men generally treated the volunteers on the van with respect and they got to know them as they gathered around for their tea, clearly enjoying the company. Ian, the Australian, always had a warm smile for Helen, followed by a comment about how nice it had been to see her Aunt Lily again yesterday. And when Lily was known to be suffering with a bad cold, he presented Helen with a small bouquet of blowzy autumn roses, grasses, and leaves. "An old lady let me have them from her garden," he said, as he showed Helen.

"For me?" she asked, in mock surprise.

"For Lily!" he replied, knowing she was joking.

"She'll love them," Helen said, and she meant it. There was something special about this man and she thoroughly approved of his interest in her aunt.

Sometimes the men from the airstrips were able to find the petrol to journey into one of the towns on a Saturday evening and attend a dance. Used to the army being in Lydd, the RAF men in their dark blue uniforms caused a bit of a stir amongst the local women, there being a general agreement that there was something rather exciting about being a pilot. Helen and Lily attended the dances on a regular basis. A neighbour looked after Jack as Elsie now came with them. There seemed to be an urgency to have fun. The members of the forces never knew if that dance would be their last and the people who stayed at home felt an obligation to entertain these brave men. Re-working old dresses into new styles became something that regularly absorbed the women during the evenings.

Helen cradled Ian's flowers on her lap as Annie drove them back to Lydd and reflected on Lily who had been a widow since the October of 1940. At forty-three years old she was still an attractive woman, with little grey hair amongst her auburn waves and only thin laughter lines around her eyes and mouth. There had been a new glow about Lily recently, a suppressed excitement as she prepared for work or dressed up for the local dance. Helen hoped it was the gentle Australian who had brought a new pleasure into her aunt's life. But with it came fear and uncertainty, and she was sure Lily would dwell on these anxieties while enjoying the new experiences.

"For you!" Helen handed Lily the flowers, glad that they were alone, apart from Jack who wasn't likely to offer an opinion.

"Oh, *lovely*! From Ian?" Lily coloured a little.

"He asked after you," Helen told her. "He's delightful, isn't he?"

"He is!" Lily relaxed a little. "But, well… you know..."

"Charlie?" Helen asked. "It's been a while and you'd never forget him."

"Not likely!" Lily grinned. "But Ian will be gone again in no time, posted somewhere else, and what if..."

"Yes, he'll move on with his squadron," Helen agreed. "But he doesn't strike me as one of those men who pick up a new woman at every airstrip. He's not like that, is he?"

"No." Lily pondered the matter. "No, he isn't"

"And he doesn't have a wife at home, does he?"

"No, he says not."

"And not every pilot will die. And the war will be over one day," Helen persisted.

"No, and yes it will."

"So, no harm in inviting him for dinner one

Sunday?" Helen suggested.

"Oh gosh..." Lily's eyes widened.

"Or go out, just the two of you. To The George or somewhere? Perhaps further afield?"

"On the train perhaps?" Lily wondered. "Maybe we will… if he asks."

On Saturday evening, Lily's smiles were radiant when the truck from Newchurch pulled up in the High Street as she and Helen walked towards the Guild Hall. The men from the RAF 19th Squadron poured out of the back and Ian immediately bounded over, giving each woman a kiss on the cheek.

"G'day. I hope you're both going to save a dance for me."

"I will – what about you, Lily?" Helen felt completely at ease with the Australian. She hoped everyone in the family would feel the same; she was certain he was here to stay.

"Well, I've already got them queuing up..."

"I'll have none of it; they'll have to line up behind me!" And he placed his arm around Lily's waist. "Let them try to take you from me!"

Walking upstairs to the dance hall, Helen felt invigorated to hear the beat of the music and the soft tones of the singers. Recalling her first dance when she was reluctant to move onto the dance floor with anyone, she realised how much she had changed. Now she was there to have fun, and she had learned to enjoy the lively atmosphere without fear of any expectations of forming an attachment with anyone. She particularly enjoyed the American influence in the music played, with the Andrews Sisters being a great favourite. Like many of the local women, Helen was keen to learn new dance steps and spend a moment or two engrossed in something that had nothing to do with the dreadful war, which now seemed as if it had been going on forever.

The NAAFI van girls were all there. Denny had formed an attachment to an older man who was one of the officers based at the army camp. She confided in Helen, as they drove along the country lanes or the coast road, that she and the officer had reached an understanding, or at least she felt sure they had. Denny wondered about the distant towns and villages of Wiltshire where he came from and, if he were to ask, would a wedding take place there in some unknown town, or here in Lydd, where the church was partly destroyed so that services now had to take place in the Hardy Hall – a rather insignificant corrugated iron hut.

That evening Helen noticed that Annie was subdued. Her laugh still rang out, but it was less raucous. Usually the first to line up at the supper table, she picked at a few things but seemed uninterested. David Mason, the man who she had declared to be “all my dreams come at once” asked her to dance and she accepted, but with no enthusiasm. Helen looked on, feeling puzzled as she had never seen her fellow tea-lady in low spirits before. Happy or sad, her emotions were usually freely expressed, leaving others in no doubt as to how she was feeling.

“Is everything all right?” Helen moved close to Annie as they walked off the dance floor.

“I'm just feeling a bit tired,” Annie said. “You know how it is...”

“It's not like you,” Helen linked her arm through Annie's. “Shall we move out into the hallway, where it's a bit quieter?”

“Somewhere cooler. I'd like that.” The new docile

Annie allowed herself to be led out of the room.

They walked down the stairs and found a couple of chairs in the hallway. Annie slumped on one and yawned. She closed her eyes for a moment, then opened them and said: “I've been knocked up as they say. Can you believe it? Me, thirty-nine years old and in the family way!”

Chapter Twenty-One
June 1944

Driving along the lanes to Newchurch, Helen reflected on the contrasts all about them: the sky was a pure blue; the grass was a lush green in the fields; swans clustered by a pool; lambs were stocky and white in the fields. Yet above them, one by one the Spitfires and Typhoons were taking off from the airstrip. Not to fly across the Channel to Germany or France, but to face a new terror in the skies above them.

It had been rumoured, but who would have believed it, that there could be such a thing as flying bombs? When Helen had cut *Nancy's* engine at the previous airstrip, the rhythmic ack-ack-ack of the guns on the coast could be heard. Pointing over the sea, the gunners tried to shoot down the rocket-like missiles with their flaming tails, but any they missed then had to be faced by the fighter planes. Day and night the huge guns pointed to the sky and the cacophony, as bullets blazed through the skies, travelled far inland and rang within people's heads long after the firing had ceased.

D-Day had passed just two weeks beforehand; the Allies had landed in Europe and after months of heavy bombing it seemed that the people of Romney Marsh could allow themselves to hope for peace. But it was not to be, as Hitler's new weapon, the flying bomb or doodlebug, was sent to kill and cause panic.

"You've got the hang of this driving business!" Maeve said. "You take it nice and steady."

"It's not easy in this great beast," Helen replied. "I'm sure Annie would be complaining that I'm too slow."

"Well, Annie isn't here and I'm not complaining about feeling nice and safe, not tearing round corners and being flung about in my seat!"

"I'm going to call in to see her tomorrow," Helen said. "Isn't little Sylvia a beauty?"

Annie had stunned them all by marrying a local man, John Harvey, who was a carpenter as well as serving on the home guard. How romance had flourished, no one was sure, for he had never been seen at one of the dances, and Annie had not mentioned a trip to the cinema or a walk on a Sunday with him in the weeks before her marriage was announced. In fact, she continued to flirt with the men on the airstrips until the thin gold band was firmly on her ring finger.

The wedding had taken place in the December of 1943, just before the swell of her stomach became obvious. Annie had continued to serve on the tea-van during the winter months until it became cumbersome for her to drive *Nancy* or to squeeze into the rear. Then she had settled down to run the home and to meet with local women who knitted for the soldiers. Her laugh was just as coarse and the slash of red across her lips just as bold, but Annie had relaxed into the role of wife and mother in a way her friends could never have imagined.

Any thoughts of Annie and her beautiful baby daughter were lost as the planes started firing at doodlebugs. Helen had to concentrate on the road, but

Maeve, her new companion, craned her neck to see as much of the sky as possible.

"They've got one," Maeve reported, "And another...Oh, my Lord, it's coming down." The bomb landed in a field to their right and exploded.

Helen, her knuckles white on the steering wheel, had no choice but to carry on. "Did I do the right thing, staying here with Jack?" she asked, knowing Maeve couldn't possibly answer.

"You did what was best for you both at the time," Maeve replied. "Who would imagine we'd have all this going on above our heads?"

"I know."

"I ask myself the same question." Maeve said. She was mother to two boys who had been evacuated at the beginning of the war, only to return when it seemed that there was no real threat from the Germans. Her husband was the local postman, as well as carrying out home guard duties. She frowned, looked ahead, then said: "They missed one."

The flying bomb was almost as big as a small fighter plane, with its streamlined body and engines perched on its wings. Packed with ammunition and no pilot on-board, it was set on a path to destroy someone or something unknown to the women in Nancy-the-NAAFI-van. Helen eased off the throttle and they could hear the deadly weapon overhead, not unlike a small car labouring through the summer sky. Its flaming tail shone bright, even in the sunshine. For a moment she thought of images of Halley's Comet, seen in her school text books.

A Spitfire soared overhead. Helen's shoulders tensed and she felt slightly sick. "It's going after it."

Now the action was directly in front of the van which had rolled to a halt. Helen's mouth was dry as she became mesmerised by the scene unfolding. Rather than shooting at it, the Spitfire pilot was tracking the flying bomb, keeping steady and closing in on it. The fighter plane moved alongside. Then, in a flash, the pilot tipped his wing and caught the doodlebug, sending it off course and plummeting to the ground. A fountain of water erupted upwards as it hit the ground.

"It landed in a dyke then," Maeve commented, her voice quiet.

"I can't believe we just saw that," Helen replied. "How could he… how could he take the risk?"

"I guess he knew what he was doing," Maeve said. "But imagine if it hadn't worked."

"We'd have seen him blown up in front of us," Helen said shakily. "It doesn't bear thinking about."

They were driving through the village now. People were standing at their doorways, looking skywards. This was all new to them; they were used to the RAF and the Luftwaffe fighters and bombers, but the sinister doodlebugs brought a new twist to the war.

At the airfield, the mood was sombre. The ground crew were agitated, their faces turned to the sky. The crew included riggers and fitters who had only just prepared the pilots for flight, knowing some of them might not survive. There were engineers too, and the armourers who had ensured the fighter planes had all the ammunition they needed. The team had done all they could, and now there was nothing to be done but look on, wait and pray all the pilots would return safely.

Ian was up there in one of the Typhoons. *Should I have encouraged his romance with Lily?* Helen wondered as she put the kettle on the hob. *Surely these flying bombs will cause the death of many good pilots.* Tin mugs were raised to lips and chunks of Ration Chocolate snapped off the small bars, but this was not a day for light-hearted banter and the two women left in low spirits.

"We're meant to be cheering them up." Maeve slumped in the passenger seat.

"Sometimes we just can't," Helen replied as she turned *Nancy* on to the country lane and pointed the van towards Brenzett.

Here it was the same: the ground crew were looking to the sky, then wandered over to the tea-van minus their usual smiles.

"It's all going on up there, girls," one said, jerking his head to the heavens.

"It's terrifying," Maeve said. "All that awful noise coming from the guns on the coast... it's a living nightmare."

"Some of them are tipping the doodlebugs with their wings and that's not the way it's meant to be done," an engineer informed. "Damned clever of our men up there, but the bosses aren't happy."

"Tipping the doodlebugs?" Helen repeated. "Golly, we just saw that; it was terrifying."

"But it worked?" the man asked.

"The bomb ended up in a dyke," Maeve told him. "I guess it saved someone in London losing their life or their home, but it's not doing our countryside any good."

"Fair enough." He took his tea and stepped away.

Without all the banter, and fewer men to serve, they were soon tidying away, but one man approached Helen as she wiped out the cups. "There was someone asking after you," he said. "One of the new pilots; he was asking if you came here in the tea-van."

"Oh?" Helen frowned. "I can't think who..."

"James his name is."

"James? Gosh, James with the broken leg?" It had been a year since he had left The Shrubbery and returned to his squadron. A couple of letters had followed, and James had told of being on light duties while he returned to full strength. The last she had heard the pilot was about to start flying again. There had been nothing more; Helen often wondered if he had survived the past year.

"He hasn't got a broken leg now!" the man said. "In fact, I got his plane started just an hour ago.

"So, he's up there." Helen gazed into the distance where the shapes of the Spitfires and Typhoons could just be recognised.

"That's right. He asked to be remembered to you if I saw you before he did."

"Give him my best wishes, please." It seemed rather inadequate when Helen considered the danger James was in. "I… I'll see him soon. I hope."

Helen and Maeve journeyed on to Midley, the final airstrip of the day. Both sobered by the day's events, they had little to say as Helen negotiated the twists and turns in the narrow lanes. The planes, although not overhead, could still be seen. But as they approached the airstrip, it seemed as if the threat was over for the day – the fighter planes were coming into land one after the other. By the time they had parked up and the kettle was boiling, a couple of the pilots were sauntering over. The strain showed on their faces as they shrugged off thick flying jackets, but their comments belied the intense stress endured during the couple of hours they had spent in the air.

"We arrived just in time then!"

"Got the tea ready, ladies?"

"And a nice bit of fruit cake?"

"It's a Victoria sponge for me, my love."

Helen poured the tea, while Maeve placed the mugs on the shelf at the hatch. "If I could bake you men a nice cake, then I would," Maeve told them. "But in case you hadn't noticed..."

"There's a war on," one of the pilots finished. "I thought there might be!"

"Good of you to drop by and see us," Maeve continued. "They weren't so sociable at the other airstrips."

"Let's hope it's over for today," the pilot said. "You'll wait for all the planes to come in, won't you? We'd appreciate it."

"Of course, we will." Helen stepped out of the van, her own mug of tea in her hand. "We've got plenty of time."

After a tense and difficult day, the NAAFI volunteers felt a little more cheerful when they left Midley. They had seen all the pilots arrive safely back and there had been no reports of any fatalities in the skies that day.

That weekend there was another dance, but Helen stayed at home while Lily and Elsie went out to enjoy themselves. With Jack in bed the house was quiet, and she sat at the table and wrote letters, first to her grandparents and then her parents. She told of her increasing confidence as she sat behind the wheel of the tea-van and of the wildlife she saw as she travelled along the Marsh lanes. Helen wrote a little about the men on the airfields and how pleased they were to have the van arrive. She said nothing of the distant *patter-patter* of guns firing or what it was like to see the Typhoons and Spitfires in the skies above, gunning down the flying bombs. She didn't write about the horror felt when watching the wing-tip of a fighter plane push the bomb off-course and how sickening it was to see it plunge to the ground where it could kill or injure.

Helen wrote a little about going along the coast; she told how the sea sparkled in the sunshine and that, sometimes, the white cliffs of Dover could be seen. She didn't mention that here the sound from the guns could be unbearable and how the shattered bombs rained down upon the sea. As she signed her name at the end of the letters, Helen felt relieved. It was still early but she changed into the comfort of her nightdress and slippers before making a cup of tea and settling in an easy chair with a book and a blanket. As she thought of going to bed, Helen's eyelids began to drop, and she dozed off in the chair.

Lily and Elsie returned home at about eleven o'clock; the sound of the front door closing, and their loud whispers woke Helen.

"You're still up," Lily said as she sat down in the second easy chair. "It's a beautiful night out there. So quiet. No guns."

Helen nodded her understanding, still a little confused at finding herself in the chair, rather than in her bed. "Good evening?" she asked.

"It's always good to dance!" Elsie said.

"And was Ian all right?" Helen asked Lily. "It's not easy up there."

"A little quiet. All the pilots were," Lily replied.

"But there was one asking after you, Helen," Elsie added. "It was James; he's come back."

Helen frowned a little. *What would it have been*

like if she had been there? Perhaps a little awkward? For a time she had wondered if there might be something between them but, despite his good nature, Helen had felt herself holding back and she didn't know why. Perhaps he felt the same; her last letter had gone unanswered. Yet there was the memory of another pilot still flitting into her mind occasionally and she scolded herself whenever she dwelt on Karl who, as far as she knew, was in a prisoner of war camp until he returned to his home at the end of the war.

"He sent his best wishes and hopes to see you soon," Lily added.

"That will be nice," Helen replied, reluctantly pulling her thoughts back to James. "I hope he had no trouble from his leg."

"He looked well enough." Lily said. "You're sure to see him at the airstrip within the next few days." She gave a long yawn. "It's bedtime for me."

The next couple of days that Helen spent on Nancy-the-NAAFI-van were on the coastal route. Whether the guns were silent or firing, there was tension amongst the men. Their skin looked grey and faces gaunt. "It won't be long now," everyone said to each other, but the words did little to ease the strain.

"I saw James again," Lily told Helen; she had been on the rural run. "He was hoping to see you."

"I daresay he will soon enough," Helen replied. She was folding the bedsheets which were crisp and dry from being on the washing line all day.

"He mentioned the dance at the weekend and hopes to be there."

"Perhaps I'll see him then," Helen said, picking up the pile of linen. "I'll just put these away in the cupboard."

Helen and Denny took the countryside route the next day, this time with Denny at the wheel. By the time they reached the St Mary in the Marsh landing ground, the fighters had already taken to the sky and the guns on the coast could be heard.

"Here we go again," Denny muttered.

Driving on to Newchurch, they spotted a couple of doodlebugs that had evaded the coastal defences and now had Typhoons in pursuit. Both flying bombs exploded in the sky, raining debris over fields, roads and people's homes.

Just as they reached the village there came a sound so violent that, even above the noise of *Nancy's* engine and the rattle coming from the back of the van, Helen and Denny both gasped and turned to look at each other.

"That was close." Helen felt her body go cold.

"Doodlebug?" Denny questioned.

"I hope so."

There was nothing to be seen. The back of the van was bulky, obscuring any view of what was happening in the sky behind them. They could only assume it was a doodlebug and knew it had come down not far away. As the road twisted and Helen could see back towards St Mary in the Marsh, she spotted a spiral of smoke slowly swirling upwards.

They were soon in Newchurch and pulling into another airstrip that was free of fighter planes. The men came forward; they had news to share and their distress was clear to see.

"There's a plane down," one of them said. "Did you see it?"

"No," Denny replied, as she filled the kettle. "But we heard an almighty bang; we thought it was a bomb."

“It was a plane.”

“What happened?” Helen asked.

“Too soon to tell. Perhaps the pilot tried to wing-tip and it went wrong, or perhaps… it could be any number of things.”

Another one of the ground crew approached. “Word has just come in,” he said. “They say it was two planes that collided.”

“No, it was one,” the first said, his voice agitated. “That's what I heard.”

“It's two. That's the latest. I wish it weren’t, but it just came over the radio.”

Helen placed mugs of tea on the serving shelf. She said nothing. Two planes down; two pilots killed or critically injured. Was this why she steered clear of any romance?

As the men drank the last of their tea in near silence, all faces were raised to the sky to follow the path of a lone Spitfire heading for the airstrip. “Engine sounds a bit rough,” one of them commented and the others nodded their understanding.

“I'd like to know who it is,” Helen said to Denny. “Let's see if there is any news. Whoever was in those planes, we were bound to have known them.” She was thinking of Lily and in her mind the words ran over and over: *Don't let it be Ian; please don't let it be Ian.*

The aircraft touched down and a couple of the ground crew approached it. The two women, standing beside the NAAFI van, looked on. With the heat of the summer sun beating down, the pilot was soon removing his bulky jacket and speaking to engineers, pointing towards the engine as he did so. Then he walked away and came towards Helen and Denny.

“It's Ian!” Helen said.

“Thank God for that,” Denny let out a long sigh.

They watched the Australian approach. He offered a brief smile and put an arm around Helen's shoulders, giving her a quick hug. “I'm glad you're here,” he said. “You can tell Lily that I'm all right.”

“So am I,” Helen replied fervently.

“It's bloody awful up there.” He nodded to the sky.

“I know.” Helen looked at him, not wanting to ask, or knowing how to express the words. “Do you…? It was all so quick: do you know who it was?”

“I'm not sure, but I think it was two of the lads from Brenzett. They were Spitfires you see, and it's only us and Brenzett with Spitfires; the others have Typhoons. I don't think it was ours, but I could be wrong.” Ian shrugged his shoulders. “There's nothing to be done but wait until word reaches us. The ambulances will be there by now.”

“We've got to go to Brenzett next,” Helen said, her heart heavy.

By the time they arrived, the fighter planes were returning. Helen and Denny started to make the tea; they spoke little. There was an awareness that not all the Spitfires would be back.

The men came over. The smiles they gave were brief; there was no laughter in their eyes. “It was that new lad, James,” one of the pilots said. “I saw it happen. And David, the Yorkshireman.”

“Are you sure it was them?” another asked.

“Well, they're not here now, are they?”

Helen turned white. “He'd been asking after me,” she said, partly to herself. She clutched the shelf as a support while her other hand pressed against her forehead. “He was going to the dance tomorrow. I was going to see him there.”

Chapter Twenty-Two
May 1945

Helen was wiping the porridge from four-year-old Jack's hands and face when Lily came bursting in through the front door. She almost ran into the dining room and stood there, her eyes bright and a little breathless.

"I had to come back," she said, the words tumbling out. "It's in the newspapers. He's dead! Hitler's dead!"

"Dead?" Helen repeated. "How can he be? I mean..."

"It's here in the paper." Lily flung the *Daily Express* down on the table.

"Germans put out the news everyone hopes is true," Helen read aloud the first of the banner headlines. "Drum roll heroics."

"Surely it will be over soon," Lily said. "It has to be. The Americans are advancing through Austria."

"But Doenitz is to continue the fight." Helen scanned the words, unable to take it all in.

"Not for long," Lily persisted. "So many of the coastal defences have been moved over the last few months, and the black-out restrictions have been lifted. That would not happen if we were still under threat."

"You're right, of course," Helen said. "I can hardly remember there not being a war on. It will be strange to go back to normal life. I don't even know what that is any more."

"I must dash." Lily moved towards the doorway. "But talking about normal life, please do think about that job I told you about."

"I will." Helen's heart sank a little. Then she thought of the men who had been imprisoned by the Germans. There were several women in Lydd who knew little about where their husbands were and how they suffered in the camps. "I suppose the men will come home now, those who were captured."

"It will take time," Lily said. "They'll be in a bad way, I imagine."

"And the ones here, they'll go back too."

"Are you thinking of your German pilot?" Lily asked.

"I was." Helen frowned. "We'll never know what happened to Karl, but at least we can be fairly certain that he survived the war."

"I'm sure he did, and he'll remember how kind an English girl was."

"I hope his sweetheart waited for him." Helen recalled mention of a girl from his village and letters exchanged when Karl left home. The thought of this unknown woman left a heavy feeling in Helen's stomach.

"We'll never know," said Lily and Helen realised that she was probably right.

It was a week later, on Tuesday 8th May, that the Allies accepted Germany's surrender. Denny and Helen had gone no further than Galloways when the news came.

"They've surrendered," one of the home guard said, as he approached *Nancy* and the women.

"It's over?" Denny asked.

"That's what they say."

Denny and Helen looked at one another. After all this time, could it really be the end? The Allies had been gaining strength for some time and the threat at home was diminished, but to hear those words brought feelings of wonder and disbelief and confusion all at once. Slowly, broad grins spread across their faces and the two women embraced each other, and then they hugged the small group of men, who still stood waiting for their tea.

That day, as they drove along the coast, they got to hear people's stories of the war – of missing family members and friends and the fragile hope that they would be reunited with them soon. Helen, who was driving the van, turned back to Lydd. Suddenly, a strange sense of depression settled on her.

"What will you do now?" she asked Denny. "We won't be needed any more, will we?"

"I'm going to get married," Denny announced. "My Stanley is returning to Wiltshire, and I'll go with him. We'll get married here first. He asked me a few days ago."

"Gosh, that's wonderful!" Helen said. "How exciting for you. I wonder what it's like in Wiltshire."

"It's not flat," Denny told her. "And there's no sea. There's big rolling hills and lots of countryside."

"Lily says I should work at the solicitors' office, *Scott and Browning*. The receptionist is leaving, and Jack will be at school soon. It's a part-time job and one day Bobby will be there as well; he wants to be a solicitor, just like his father was."

"It sounds like a great idea," Denny replied.

"It does. It is." Helen faltered, "Not the same though..."

"But this is all over," Denny stated, and she was

right.

The airfields were now deserted; the pilots gone once the threat of the doodlebugs had passed. On the coast the defences were being dismantled; mines were being cleared from the beaches which were then open to the public once more. Only at Dungeness the restrictions remained, and with them secrecy as to why the area was still out of bounds to anyone without a pass.

The tea-van was left at the army camp. “They might want us for a while longer, I suppose,” Denny said as they walked away. “There's all the men on the coast removing the defences; they'll like a cup of tea and a bit of company.”

“Yes, of course they will.” But Helen frowned; life seemed very uncertain.

When Helen arrived home, there was a crowd around the dining table and even a pile of rock cakes on a plate in the centre. Lily was pouring tea for Allie; Grace was there with her daughter, Eva, and Elsie must have just finished work because she was in her uniform still. Jack was perched on Cousin Elsie's lap, his small fist full of crumbs and currants. The little boy clambered to the floor and ran into Helen's arms.

“Hello Jack, have you been good today?”

“I played on the Rype and Bobby is coming home from school soon,” Jack informed her. Bobby had been at the grammar school in Ashford since the September of 1944. During the week he stayed overnight with his grandparents, occasionally travelling back by train. Being Bobby's greatest admirer, anything he did was of great interest to Jack.

“Tea?” Lily asked Helen.

“Yes, please.” Helen took the spare seat.

"Did you have a good day?" Allie asked.

"It was quiet. Strange to see the defences being taken down," Helen said, before quickly adding, "Good though. Good the beaches are clear again." She turned to Eva who had been away for a few days. "How was Dennis? Have they taken any of the bandages off?"

"He tries so hard to be cheerful," Eva gave a weak smile. "But I know it hurts. They have put some lighter dressings on and are hopeful he'll make a good recovery." Eva and her mother-in-law had been to visit Dennis, who had joined the Navy days after their wedding. He was currently in hospital at East Grinstead, having suffered from burns to his hands and arms a couple of months beforehand.

"But they are hoping he'll come home soon," Grace added.

"Yes, there should be news any day now," Eva agreed.

"That's wonderful." Helen gave a big smile, then asked Allie: "And have you heard from David?" At eighteen years old, Allie's elder son had only just joined the army.

"He's still off doing his training," she said. "Never got to go to war properly, thank goodness. He won't be out of the army for a while now, but I know he's safe at least."

Half an hour later and it was just Helen, Lily and Elsie at home with Jack and a pile of cups to wash up. The evening was spent doing the usual household chores, and later with a book by the fire. Helen felt ill at ease. What was her role now that the NAAFI tea-van was to be redundant, and socks would no longer need knitting for the troops? Elsie had already moved from the ambulance service and was now an auxiliary nurse in the convalescent home; there would be soldiers recuperating for a long time, so her job was secure. Helen felt herself frowning as she tried to concentrate on the book, and when she got up to get ready for bed, she said, "I'll walk along to *Scott and Browning* in the morning, to ask about the job."

"There's to be a service of thanksgiving," Lily told Helen, a few days later. "In the church."

"In the church?" Helen repeated. "Gosh." Since the chancel had been destroyed in 1940, the Hardy Hall had been used for services.

"It's being given a good tidy up and made safe," Lily informed her.

It was a Saturday morning and Helen was playing in the garden with Jack. The game was pushing or throwing a ball over the Anderson shelter. Lily had just returned from the local shops.

"I wonder how it will feel?" Helen thought of that day in October 1940.

"The first time will be difficult, and then it will get a little easier every time we go there," Lily said.

"I hope so." Helen pushed the ball back towards Jack and called out: "It's coming…!" She wondered about the shelter, should it stay there – just in case? "Will we keep the shelter a bit longer?"

"I don't know," Lily frowned. "Charlie built it, didn't he? I don't know that… I guess it's no good to us now."

"Jack likes playing in it," Helen offered.

"He does, doesn't he?" Lily smiled. "It can stay here for a while then. Oh, it's tomorrow – the church service! At least we won't have much time to think about it beforehand. And there's a dance in the evening. Shall we ask if Mrs Gossings will have Jack?"

"Oh yes, I'll pop around to see her in a minute," Helen replied. "Come on, Jack. Throw the ball back to me!"

It was good to have Jack skipping along between them as Lily, Helen and Bobby walked to the church the next day. He demanded their attention and kept their thoughts from dwelling too much on the awful day when they had last been there, However much Helen tried to think of October 15th as the date Jack was born, rather when her Uncle Charlie was killed, she felt that today was a time to face the reality of what had happened. It seemed that Aunt Lily and all she had suffered were in the thoughts of her dear friends too, for Allie was waiting for them in Church Road with her husband, Ernie, and younger son, David.

"Thank you for coming," Lily said gratefully, linking her arm through Allie's.

It was dark inside the church, despite the candles and electric lighting. With the chancel boarded up, natural light from the east end was missing. But the organ was playing, and the fresh spring flowers were colourful. The seven of them filled a pew and waited in silence, watching the movement of people around them. As the church filled, a young, dark-haired woman in a nurse's uniform rushed in. She looked around and spotted her family, then squeezed in next to them

"Elsie!" Lily smiled at her daughter.

"I had to come; they said I could have an hour off work."

The rector, mayor and local dignitaries appeared at the open doorway. Whispers ceased and the only sound now came from the organ as the men progressed along the central aisle. The rector's cassock flowed, and the mayor's chain of office glinted. The music stopped and the service began with a prayer of recognition for those men and women of Lydd lost at home and away during the years of war.

It was mid-afternoon when a jubilant rat-a-tat-tat was heard on the front door. "Who could that be?" Helen asked Jack, as the pair of them went to answer the door.

Two men in RAF uniforms stood side by side on the doorstep. The younger was slim with very dark brown hair and dark eyes, his smile was cheeky, but he looked beyond Helen as if hoping to see someone else. The second man was older, in his mid-forties, much stockier, with shining blue eyes and a relaxed posture.

"Oh golly – two of you! How? But you don't even know each other?" Helen turned and called excitedly: "Lily...!"

"Hello Helen," Ian gave her a kiss on the cheek. "It's amazing who you can meet on a train!"

"But Elsie's not here," Helen apologised, leading them through into the living area, "although she is due to finish work soon."

Then everyone was talking at once as Lily came through from the kitchen and flung herself into Ian's arms and gave Ben a huge hug. And the men were explaining how they started talking on the train and couldn't believe that they were both heading for the same household.

"When does Elsie finish?" Ben asked.

"Four o'clock," Lily said. "In fifteen minutes. Have a cup of tea and she'll be back in no time."

"I think I'll walk along to meet her," Ben turned to the door. "And maybe go into Elderkins or the Beehive for tea and cake?"

"She'll love that."

"Lily, shall we do the same?" Ian asked. "I need to see if there's a room at the George Hotel for a few days."

"Of course." Lily looked up at Ian, her face was radiant. "How long are you staying for?"

"Ten days!"

"Really? That's fantastic!"

They invited Helen to go with them, but she declined, not wanting to intrude on their time together. "I'll take Jack along to see Bobby at the allotment," she said. "He'll want to know the news."

"Oh, and there's a dance tonight," Lily remembered. "You'll come, won't you?"

It had been a wonderful evening. Helen looked on and wondered how Lily's and Ian's relationship would grow over the next few months. They were so happy, but surely there would be long discussions ahead of them, as she knew Ian to have property and commitments nine thousand miles away. *What is it like, this home of Ian's in the hills above Perth, and would he be willing to leave it for Lily and a life here in Lydd? It sounds like a beautiful place with views over the city and across the coast.*

Helen's thoughts moved to Elsie and Ben, still so young and him with time left to serve in the RAF. They had shown such commitment to each other and although Lily worried about Elsie not being twenty yet, it was a marvellous thought that the families, brought together at the end of the last century, would possibly be joined by marriage.

As for Helen, the dubious influence of women such as Annie and the strong bond she had with Lily, had enabled her confidence to grow through each year of the war. That evening, as music from loudspeakers blared military-band music through the centre of Lydd, Helen danced non-stop with both local men and those from the forces. She didn't expect any of the men to ask her for a walk, or tea and a bun on a Sunday afternoon. She just enjoyed the moment and tried hard to look forward to a new episode in her life.

Chapter Twenty-Three
November 1945

Five-year-old Jack, his knees grubby and his cheeks red, bawled his frustration and stamped his feet as he missed the football Helen had aimed at him. He turned and ran after it, then kicked it as hard as his stout little legs would allow. It moved a couple of yards across the rough grass on the Rype; the rage passed, and he had a big smile across his face. Jack kicked the ball again and this time it almost reached Helen who ran forward to meet it. She was about to kick the ball back to her son when she saw his attention had wandered and followed his gaze across the open green.

"Aunt Lily," Jack roared, and he started running in the direction of home.

Feeling a little uneasy, Helen followed kicking the ball along as she went. It wasn't usual for her aunt to meet them as they walked home from school. Lily had been glowing recently. Ian, her Australian, had returned safely from the war and the two of them had been spending a lot of time together. He needed to return to his home in the new year. Rather than Lily seemingly crushed by this, there were plans for her to travel with Ian and her enthusiasm to see this country on the other side of the world was clear to see.

Today, even from a distance, Helen could see that Lily was lacking her usual vitality and, on nearing her aunt, she could see her pale face looked drawn and the fine lines around her grey eyes were accentuated. Then she saw it, the small square of an envelope in Lily's hand, and Helen quickened her pace. Jack had skipped into his aunt's arms and was being swung up high but, over his dark curls, the women's eyes met.

"Bobby is at home, darling. He finished school early," Lily was saying to Jack. "He's found an old truck he wants to show you." She put Jack down and he trotted off.

"A telegram?" Helen asked. "It's meant to be over."

"I know. It has both our names on it."

"From home then." Helen still called Ashford home, despite having lived in Lydd since the day she gave birth to Jack.

The family and extended family were gradually getting used to their post-war lives. For Helen and Lily, their days on the NAAFI van were finished. Incredibly, *Nancy* had survived both the occasional gunfire from enemy planes and the erratic handling from Annie. Helen had stopped her WVS work a couple of months before the war was declared to have officially ended in September 1945. She took up Lily's suggestion of filling the post left by the retiring receptionist at Scott and Browning Solicitor's office. With some reluctance, she exchanged her khaki outfit, with sturdy lace-up shoes, for plain A-line skirts and neat pumps with square heels and toes. She missed the banter that came with her role on the tea-van but was conscious that the war was coming to an end and she needed to think about providing for herself and Jack over the coming years.

While Lily's romance flourished, Helen's heart did not sing for the soldier who had occasionally escorted her to dances or for a Sunday afternoon walk. He went home to the south-west of the country, with talk of letters being exchanged, but no words of marriage, thankfully. Her thoughts sometimes wandered to her husband, and she wondered what it would be like if he had returned from the war. She felt so much more grown-up than when they had married in early 1940 and, try as she might to imagine life with him, to her regret his image was fading in her mind. The loss had become a small ache in her heart, not the all-consuming grief she once felt. She realised that Lily's future seemed secure with Ian and, on their return from Australia, it would be time for Helen to set up her own home with Jack.

“I couldn't just sit there, holding it,” Lily said, looking down at the envelope. “And it has both our names on it so...”

“Look at Jack, running on ahead. We'll be back in no time and Bobby will keep him occupied.”

They walked briskly, saying nothing, not wanting to speculate on the words they were sure would bring upset and changes to their lives.

It will be Grandmother, Helen thought. *But she seemed so well, and Grandfather too. It could be Grandfather though. I imagined they had a few more years ahead of them.*

Walking into Mill Road, there were a few changes. A bungalow damaged, but not destroyed, by a narrow miss with a bomb was now being repaired and another, part-built before the war, was being worked on again. Lily's red-brick bungalow had survived the five years, only suffering some broken windows on two occasions when they gave in to the blast from a bomb landing nearby. Lily opened the front door and Jack charged ahead, looking for his much-loved big cousin, Bobby.

Helen sat on the edge of her aunt's bed while Lily eased the telegram open and read the words: "Richard badly injured STOP in Cottage Hospital STOP come immediately STOP."

"Father! Whatever can have happened to him?" Helen whispered.

"Gosh, I thought it would be… well, not my brother. I hadn't thought of that," Lily said.

"I know," Helen replied. It did not need saying that they had both been concerned about the more elderly relatives.

"I've had time to think about this, since it came," Lily said, as she took charge. "Jack can stay with Bobby and Elsie will be home within a couple of hours. The train to Ashford leaves in forty minutes, and we can take a taxi to the Cottage Hospital."

"Of course." Helen stood up, and then sat down again. Suddenly she felt a bit wobbly. With her husband, Jack, and then Charlie dead, and Eva's husband injured, was there to be no end to the grief?

"We need to pack a few things, for an overnight stay." Lily put her arm around Helen.

"Yes, we must."

"And I'll have a word with Bobby," Lily continued. "Jack will be fine, you know."

Within an hour, Lily and Helen were nearing Ashford on the steam train. They spoke little, every now and then blurting out their frustrations.

"It's not knowing that is the very worst of it," Helen complained.

"We are making good time," Lily said. "Even in a motor car it would have taken just as long."

“I know, I know. But whatever can have happened? Injured it said, an accident of some sort?” Helen scowled as she spoke, “What sort of accident could Father have? He is just so… so sensible.”

“He always was sensible,” Lily reminisced. “Both of my brothers caused no trouble at all to my parents. It was me who worried them.”

This caused a smile to flicker, and the strain momentarily fade from Helen's face. She had always been so fond of her aunt. As a child, when listening in to her parents talk of Lily and the family in Lydd, she had secretly hoped that she would be as adventurous when she grew up.

As the train moved into Ashford Station, both women moved to the edge of their seats and were standing before it stopped. Then they were on the platform and walking at a fast pace through the crowds. Lily hailed a taxi as soon as they were outside and they swung themselves into the back of the motor car, while the driver placed their bags in the boot.

“The Cottage Hospital, please.” Lily's voice was a little breathless. She turned to Helen: “We'll know very soon now, very soon.”

Within a few minutes the hospital came into view, the taxi stopped, and the women were getting out. They paid the driver, and he was pulling away when Helen noticed her mother walking through the wide entrance doorway from the hospital. She was on the arm of Helen's Uncle Henry, Lily's younger brother. He looked pale and sombre; she appeared to be wiping tears from her eyes.

“Gosh, Henry is here too,” Lily said. “I suppose he would be.”

Helen's mother looked up, and recognition showed in her eyes. Letting go of her brother-in-law, she scurried forward. “Helen darling, and Lily, it's… you're too… you're too late.” She took Helen's hands in her own. “He just couldn't hold on; it was too much for him to bear. I'm so sorry, your father…it was all a terrible accident.”

“Perhaps we should do this inside,” Henry said, taking the elbow of his brother's wife and turning her back towards the door. “There must be a place for this sort of thing...a room, you know. Or at least a seating area. Somewhere private.”

Helen's hand was still in her mother's. She looked back at Lily, who was pale, with a slight frown on her face. Helen reached out with her spare hand and Lily took it. Together, the four of them walked back towards the hospital, only parting a little to move through the doorway. Henry ushered the women to some vacant chairs, not strictly private but the space was empty of other people.

“It was a bomb!” Helen's mother announced.

Helen and Lily looked on in stunned silence.

“It was a bomb… Can you believe it? There in the ground. At the allotment.” Now the words poured out, her voice was high, almost hysterical. “There he was digging. You know how he liked it… how he liked to do his bit for the war effort. There's still rationing you know… of course you do. It's no different in Lydd. You must be careful. Tell Bobby. Tell Bobby to be aware.”

“Anne, I think that's enough,” Henry spoke, his tone calming.

“Of course.” Helen's mother fell silent.

“That's how it was, or so it seems,” Henry confirmed. “His legs were shattered, and although they got him here as quickly as they could… Internal bleeding, you know.”

“Damned war,” Lily muttered. “Didn't it take

enough of us?"

"It's not right, not right at all." Henry patted Lily's arm.

Helen stood beside her weeping mother, her arms around her shoulders. "Perhaps it's time to go home now?"

"Of course," Henry agreed. "My car is outside."

Three weeks later and Helen was at the doorway of the bungalow in Mill Road, her heart heavy and eyes swollen. "Just don't say another word," she said to Lily. "I don't know that I can bear it. But life has to change, and you're off on a journey across the world."

"You'll have your own adventures soon enough," Lily replied, as they clung together before leaving. "I'll walk to the station with you and Jack, but you're right, we've talked enough."

"I don't want to take Jack away; it's all he knows," Helen said for the umpteenth time.

"Children are so resilient. It will be exciting for him," Lily replied, biting on her lip to fight back her own tears. She had been a second mother to Jack; Helen had been a best friend and favourite niece rolled into one. The bond between them was unbreakable.

Helen's mother just wasn't going to cope – that was clear enough. She had always fussed and worried over every little incident in her life. Helen knew the decision to stay with her mother would have to be temporary, perhaps for six months. After that she and Jack could find their own little home in Ashford, or even back in Lydd. It was too soon to look that far into the future.

The two women and the little boy walked along Mill Road and through the cemetery in silence. They looked at the graves, remembering so many terrifying incidents over the past five years. It was bleak there in November: the trees bare, with leaves brown and decaying beneath them. The grass was damp and tatty.

Before long, they were approaching the station; each step became harder to take. Helen's limbs were leaden, her heart tight. She looked at Lily and gave up the fight to hold back the tears. "I don't know how I'll cope," she said as she threw her arms around her aunt.

"You just will. Really you will."

At the station they concentrated on Jack, chattering about the trains and the station staff in their uniforms, reminding him of trips to Ashford to see Grandmother and Grandfather, as well as his great-grandparents. They did not notice a man sitting on a bench at the far end of the platform. He had arrived on an earlier train, determined to seek out the young woman whom he felt a need to thank for her kindness. Yet there was more than that: he felt a connection, a bond, which had remained with him over the past few years. But on arriving in Lydd, he had allowed his fears to flood through him and was considering returning on the next train. Perhaps he could send a letter and could only hope it would find her in a small town such as this. He sat with his head in his hands, feeling foolish and very alone in the world.

Helen looked down the platform; she spotted a kestrel hovering and wanted to point it out to Jack. These things kept her busy and distracted. Jack tugged at her hand, and they walked along the platform. She saw the man on the bench and briefly wondered at his rounded shoulders, and his head resting on gloved hands. Everyone had a story to tell;

she wondered what made him look so sad? She saw him lift his head; no doubt disturbed by the excitable words coming from the small boy.

Helen frowned. It couldn't be? She saw the man straighten and then stand. Slowing her pace, Helen felt her heart begin to pound and a flush spread over her face. But she still wasn't sure; how could she be when she had only seen him a few times, and that was several years before? Yet there seemed to be recognition in his face, and he took a couple of steps towards her.

He looked well, Helen thought. His face was clean-shaven, and his hair cut neatly at the back and sides, although his blonde waves still curled about one another. He was slim, but not too thin. Healthier than before. Wherever he had been they had treated him well.

"Do you see it, Mummy?" Jack was still following the kestrel's flight.

"Yes, over there," Helen replied, barely hearing her own words. She took a step closer, her eyes fixed on the face of the man who still walked towards her, his own gaze unwavering. Now they were within yards of each other and afterwards she never knew how she managed to say his name, her mouth was so dry. "Karl…?"

"I came to see you… but I couldn't… and here you are," he replied, his face full of wonder. Then he turned to the small boy. "Hello, you must be Jack. I'm Karl. That's a fine kestrel you have spotted."

"Actually, Mummy saw it first," the boy replied.

Karl turned back to Helen, he saw her swollen eyes and the strained look on her face. Words of affection slipped out, "My love, whatever is wrong?"

"Nothing. Nothing at all," Helen said. Then she

flung her arms around his neck, buried her face in his coat and started sobbing.

And Lily, who was not far behind, and had heard the hint of a German accent, took Jack's hand. “Come along darling, everything is going to be all right now.”

Part Two
Chapter Twenty-Four
The Artist
July 1958

The Kentish Express was spread out over the Formica topped kitchen table. Nowadays, it was the deaths column that held the most interest for Arthur. "We're top of the queue now," Beryl had said numerous times, until the Lord had seen fit to take her just a year ago. But what was this? The old man reached across for his magnifying glass: something about Lydd and the poor church.

"Fund raising," he muttered to himself. "Well, something needs to be done about it. What a carry on – a church half-repaired after all these years."

The parish church, All Saints, had been partly rebuilt and then re-hallowed in 1953. But the chancel remained in ruins, the plans for its restoration being put aside due to lack of funds. Where there should have been an eastern window there remained a solid wall of concrete blocks and the altar had been moved forward to the end of the nave. The 'Cathedral of the Marsh' had been robbed of its full length and more money was needed to complete the renovations.

The mayor and rector of Lydd were seeking support from the people of Romney Marsh. In the thin pages of print, they asked for donations and for support at fund-raising events. Arthur had no money to offer; he lived a frugal existence. He could buy a cup of tea at a fair or have a go on the tombola, but what good were his shillings when there was all that work to be done? But he had seen the bomb fall on the church; it seemed only right that he should do his bit towards helping with the restoration.

Frowning, Arthur pushed back the kitchen chair. Where had he put the painting? Somewhere he hoped Beryl wouldn't find it. Under the stairs, was it? Holding on to the banister, Arthur lowered himself to his knees, then leaned forward into the dark space, fingers creeping along until they closed in on some cardboard. He gave a tug and the slim package slid out.

Sitting back at the table, Arthur felt a warm sense of pride to see his image of the chancel at the time of its destruction. It was a good painting; he was sure of it. The words of a letter to the mayor began to form in his mind:

Dear Sir, I saw your appeal regarding funds for the chancel of All Saints and although I have no money to offer, I have something you are welcome to sell...

Chapter Twenty-Five
Lily's Story
August-November 1958

"Who would have thought that such a lot of money would be raised by selling a painting by an unknown artist," Lily said to her husband, Ian, as she pored over the letter from England.

"It must have been quite special," he replied.

"It must have been," Lily agreed. "I remember the man who painted it; I had no idea he was so talented. Such a quiet chap, not the sort you would really notice."

"Perhaps this is the excuse we need to pay a visit? It's been three years."

"To go back for the re-hallowing? To see the church restored?" Lily looked up from the letter, her smile wide and eyes bright. "Really?"

"Why not? We've been saying for a while that it would be good to go back."

Lily pushed back her chair, stood up, wrapped her arms around Ian's neck and planted a firm kiss on his lips. "Thank you, darling."

The Australian gave a smile, his blue eyes dancing. "We'll drive down to the airport and see how often the flights go; I believe it's twice a week. Or would you rather go by boat?"

"I'd be terrified, but I think we should fly," Lily replied. "If you'd like to?"

"That's what I was thinking. Anyway, it has to be more comfortable than a Hurricane or Spitfire!"

"I guess so..." Lily wasn't too sure.

Give me another kiss and I'll finish work for the day..."

Lily willingly complied. "I'll make us some fresh lemonade; look how many lemons I picked from the tree today!" She pointed to the bowl on the table with five enormous yellow fruits in it. "They'd never believe the size of these, back on Romney Marsh!"

"They wouldn't," Ian agreed. "And will we have lunch with the lemonade?"

"We'll have lunch," Lily said, with a smile. "Who'd have thought that by the end of the day we'd be planning to fly to England?"

"You never know what's about to happen!" Ian dropped a kiss on Lily's head before walking out to the veranda and continuing: "I'll just go and sweep up, tidy the tools away and then I'm all yours."

Ian and Lily lived in the small hillside settlement of Kalamunda, close to the city of Perth. It was a town that still held on to the feeling of a traditional settlement, while on the flat lands below, the city of Perth was steadily growing around the banks of the Swan and Canning rivers. In contrast to the rambling villages and towns of England, here the red-roofed properties, each with their own plot of land, were laid out on a uniform grid pattern. And directly below the Darling Ridge, on which Kalumunda had emerged, there was another geometric pattern: the runways of Perth Airport, now operating international flights, with planes from Sydney landing there on a regular basis, before flying on to foreign lands.

Their home was a traditional wooden bungalow, with deep eaves forming a veranda at the front and back. While keeping the summer sun at bay, the eaves also prevented the piercing light from spilling in, so Ian had painted the walls white, and Lily chose bright furnishings that brought their own sunshine into the building.

Taking the plates of cheese and salad out to the back veranda, Lily looked up at the eucalyptus trees: she loved their elegant shape, dappled trunks and the subtle scent they released when the sun beat down through the summer months. A couple of green parrots flew from one branch to another. Scanning the table and chairs for spiders or flying insects, Lily put the food down and returned for the bread.

It was wintertime and she wore a light cardigan. The days were still warm, but the nights were cold, and Ian would light the log stove by late afternoon. In the evenings, they sat with blankets over their knees and often said that the family back in England would never believe how chilly it got here in Western Australia.

Lily paced about the room, checking and re-checking everything was ready. Two suitcases were stood by the front door and two smaller bags slumped beside them. “I know it's a little early, but can we leave now?” she asked Ian.

“We'll only be waiting about at the airport,” he replied, understanding her impatience. “They said to arrive fifteen minutes before the flight leaves.”

“But at least we'll be on our way...”

Ten minutes later and Ian was carrying the cases with ease into the airport foyer. They joined a short queue to have their baggage weighed and paperwork checked, then stood at the window of a lounge area awaiting the arrival of the Qantas plane from Sydney. Ian went to the bar and returned with a couple of glasses of wine. “Something to ease your nerves,” he said, handing her the glass.

In no time at all the small group of passengers was looking skywards, tracking the descent of the slender plane that was to take them all the way to London. Its four wing-mounted propellers glinted silver in the afternoon sun and a bold red stripe revealed itself as the aircraft neared the runway. Within minutes the plane's wheels were touching down on the Tarmac and men in overalls were pushing a staircase towards it. A young man in a smart uniform opened the door and stood aside, allowing men in suits and women in neat skirts, pretty blouses and heeled shoes, to stroll past clutching their hand luggage. There were eight of them travelling on the next stage of the journey; Lily wondered how many others were embarking on their first flight.

The cabin reminded Lily a little of the interior of a theatre. There was a wide carpeted aisle and pairs of seats with chrome fittings, velour covers and plenty of room for passengers to stretch their legs out. A slim airhostess, with glossy dark hair in an immaculate bun, pointed to their places with her white-gloved hand. Gazing about at her fellow travellers, Lily noted that those who had flown from Sydney were already very much at home with Champagne glasses on their small tables and a haze of cigarette smoke above their heads. Ian indicated for Lily to sit by the window and placed their bags in the rack above their seats. She made herself comfortable, pulling her skirt into place and removing her hat, which Ian also placed in the rack. The hostesses, attentive but aloof, ensured that everyone had their seatbelts securely fixed and all bags were safely stowed away.

A slight vibration moved through the body of the plane, as the engines started. “Next stop Singapore,” Ian said, reaching out for Lily's hand.

“And in three days we'll be in England!” Lily replied, hardy believing that it could be possible.

The 1958 Rover P5 in maroon with a silver roof, purred along the lanes from Ashford to Brenzett before turning on to the wider, straighter road leading to New Romney. Ian put a little more pressure on the accelerator and the car picked up speed, passing through the village of Old Romney with ease and gliding on towards the turning to Lydd. With every mile that passed, Lily's excitement mounted as she pointed out familiar landmarks and voiced her displeasure at any changes. Ian flicked out the indicator and they turned towards Lydd. Then the church tower was in sight and before long they were passing over the railway bridge.

Ian glanced towards the cemetery. “Did you want to stop?”

“No darling.” Lily reached out and placed her hand on his arm. “I'll walk along later, perhaps with Allie.”

Then they were driving along Manor Road on The Rype, and she was exclaiming that it all looked just the same. The Rover came to a stop outside a row of Victorian terraced houses and Lily was opening the passenger door almost before the engine had died. And there was Allie, at the front door before Lily had raised her hand to the knocker.

“I've been looking out for you!” Allie said, as they

flung their arms around each other before standing back to look at each other.

Both in their late fifties, the two women had first met not long after the Great War, when in their mid-twenties. Allie now had iron grey hair, thick and wiry; her figure had always been slim, and it remained so. Her face was lined but her dark eyes shone with the excitement of seeing Lily.

"Oh, look at you, with your lovely tan and still as beautiful as ever." Allie looked over to Ian: "Australia certainly suits her!"

"I hope so!" Ian replied. "Good to see you Allie."

"It's just wonderful to be here," Lily couldn't stop the smile from spilling over her face. "I've seen so many changes over the last few miles, but look at this – The Rype, and all the houses and the church tower over there – it's all just the same!"

"I suppose it is, in some ways," Allie said. "You'll see plenty of changes, but standing right here, it's much the same as it was. Anyway, come on in. You must be tired. I'll put the kettle on and call Ernie in from the garden."

"I'm here! I heard the car." Ernie, slightly overweight and balding, with a warm smile and kind eyes behind thick glasses, gave Lily a quick hug then extended his arm to shake Ian's hand. "Wonderful to see you both: I can't tell you how excited Allie has been!"

"About the same as Lily, I imagine!" Ian replied.

"Let me give you a hand with the bags," Ernie said, walking towards the car. "We'll leave the women to catch up with their news for a moment."

Lily and Allie walked through to the kitchen. The gas hob was lit, and the kettle placed on the flames. A tray was already prepared with cups and saucers; a plate held a selection of fruit cake and a Victoria sponge. Looking towards it, Allie said: “We're still grateful rationing has ended; it just seemed to go on forever, didn't it?”

“It did, although I managed to escape it!” Lily gave a guilty smile. There had been no rationing in Australia!

With the tea ready, Allie carried the tray and Lily the plate of cake through to the dining room. “I've invited Elsie, Ben and the children here for supper,” Allie said, as they laid everything out on the table. “I knew you'd want to see them as soon as possible. Little Sandra is the spitting image of you, with her red hair and pointed chin! The other two are dark haired like their parents.”

“I can't wait to see them all,” Lily beamed. She turned to Ian as the men walked in, “Did you hear that? Allie says that Sandra looks just like me and they'll all be here for supper!”

“That's wonderful,” her husband replied. “Thank you so much; they will have grown so big in the last few years, and we can't wait to see them. Sandra was just a baby last time we were here.”

“Elsie and the family today, and then Helen and her family in two days’ time. It really is wonderful,” Lily agreed as she reached for a slice of cake.

Chapter Twenty-Six
Helen's Story
November 1958

"Of course I was practically born in the church!" Jack Meyer said to his younger sisters, as the train left Appledore Station, bound for Lydd.

"You were born in Aunt Lily's house," his mother, Helen, reminded him.

"But I could have been born in the church," Jack persisted. "It makes the story far more interesting for the girls." He reached across and tickled the stomachs of both his younger sisters, making them squeal with excitement. They loved having their big brother with them for the day. He was usually so busy, working at his apprenticeship as an engineer at the Ashford Works or out with one girl or another in the evenings.

They could have travelled by car of course, but Helen was feeling quite nostalgic and, for some reason she could not explain, it seemed important to journey to Lydd by steam train, just as she had in 1940. Karl, her husband, seemed to understand. They hadn't spoken about it much; there were some things about the war that you couldn't quite put into words. Not even now, over a decade since it had ended. Karl reached out and took Helen's hand; she squeezed his back.

"Tell us about the bomb, Jack," nine-year-old Avril Meyer said, looking up at her dark-haired brother. Avril and her sister, Christie, both had the blond curls and freckles of their father.

"Well, it came out of nowhere..."

"Of course it didn't," Avril laughed.

"It came from the sky, from a fighter with bombs." Christie, the elder sister, wanted to show her superior knowledge.

"Boom!" Avril put her hand up high and swung it downwards.

"That's enough," Karl spoke, his voice low but commanding attention. "Your mother's uncle was killed. Lots of people were killed just in that one small town during the war and millions were killed around the world. I'll not have you making fun of it."

"Sorry Daddy," the girls spoke in unison. Their father was usually so gentle, so calm; they knew when he was being serious and when something was important.

They were silent for a minute or two, as the train steamed across the low-lying farmland of Romney Marsh. Then, as they neared Brookland, Christie spoke: "I wish you had been at the church fête last month, Jack. It was such good fun, wasn't it Daddy?"

"It was," Karl replied with a smile. "The model church was fantastic. The tower must have been at least three times my height."

The girls began to chatter to their brother about all the activities on offer at the fête: the thrill of the merry-go-round, the competition between them when they challenged their father to miniature golf, and the fun of a donkey ride. "Just like being at Dymchurch," Avril said.

Helen and Karl, sitting across the aisle from their family, were able to talk in private. "I remember the first time I sat on this train," he said. "I should have been nervous. I only knew your name, and that you had a son, Jack. A baby!" He looked towards Jack and gave a smile.

"Perhaps you had been through so much, you had no more energy for nerves?" Helen suggested, thinking of the moment when his Messerschmitt had swooped low in the sky over the Dungeness coastline.

"Maybe." Now Karl looked back at his wife and their eyes met; she smiled at him. "Or maybe I just knew you'd be waiting for me."

"With all those young servicemen in the town and dances held every weekend?" Helen grinned.

"And all those lonely soldiers buying tea from your NAAFI van!" Karl rolled his eyes, "You're right, I was lucky no one else had snatched you away while I wasn't looking! I don't know why they didn't."

"I don't think I was ready to be snatched!" Helen leaned across and kissed him gently on the lips.

"Euch!" Avril cried out, prodding her sister and looking across at their parents.

"I was just saying how lucky I was to find your Mummy!" Karl told them. "I came on this train, you know. From Ashford to Lydd, and I was going to look for her. Walk every street and knock on every door."

"But she was going back to Ashford!" Christie shrieked, loving the well-worn story. "You could have stayed in Ashford and found her."

"Or he could have been stuck in Lydd, looking and looking forever..." Avril laughed.

That was how the Meyer family story went. In 1945, Karl had been released from the Prisoner of War camp in an area south of Ashford, known as Stanhope. It was now gone, and the area was destined to have rows of modern council houses built for people whose homes had been lost. The former German pilot had been detained for four and a half years, and in that time his good behaviour had led to him being allowed to work in the local community. On his release he had continued to work in the grounds of Godinton House but, rather than growing vegetables, he was restoring the grounds to their former elegance.

As he laboured, Karl thought of the young woman who had taken him to the safety of the deserted school and later fed him sandwiches from her precious rations. One day he put on his smartest shirt and jacket, scrubbed the earth out from under his fingernails and caught the train to Lydd in order to seek her out.

When Helen and Karl married, they lived in a rented terraced house in Ashford for a few years but, shortly after their second daughter, Avril, was born, the family moved to the beautiful village of Appledore. For Helen, it brought her closer to the flat lands of Romney Marsh with which she felt such an affinity. They only needed to walk along the village street and across the Military Canal, and the open countryside stretched out before them. This was an area that had not even been ploughed for crops to help feed the nation during the war. Fields stretched for miles, dotted with sheep and criss-crossed by ribbons of reed-lined drainage ditches.

Karl, having grown up in a wooded area of Germany, fell in love with the open skies and wide views. He took his young stepson cycling along winding lanes, a favourite route taking them to the tiny church of Fairfield. Here they puzzled over the reason for it being there, with no village to speak of and the access being across sheep fields and an old wooden bridge crossing a narrow dyke.

As a family, they walked the banks of the canal and picnicked looking out over the waters, enjoying glimpses of wildlife. Chickens lived in coops in their garden and Karl grew vegetables in small plots.

The shadows of the war lived on and, as Karl decided to start his own gardening business, he found some people would not consider employing him once they detected a faint German accent. But most welcomed the young family into their community, exclaiming over the pretty girls with their golden curls and liking the older brother, who was always polite and clearly loved his little sisters.

The steam train trundled along the tracks. Helen, lulled into a peaceful mood by the clanking of wheels, peered ahead for the remaining arch of Midley Church. She spotted it, stark and alone in a rough field. The train passed by. But then looking back, the low October sun shone on ancient stones. It was no longer grey; the ruin glowed a soft golden colour.

Lydd Town was the next stop and Helen craned her neck to see the slender tower of All Saints amongst the trees and roof tops. The train began to slow as it approached a tunnel under a bridge and then the station buildings lined either side of the track.

"Lydd Town, Lydd Town. Next stop: Lydd-on-Sea, then Greatstone-on-Sea and New Romney." The station master, a retired soldier, limped forward, dragging his wooden leg.

"Come on, girls." Karl reached for Avril's hand. "Be careful stepping down onto the platform."

In the sky, the swathes of palest grey clouds

parted, and the sun's rays broke through, casting a mellow light on the soft orange bricks of the station buildings. They looked a little tired though, Helen reflected, as if the staff no longer had the energy to maintain the flower boxes or repair broken roof tiles. There wasn't quite the hustle and bustle she remembered from the past. But of course, many people used cars now; Karl took a great pride in his own Rover.

She was the last of her family to step out of the carriage and as she stood, surveying the platform, her gaze met that of a woman whose greying hair, was still flecked with an auburn that shone in the autumn sunshine. Even from across the platform, she could see the pointed chin and slightly tipped-up nose she knew so well, and something new – a warm glow to the skin. The woman stepped away from the man standing behind her and a wide smile lit up her face.

"*Lily*!" Helen shrieked, causing her girls to look at their mother in wonder. But Karl knew and understood; he recognised the aunt to whom Helen was so close. Even nine thousand miles couldn't break the bond. And Jack, although his memories were fragmented, knew as well.

The two women, frustrated by the barrier of other passengers, side-stepped and jostled until they met and flung their arms around each other. Helen felt tears filling her eyes and she tried to blink them back but, when they finally managed to let each other go, she saw Lily was reaching for a handkerchief.

"I really didn't want to cry," her aunt said, shaking her head. "But I knew I would."

"It's marvellous you could come." Helen felt her words seemed so ineffectual. "How was the journey? Was it awful?"

“It was fine.” Lily brushed away the many hours in the skies and the airports in foreign lands. “I'll tell you later.”

Now Lily's husband, Ian, was with them and he too gave Helen a big hug, before shaking Karl's hand with enthusiasm. And Lily was looking at Helen's family, at the baby who had grown into such a lovely young man and the two girls she had last seen three years beforehand.”

“Oh Jack, so handsome.” Lily gave him a huge bear hug. “Do you remember the years we lived together?”

“Of course, I do!” The young man said. “And I don't think a day passes when Mother doesn't mention you. I remember every time you pushed me in my pram across the Rype or fed me a biscuit when Mother wasn't looking!”

“Jack, you were just a baby,” Christie objected. “You don't remember.”

“Oh, very well, I don't remember it *all*,” Jack conceded. “But I wasn't always a baby when we lived with Aunt Lily,” He turned back to Lily and continued, “I know I was small, but of course I remember. Wasn't I the luckiest little boy to have a mother and an aunt to look after me?”

“They were good days.” Lily looked at Helen for confirmation. “Despite everything...”

“They were,” Helen agreed.

“And let me look at you two.” Lily bent down a little before Christie and Avril. “You've got your father's hair and freckles, but I can see your mother in you as well. It's just wonderful to see how you have both grown. Do you give hugs to an aunt visiting from Australia?”

“Of course, we do!” Avril replied and launched herself into Lily's arms.

"I'd love to walk into the churchyard from Church Lane, to see the window from the outside." Helen had to raise her voice above the general hubbub of noise, as the family group walked along the narrow pavements towards the town.

The girls were in front; they knew the way, having been to Lydd so many times throughout their young lives. Then there were Helen and Lily and Jack, almost like the old times, Lily had commented, apart from the fact that Jack was now standing a few inches taller than his mother and aunt. The men brought up the rear; they too spoke as if the gap of three years was nothing, as if Lily and Ian had merely migrated across the border to Sussex, rather than voyaged nine thousand miles to Western Australia.

"Of course, it's the best way," Lily agreed. "Girls, we are turning left now and into the churchyard."

"We wanted to go this way before," Avril commented.

"But Mummy wouldn't let us. Not until it was finished, she kept saying," Christie added.

"I just wanted to wait until it was completed." Helen gave an apologetic grin.

They passed ancient cottages in the narrow lane and gradually more of the church came into view, at first the tower and rooftops stretching towards them, and then the triple end of the chancel and aisles. There was All Saints, laid out before them and all seven of them stood, taking in the details of the restoration.

"It's so beautiful," Helen whispered.

Where the previous window had been fussy, with stone mullions rising upwards to divide it into five lights, then branching out at the top to create many smaller windows, this new creation was breathtakingly simple. Now there were three separate windows, each one of them very tall and slim with a rounded top. The central window was a little taller than the others and they were leaded with stained glass, but the impact of their colour could not be seen from the outside. It was too soon for it to blend with the rest of the building, for not only was it now in a style from the church's early English beginnings, but the ancient stones were bound with lines of bright new mortar. Perhaps its combination of new and old made it all the more awe-inspiring.

"I love it," Lily said. "I really do."

The two women moved a little, wanting to stand so they had a central view. And Jack, whose interest was focused on the tower, the place where the look-out had cowered, moved with them. The churchyard was busy – people would come and go all day, looking at the church and exchanging memories – but they seemed unaware of them. Lily and Helen stood with Jack between them, his hands resting lightly on their shoulders.

"What would he have said about me going off to live in Australia?" Lily asked, half to herself.

"Uncle Charlie? He would have probably laughed at you," Helen replied, she felt tears threaten and bit in her lip.

"I'm sure he would have done." Lily tried to smile. "That's what life does: you think you're following one path and it sends you down another. The war left so many widows and..." she turned a little to look at Jack, "…and children who grew up without their fathers."

"But now we are settled again and look at what the people of Lydd have done – they raised thousands of pounds in order to restore their church," Helen said. "For one small town to do all this… it's amazing."

Karl held his daughters' hands. The young girls, interested in the aunt who may have seen koala bears and kangaroos, started to edge away from their father. But he called them back. "Stay with me, Christie, Avril. Let them spend this moment together; it's their history. It's what brought the three of them all their shared memories."

And the girls, not fully understanding, for they had no memories of the war, stepped back towards Karl. It was all stories for them, tales of horror and hardship from before their time. But they knew their brother had been born just after this church was bombed, and their own arrivals in the world were not nearly as dramatic.

"Worth coming all this way to see?" Jack asked Lily. He recalled that, as a small child, whenever he passed by, this end of the church was just piles of rubble.

"I didn't just come to see the church," Lily replied, reaching out to put her arm around his waist.

"Shall we go in now?" Helen asked. "It must be time."

"Come on then." It seemed as if Lily was bracing herself.

The family group walked forwards, circling the east end of the church, and then moving towards the tower.

"Gosh, look at them all," Avril exclaimed. The clergy of all ranks were gathering, their layers of robes flowing and lifting slightly in the breeze.

"That one is the Archbishop!" Christie announced, as the churchmen, with their own dear rector from Lydd, took their places for a photograph outside the double doors leading into the church.

The Archbishop really was the most splendid of them all, with his mitre and cope of a gold brocade, pectoral cross and golden staff with a scrolled end.

The family group paused, uncertain of how to pass by and into the church, but the clergy parted and allowed the congregation to flow into the ancient building.

Looking about, as they joined the river of people, even the children were silenced by the volume of the crowd, their smart clothes, and the noise emanating from so many worshippers. Helen now had her hand in Karl's. *I hope someone scrubbed the mess away;* she thought of her fluids staining the tiles in the seconds before she realised Jack's arrival was imminent. Lily, moving on ahead, had spotted her daughter on the pews reserved for the family. And, as Elsie's youngest daughter saw them, her joyful cry of "Nanna!" could be heard all around the church.

Chapter Twenty-Seven
Elsie's Story
1958

Elsie sat on the wooden pew with her three-year-old daughter, Sandra, on her lap, running her fingers through the child's red curls. She loved the way the ringlets sprang back into place. "Where's Nanna?" the little girl would ask every few minutes.

"She'll be here soon," Elsie replied every time. "She's gone to meet Auntie Helen at the station." Helen was not strictly an auntie, as she was Elsie's cousin.

"I wanted to go to the station," Sandra persisted.

"Well, you couldn't. We went in Daddy's car," her brother, Robert, told her.

"But I wanted to."

Robert scowled at Sandra and looked down at the Dinky car in his hand. Two years older than his sister, he knew so much more about life!

"And Christy and Avril and Jack," eight-year-old Susan chanted.

"Yes, they'll all be there," Elsie agreed. "And Uncle Karl. Look, there's space for them all to sit behind us.

"Mummy, can I sit with them?" Susan asked.

"No, because Nanna and Grandpa will be wanting to sit with you. There will be plenty of time to play with the girls afterwards."

Elsie smiled at Ben, sitting at the far end of the pew. "I don't know how they are going to sit quietly for an hour, with their Nanna here and all those questions to ask about kangaroos, spiders and snakes!"

"And commenting on Ian's accent!" Ben added with a grin.

"Can they come to our house again tomorrow?" Susan asked.

"They are all coming," Elsie reminded them. "Nanna and Grandpa, Helen and Karl and the girls. I'm not sure about Jack."

"And Granny and Grandpa from next door," Ben added. He looked towards his parents sitting behind them.

When her mother and brother emigrated to Western Australia, Elsie was adamant that her future was here with Ben. Having lived and suffered through the war years, it was so hard to say goodbye, but everything was changing. Helen and Jack had gone to live in Ashford, and then Ian was taking her mother off to visit his home. Before long, her brother, Bobby, was choosing to emigrate and continue his studies in Perth. They asked Elsie to go with them, perhaps just for a visit, but she couldn't imagine leaving her home or Ben. There were offers for her to live with Allie in Lydd or with the family in Ashford, but she chose to stay with Grace and Edward in Dungeness, while Ben continued to serve his time in the RAF.

Elsie and Ben married in the autumn of 1947, two years after the war ended. Ben had now returned to Dungeness to work alongside his father, Edward, on the fishing boat. In that time Elsie continued to be employed at convalescent homes as an auxiliary nurse. She had considered training to be a nurse, but in her heart, she knew that even before the training had finished, she would marry her childhood sweetheart and her life would take a new course. As an untrained nurse, the work was rewarding and now, although busy with her three young children, Elsie continued to visit and offer company to those who still suffered because of the war.

Their home was the wooden cottage once belonging to Ben's grandparents, Ed and Emily. It was a good size for the newly-weds and had suffered no damage during the war. In those post-war years, money was short, and they made use of furniture already in the home, along with some favourite pieces from Elsie's childhood home. In the months before their wedding, Elsie and Ben worked long hours removing floral and patterned wallpaper, then replacing it with plain lining paper, painted in pastel colours. Cushions and curtains were gradually renewed, with the help of Allie, a great seamstress.

"Nanna!" Sandra screamed, the screech almost piercing her mother's eardrums. "Look!"

The other children saw Lily too, and Grandpa Ian, whom they had discovered to be a lot of fun. But they saw their mother's warning look, and besides, they knew better than to scream out in church. Sandra was already getting a reputation as being the liveliest of the siblings and the one most likely to be scolded.

"Hello darlings," Lily sat next to Elsie, and everyone moved up to make room. Helen and her family settled behind. Sandra was soon on Lily's lap; the other children knew Nanna would be fair, and there would be plenty of time to play games with her later

A gentle hymn continued to play on the organ, and a hush fell upon the congregation as, one by one, they remembered they were now in the presence of not only their own rector and church wardens, but the Archbishop of Canterbury. Regal in his robes and carrying his crozier, he passed them as he progressed down the aisle. Then standing before the people of Lydd, he spoke of his great affection for the 'Cathedral of the Marsh' and how hugely impressed he was by the people who had raised funds with an unfailing determination. This was his sixth visit to All Saints; last time the chancel had been blocked off and it seemed impossible enough money could be raised to finance its repair. A shortened church was unacceptable to the people of the town and the money had been raised to rebuild it. An incredible feat, considering the small population.

The men, women and children looked on from under their best hats, each of them knowing that they had contributed. And from his spot, partly concealed by a pillar, the artist, Arthur, felt a small glow of pleasure. His painting had been bought by an anonymous benefactor, whose generosity had been unforeseen. It had then been placed into an ornate gilt frame and given to the church where it was hung at the west end near the tower. Not many people knew who the artist was; he didn't want or need the attention on himself. However, the Archbishop had taken a moment to seek him out, and that brought a warm feeling of satisfaction, which Arthur carried with him as he mouthed the words to the first hymn.

What time will they be here?" Robert stood at the window.

"Midday," Elsie said for the hundredth time. "When

both hands on the clock are on the twelve."

Elsie, with help from her mother-in-law, Grace, had prepared a lunch for the extended family. The armchairs had been pushed to the side of the room and an extra table put alongside the dining table. Two pots of casserole simmered on the stove, and potatoes were baking in the oven.

"I hope there's enough," Elsie said, standing back to look at the table.

"There's enough for today and your supper tomorrow!" Grace replied. "Isn't this wonderful, us all together again?"

"It's a shame Bobby can't be here."

"He's doing so well for himself; think how proud your father would be," Grace reminded her. "I'm sure he'll visit within the next few years. It just wasn't the right time, was it?"

"No, not with the baby and him just being promoted. Hard to believe that my scruffy little brother is working as a posh city lawyer!" Elsie gave a smile, "At least Ma and Ian came."

"They're here!" Susan called.

"Look at their car," Robert spoke with awe.

"I can't see..." Sandra wailed, while her sister tried to lift her up. Her eyes were raised above the windowsill, and she gave a jubilant cry, "I *can* see!" before Susan's strength ran out.

Elsie was at the door, and then everyone was talking at once. Lily and Ian, Allie and Ernie filled the room, and when Edward and Ben arrived, having been out since early morning in the boat, the room was filled to the limit. Five minutes later, Helen, Karl and the two girls had arrived, and Elsie wondered if the timber home could possibly take any more people. Coats were removed and placed on the double bed and in no time at all, Lily was sitting, surrounded by the children. With a rhyming picture book open before them, she began to read *The Oyster and the Snail,* one of the gifts she had brought for the children.

A couple of hours later and Sandra was fast asleep in her bed. The other girls played with dolls while Robert and Ian assembled a wooden truck, complete with its own tools.

"It's just like Christmas!" Ben said, reaching across to squeeze Elsie's hand. "You've done a wonderful job, love."

"I didn't do it on my own," Elsie said. "Your Ma helped out and she had the children next door for an hour this morning."

"Thanks, Ma," Ben gave Grace a warm smile.

The washing up had been done and now a large pot of tea sat in the centre of the table. With the warmth from the stove, eyelids were beginning to droop. "I know it's a bit breezy, but I'd love to walk over to the school," Helen announced. She looked towards Karl: "It's part of the family story."

"I'd love that too," Lily said. "I've often wondered what it was like for mother living and working there." One of her regrets on moving to Australia was knowing as her parents aged, she could offer no support to them. Alice had passed away a four years earlier.

"Let's make it an outing for us girls," Allie suggested. "I had some happy times there."

"It looks as if the dads and grandpas are in charge of the children," Elsie announced. "Let's go now; the sun will be getting low in an hour or so."

Once outside, having been spoiled by the heat from the range, hats were pulled further over their ears and scarves wrapped securely. But the sun was shining and the sky blue, so it was with good spirits that the five women began their trek; they knew they would soon be warmed by the exertion.

The route they took was close to the path Helen had taken on that day in 1941 when, having gazed in horror at the remains of the burned-out German fighter plane, she had then set off towards the school, only to come across the injured pilot. First, they crossed the narrow-gauge railway track, and then the cottages were behind them and only the shingle wasteland stretched out in front. Walking over a ridge, they passed through the dip where all remains of the crashed plane had been removed many years before. The carcass of the school came into view and the women trudged on. The stones beneath their boots were mostly free of plants and what flora there was had been ravaged by the wind over the autumn months. Broom was woody and grass bleached; seed-heads had scattered.

"Gosh, it still had the roof intact last time I was here," Lily said, as they came close enough to study the features of the tattered building. With unspoken agreement, they all paused to recall old memories and take in the changes.

"When was that?" Grace asked.

"Before I left for Australia," Lily replied. "Over ten years ago; mother and I walked out here to see the damage caused by the bomb. It was already decaying of course, but the tiles were still clinging on."

"Karl and I came here about five years ago," Helen said. "The roof tiles were gone and there was timber strewn all over the place." She gestured to the ground in front of the school, now free of debris. "It was if it had all blown off and was cast about like matchsticks.

The main structure was still in place, but the windows were broken, every one of them."

"The wood has been reused or burned," Grace told them. The others nodded, understanding that it was sparse at Dungeness and could not be left to rot.

The five women walked forward until they stood almost in the shadows of the broken-down walls. The whole of the roof had now gone and just a few shattered tiles lay scattered around the perimeter of the walls. Much of the white paint had flaked off the rough exterior and the concrete blocks were crumbling; the tops of the walls had become a row of jagged teeth, some missing altogether.

"Mother held secrets about her time here," Lily said. "She never spoke about it when I was younger."

"It's strange because we knew all about you and your family living in Ashford," Allie said. "But you knew nothing about us until you came here."

"I wonder why that was," Grace said.

"Perhaps because she thought we wouldn't be able to imagine how different it is here?" Lily suggested. "Perhaps because once she had gone, it barely seemed believable. Dungeness is only fifteen miles from Ashford, but so vastly different."

Elsie went to the empty window socket and peered inside the building, her eyes scanning the schoolroom. It was a miserable picture: the floor thick with dust, broken concrete, splinters of glass and roof tiles. Seagulls soared above, their cackles echoing amongst the abandoned shell, adding to her sensation of unease. "It's so bare," she almost whispered. "Imagine that Grandma Alice taught there, and this space was once filled with children reading and doing their sums. There's nothing left at all. It all seems terribly sad."

"And on a Sunday, they pulled back a curtain and

there was the altar!" Allie said, more cheerfully. "We were at school here five days a week and back for church on a Sunday!"

"And sometimes on a Saturday there was a party or some social gathering," Grace recalled. "We were never away from the place! It was the only area big enough to hold a crowd, other than the pubs."

Moving along the outside of the building, they peered into another empty space. "I think this was Mother's bedroom," Lily said. "What must it have been like, nineteen years old and living out here so far away from the other properties?" There was nothing left, no scrap of curtain, no old chest, or fragment of a diary. Nothing to tell the curious onlookers about the life of a young teacher living in the adjoining schoolhouse.

They were silent for a moment, reflecting on Lily's words, looking through other windows and doorways. With the toes of their boots, they nudged at shards of broken slate, a piece of coloured crockery or fragment of glass. Each one of them hoped to spot an item that gave away something of the school's past.

"I'd love to see it how it was then," Helen broke the silence.

"And to think that this is where the story of our families began…" Elsie said, "or did it? No, it began when Grandmother found Emily washed up on the shingle. That's when it began." Eventually she turned her back on the crumbling building and said: "Time to head back now; the wind's getting stronger. This place feels a bit creepy; let's just remember the times when it was full of life and get back to making our own happy memories for the future."

*

In Lydd, the artist stood inside All Saints beneath the white vaulted ceiling, with its colourful bosses in the form of oak leaves and Tudor roses. He gazed in silent appreciation at the simplicity displayed in the slim windows recreated in the Early English style. He hadn't painted for years but suddenly he felt a strange urge to rush home and return with his sketchpad.

He hadn't heard the quiet steps of a small dainty woman, with a wash of pale blonde over her greying waves, a neat navy twinset and a string of pearls.

"Excuse me, are you... I don't like to intrude; are you the artist, the one who...?"

Arthur smiled, liking her diffident manner and her soft blue eyes. "Yes... yes, I am," he admitted.

"I dabble a little myself, although nothing as good as yours. I was thinking of painting this window."

"I was thinking the very same thing myself." Arthur noted a pad of paper peeping from the woman's straw bag and gave his warmest smile "In fact, I was just going to go home and fetch my sketchpad."

"Well, you could have a piece of my paper; that is if it's... suitable?"

"I'm sure it would be," Arthur replied. That's very kind. Thank you. Thank you very much."

In comfortable silence, the two spent the next hour creating their different impressions of the new window. Arthur thought how good it was to spend time with someone who enjoyed art; he recalled his unease when Beryl used to complain about the mess.

Each of them thought what a pleasant companion the other was; what an enjoyable afternoon they were having – and couldn't help wondering quietly to themselves if this might possibly be the first of many...

The End

Further information and references

(RMW = Edward Carpenter's *Romney Marsh at War*)

Chapter One: The scene where Lily and Helen pause to look at fresh graves in the cemetery was based on reports of bombing on 5th Oct 1940 (p.34 RMW). On 15th October, Lydd was again bombed, resulting in the chancel of the church being destroyed. In real life, no one was killed (p.36-37 RMW).

Chapter Three: The idea to put Lily and Helen to work on the NAAFI van was inspired by a photo (p.49 RMW), but no further information could be found about the women who worked on it in the Romney Marsh area. The caption states they were at Dengemarsh, so I assume they visited lookouts along the coast, and within the army camp.

Chapter Four: Sleigh prams are fictional, although they may have existed. In this chapter Helen goes to Dungeness; this would not have been possible during the war as the area was restricted, with only the fishermen allowed to stay. Most likely the older women, such as Emily and Connie, would have been moved to Lydd. There was a checkpoint on the road to Dungeness (photo in John Wimble's *Marsh*

Memories). Descriptions of the beach and fishing during the war come from talking to local people.
The scene in which the fighter plane crashed on the shingle is based on stories that an aircraft did come down, having been flown at a low altitude. It was suggested that the pilot spotted the miniature train and assumed it was full-size, therefore thinking he was higher than he was. Internet searches have reports of this but all details about the type of plane, the pilot (Chapter Five) and the aftermath are fictional.

Chapters Six & Seven: The area surrounding the school was mined, but there were marked pathways. Descriptions of the exterior of the school are taken from photographs. All internal descriptions are from the author's imagination.

Chapter Nine: Inspired by references to a dance being organised (RMW p.55). Bobby's references to spies comes from many sources who report some being caught locally, and in particular the story of the one who tried to buy a drink in a pub before opening hours.

Chapter Thirteen: Information on Warship Week and the parade in New Romney came from Romney Marsh at War (p.66-67). I could not find out exactly when the parade was. The stories of animals in the minefields came from the same book. (p. 60).

Chapter Fourteen: Advanced landing grounds for fighter planes were built on sites at Brenzett, Newchurch, St Mary-in-the-Marsh and Midley during 1942. Midley was the first to become operational in June 30th1943, with the others opened by mid-September. The squadrons based in them are entirely

fictional; there is a reference to an Australian pilot in *Romney Marsh at War* (p.71). No evidence was found that the NAAFI van visited the airfields, but it may well have done.
The incident where the Focke-Wulf planes fired at the steam engine and the tank blew up is based on a real event (RMW p.64-65). All description of the aftermath and the pilot involved (Chapter Fifteen) is fictional.

Chapter Seventeen: On 17th January 1943, a Hurricane was fired at by anti-aircraft guns on the coast (RMW p.75). I don't know which guns fired, but I've placed Helen and Denny near Lade Fort when they see the plane flying across the coastline. The Hurricane was hit and the pilot bailed out at Hammond's Corner; the plane crashed outside Lydd and set off two mines. Looking at a map, for the plane to go from Lade to Hammond's Corner and then Lydd is rather a zig-zag route, but it suited the story to have my two young women at Lade. I know nothing of the fate of the real pilot, other than he survived the incident.

Chapter Nineteen: Wings for Victory week was a fund-raising event. There was a parade in Lydd, led by a military band (RMW p.79).

Chapter Twenty & Twenty-One: The Advanced Landing Grounds were opened from the summer of 1943. *Romney Marsh at War* mentioned the squadrons first based in them, but it seems they were only there for the summer months and there were regular changeovers. After D-Day the doodlebugs (also named V1s and Flying Bombs) became a new threat and the guns on the coast did their best to destroy them before they reached the land. Those that got past were then fired upon by fighter planes. The RAF disapproved of tipping the bombs with the wings of the planes.

Chapter Twenty-Two: On 1st March 1945 work began on removing coastal defences although Dungeness remained a restricted area (RMW p115). *Romney Marsh at War* states the Hardy Hall was used for church services during the war. As part of celebrations when the war ended the church was used for two services, but the Hardy Hall continued to be used after this until 1953. Lydd Camp hosted a dance, and the music was relayed through loudspeakers into the town (RMW p.115).

Chapter Twenty-Four: There is a painting in Lydd Church which was sold to raise funds for restoring the church. This inspired the idea of 'the artist's gift'.

Chapters Twenty-Five & Twenty-Six: All Saints was initially re-hallowed in 1953, but the chancel was still in ruins and blocked off. Information on fund-raising efforts came from church pamphlets and leaflets used to raise awareness about the money needed. Descriptions of Dungeness School come from old photographs.

About the Author

Romney Marsh writer, Emma Batten, loves to combine her interest in local history with creative writing. It is important to her that historical details are accurate in order to give readers an authentic insight into life on Romney Marsh. She enjoys giving author talks about her journey as a writer, planning unique writing workshops and meeting her local readers.

The Artist's Gift is Emma's fifth novel.

Books

Reading order and publication dates

The Dungeness Saga (also featuring Lydd and Ashford) set in late Victorian times through to WW2:

*Still Shining Bright** (2020): Cora and her daughter, Emily, are brought ashore to Dungeness by lifeboat. With no home or possessions, they rely on the kindness of strangers, and Cora must use her wit to survive.

*Reckless Choices** (2021): A chance meeting on a train upsets Emily, while on the streets of Ashford someone lurks waiting to make trouble. As tensions brew within a close family, the young woman makes a rash choice.

Secrets of the Shingle (2016 & 2020): A mystery set on the wild, windswept wastes of the Dungeness peninsula in the 19th century, and seen through the eyes of a naive young teacher.

Stranger on the Point (2018): Lily sets off to discover the remote coastal village her mother called home. A wrong turning takes her to a place where her arrival brings hope. The story of a young woman's quest to

fulfil her worth, as shadows of WW1 live on.
The Artist's Gift (2019): This tells the story of a fictional young woman, widowed through the war and living amongst real life events during the Second World War. Inspired by the bombing of Lydd Church.

*Prequels to *Secrets of the Shingle*

Stand-alone novels:

A Place Called Hope (2005, reworked 2019): Set in the 16th century, this tells the story of two young women living through the decline of a remote settlement named Hope on Romney Marsh.

But First Maintain the Wall (2019): Set in Georgian Dymchurch. Harry is passing through the village when the seawall breaches and events force him to stay. As an outsider, he struggles to be accepted and a tentative friendship is forged with a young woman who seeks answers to her past.

What the Monk Didn't See (2017 & 2021): The story of New Romney and the 1287 storm, which changed the fortunes of the town forever. As the storm breaks out, a monk climbs to the roof of the church tower. It is a superb vantage point, but what doesn't he see?

The Saxon Series introduces West Hythe, Lyminge and Aldington in 7th-century Anglo-Saxon times:

The Pendant Cross (2020): For a few days a year, the Sandtun (West Hythe) is used as a seasonal trading settlement. While they await the boats from Francia, friendships are made and hatred brews. Meanwhile four monks travel by night carrying a precious secret.

The Sacred Stone (2021): An earthquake uncovers a Roman altar buried in the foundations of an old fort. An ambitious thane and his priest are determined to secure this prize, but their actions have repercussions on the people of Aldington.

For more details take a look at Emma's website:
www.emmabattenauthor.com